Broken Boys
(The Extractor)

By L.J. Sellers

Broken Boys, The Extractor

Cover art by David MacFarlane

ISBN: 978-0-9987930-3-0
Published in the USA by Spellbinder Press

L.J. Sellers

Detective Jackson Mysteries

The Sex Club
Secrets to Die For
Thrilled to Death
Passions of the Dead
Dying for Justice
Liars, Cheaters & Thieves
Rules of Crime
Crimes of Memory
Deadly Bonds
Wrongful Death
Death Deserved
A Bitter Dying

Agent Dallas Thrillers

The Trigger
The Target
The Trap

Extractor Series

Guilt Game
Broken Boys

Standalone Thrillers

The Gender Experiment
Point of Control
The Baby Thief
The Gauntlet Assassin
The Lethal Effect

Broken Boys

Chapter 1

Sunday, June 25, 2:30 a.m., Portland, OR

Josh opened his eyes, half awake. What was that sound? A door opening? Not likely. His mom was the only other person in the home and she didn't go out late. He glanced at his cell phone on the nightstand. It was still the middle of the night. He rolled over and closed his eyes again. A moment later, heavy footsteps sounded in the hall outside his bedroom. Josh bolted upright. Someone was in their house!

The door burst open and two huge guys rushed in.

His heart missed a beat. Dark clothes and buzzed heads, they looked like military. *What the hell was this?*

He opened his mouth to scream, but the intruders came at him so quickly he never had a chance. A callused hand pressed something sticky against his mouth and a cloth bag came down over his head.

Oh fuck! This was bad. Josh swung wildly, but powerful hands caught his arms and pulled them together. Even knowing it was useless, he tried to kick his way off the bed. The strong hands grabbed his feet and shoved his legs up against his chest. The ripping sound of tape coming off a roll made his stomach heave. With terrifying speed and precision, the thugs bound his hands and feet together and wrapped him in his own sweaty sheet.

They carried him down the hall, swinging like a trussed animal. Josh called out to his mother, but the words went nowhere. Heart hammering, he scrambled to make sense of what was happening. Some kind of drug-deal payback? His oxy action was small-time and covered only a few friends—all white, middle-class high school juniors just like him—so that didn't make much sense. Whatever was going on was out of control! *Please let it be a mistake.*

They hauled him through the living room and out the open front door. Cool, middle-of-the night air enveloped him. Josh's panic escalated, and he couldn't catch his breath. He moved his mouth around, trying to work the tape loose, but got nowhere. His abductors jogged him across the lawn toward the sidewalk. His visual world was black, but his gut told him a van was parked on the quiet, dead-end street. *Waiting.*

Frantic, Josh wiggled his jaws, the only move he could make. As the kidnappers' footsteps hit the concrete of the sidewalk, the left side of the tape slipped off his mouth. He sucked in a quick breath and yelled for help.

A fist slammed into his face and pain exploded in his brain. He heard the metal click of a vehicle door sliding open, then they tossed him onto a hard floor. A moment later, the vehicle's engine started, and they rolled forward.

No! They were taking him somewhere to kill him, and he had no idea why. He would never see his mother again—and the last thing he'd said to her had been pretty crappy. Hot tears pooled in Josh's eyes.

Chapter 2

Sunday, July 2, 8:04 p.m., Southern Idaho

Red and blue lights flashed in her rearview mirror, and Roxanne MacFarlane's heart skipped a beat. *Damn!* The freeway entrance was only a hundred yards away. They'd almost made it! She braked and pulled off the narrow country road. "Stay quiet," she told the girl lying on the floor in the back seat. Lena, a thirteen-year-old, was hidden under a dark blanket, but if the officer decided to look around with a bright flashlight, Rox might soon be in handcuffs.

Lena whimpered, "What's going on? Is it Dad?"

"No. Just be quiet." Rox didn't know why the cop had stopped her, so there was no point in alarming the girl. But Lena's father and his new girlfriend were survivalists with a deep paranoia and an endless supply of weapons, so the teenager had good reason to be scared about going back to their isolated hideout.

Rox glanced in the rearview mirror. Even in the dark, she could see the double-white stripe of the state-police vehicle. Rural areas of southern Idaho didn't have their own police departments, and the man getting out wore a goofy state trooper's hat.

As he approached, Rox rolled down her window. "Good evening, officer."

"License and registration."

Even she could tell his tone wasn't friendly. Not a good

sign. Had Lena's father discovered his daughter was missing already and called the police? That would be surprising. Research into the prepper group indicated they were anti-establishment and more likely to carry out their own justice. Yet maybe the deputy was one of them. Rox's gut tightened as she reached for her glovebox. Her actions weren't technically kidnapping. Lena had come with her willingly, and Rox was taking the girl to her mother, who had joint custody. Worried that her estranged husband was off his meds and that his new girlfriend was abusive, Lena's mother had hired Rox to find the preppers' compound and get her daughter out.

Rox handed her license to the officer, forcing herself to smile and speak casually. "Can I ask why you stopped me?"

The heavyset trooper grabbed her documentation and grunted. Moonlight glinted off his sweaty face as he scrutinized her photo with a penlight. "You were driving too fast on a quiet rural road. What are you up to?" His accusation had a slight accent she didn't recognize.

Rox had prepared for this. "I'm just passing through. I got off the freeway to let my dog out to pee, and he disappeared." Lying was the hardest part of this work. Her atypical brain leaned toward compulsive honesty. But she'd trained herself to think of the necessary fabrications as *stories* she had to tell.

"What's his name?"

Who? Oh right, the make-believe dog. "Marty." Her stepdad would be amused. He'd been working this case with her until his knee gave out and his doctor ordered him to stay off his feet for a few days. She'd left without telling Marty she was doing the extraction alone.

"Huh." The cop shifted his weight. "We've had some break-ins around here, and your car matches the description.

I need to search it."

Rox's pulse escalated again. "As you can see from my license, I'm from Oregon and just passing through. I also used to be a police officer and a CIA agent." Both true. Rox paused to let him digest that information. "I know my rights. You have no cause to search this vehicle."

"Step out of the car!" His voice was no longer deadpan, and he apparently didn't believe her.

Oh hell. Rox was torn. If she complied, he might not shine his flashlight into the back and discover her hidden passenger. But if she got out, the belligerent trooper might feel compelled to handcuff her and search the car anyway. Then Lena would end up back with her crazy father and his extremist girlfriend. Rox couldn't let that happen. "This is harassment. What's your name and badge number?"

"Get out of the car!" He grabbed a heavy flashlight from his belt loop and slammed it against the metal door, startling her.

The prick! With shaky hands, Rox picked up her phone from the seat next to her.

The trooper yanked out his weapon and aimed it at her head. "Let me see your hands!"

Shit! This guy was a loose cannon. "It's just a phone! I'm calling your supervisor to report this harassment." She hit the button to roll up her window, then pressed 911.

The cop kept yelling, his face distorted with anger and his voice booming through the glass. Would she get shot and killed here today, beside the road in a bleak area of Idaho? Rox thought about Marty, the only real family she had left, and felt guilty about not telling him her plans. He would be so upset if she died! Marty had already lost his biological daughter. Jolene, her younger half-sister, had been murdered a few years earlier by a polygamous cult leader she'd been duped into marrying. And Rox had failed to get her out. Another stab of guilt seized her.

From the back seat, Lena started to cry. Rox tried to calm her. "It'll be okay." But she wasn't sure she believed it. Like most ex-cops, she kept a Glock in her vehicle, but in this situation it would only get her killed.

A dispatcher's voice suddenly sounded in the phone. "What is your emergency?"

Before Rox could respond, an SUV similar to hers blew past them, screaming down the road at a high speed. The trooper spun in the direction of the disappearing vehicle. "Holy hell!" He grabbed the radio on his collar and ran back to his cruiser. Over her shoulder, Rox watched him jump into his patrol car, pull onto the road, and chase after the red taillights.

She let out a laugh of relief and told the dispatcher she was fine. Rox started her engine and headed for the freeway. She was only five hours away from home—and safety—for both her and the girl. Another successful extraction!

Chapter 3

Tuesday, July 4, 9:40 a.m., Portland, Oregon

An intense pulse charged through Rox's brain. *Forty-seven.* Only three more to go. The magnetic stimulation therapy rippled through a coil attached to her head while the doctor standing next to her patiently administered it. This was the fifth session in her second round of treatments, each delivering fifty pulses. Rox did the math automatically in her head, glad that the magnets hadn't diminished that part of her brain. The pulses triggered her neurons to connect and fire in new pathways with the purpose of changing her thinking and emotional patterns. So far they had. She now experienced music in a deeper, more emotional way, and she'd slowly gotten better at reading people's expressions and understanding what they were thinking and feeling.

Rox counted the last three brain pulses and heaved a sigh of relief. Halfway through this course of therapy. The headaches, a common side effect, were getting to her, and her hearing had suffered as well.

Dr. Benton, an older woman with a gray granny bun, smiled. "I'll bet you'll be glad when we're done."

"Oh yes. I'm starting to feel like my head's been pried open and hammered."

"Ouch." The neurologist scowled. "You've never complained or reported side effects." The doctor detached the coil and pulled the apparatus away.

"I know. I want to get the full number of treatments and experience the ultimate results." Rox massaged her fingers into her scalp, not worried about messing up her short dark hair.

"And?" Dr. Benton raised an eyebrow. "Anything new or different from the last time we talked?"

"Not really. But I bought a purple dress, in case I ever date again, so that's some progress." She normally wore nothing but shades of blue, preferring the simplicity of choice. Plus cobalt matched her eyes and toned down her reddish skin color.

"Good to hear."

Rox stood up from the padded chair.

Her tiny doctor looked up at her. "I forget how tall you are when you're sitting."

Rox nodded. "I love being six foot, but it definitely limits the number of matches and dates I get." So did being forty. Listing her occupation as a *private investigator* and her religion as *none* worked against her too. But the screening process in online dating services was still better than wasting her time on relationships that were doomed to fail.

"I think it's brave to keep putting yourself out there." Dr. Benton moved toward the door and Rox followed. She didn't know what to say. Social situations could be awkward because of her limited ability to chitchat, but she refused to stay home alone and become a recluse. Thank goodness the treatments had helped. Despite her new awareness of other people's emotions, she still had some quirks.

"What happens after the next few treatments?" Rox asked as they walked up the hall.

"We don't know." The doctor touched her shoulder. "For many patients, the effects fade over time, but we've had a few who experienced more lasting changes."

They stopped at the clinic lobby.

"How many times can I repeat the treatment?" Rox asked.

"As many as you and your body will tolerate." Dr. Benton tipped her head sideways.

Was that skepticism?

The doctor continued, "You'll have to decide if the results you get are worth the pain and hassle of the treatment." Benton gave a gentle shrug. "There's also the cost to consider. Your insurance company may not pay for more than two rounds."

"Oh, right." Rox shook the doctor's hand. "Thanks."

"Happy Fourth of July."

"Uh, you too." Rox didn't celebrate most holidays, except for cooking a turkey for Marty on Thanksgiving. She walked out, hoping the treatments she'd undergone would be permanent, and after her next five, she would never have to set foot in the neurology clinic again. On the drive home, she put in her earbuds and grooved to Stevie Wonder, a new pleasure. She didn't trust listening to the radio, afraid she would hear a song that was too dramatic while she was driving.

Twenty minutes later, when Rox approached the duplex she shared with her stepdad in southeast Portland, she clicked off the music—and heard her work phone ringing in her purse. She grabbed it up, not wanting to miss a business call. "Karina Jones. How can I help you?" Because her actions for clients weren't always legal, she used the alias. It made her interactions—and getting paid—more complicated, but she didn't want to risk seven years in prison for a kidnapping charge.

"Are you the woman who does extractions?"

"Yes." She also offered traditional private-investigator services, but she'd been kept busy with rescue work lately. "What's your situation?" Rox pulled into her driveway and shut off her Nissan Cube, a vehicle she'd chosen for its quirkiness and now regretted.

"You have to find my son."

Rox climbed out and spotted Marty, her stepdad, standing in their shared driveway. His scowl made him look like a cranky old man. Shorter than her, with silver-blond hair and blue eyes, they made an odd pair. She headed into her house and motioned for him to follow. She focused on her caller. "Tell me your name."

"Isaac Lovejoy."

Rox smiled at its oddness. "What's happening with your son? Why can't the police help you?" Most of her extraction clients were referred to her by police officers she and Marty had worked with. They understood that families sometimes needed a different kind of help so they kept her name confidential. She trusted her buddies in blue to never betray her.

Inside, Rox kicked off her shoes and put the phone on speaker so Marty could hear.

"While I was out of town for the weekend, my ex sent him to one of those wilderness correctional schools." The man muttered an expletive about his former wife. "She won't tell me anything about the program and has stopped taking my calls."

Oh boy. Rox hadn't dealt with this particular scenario yet, and it made her nervous. "I'm sure it's a temporary situation."

"Those camps are dangerous!" His deep voice caught on the last word. "Josh is an addict. He needs drug treatment, not some testosterone-fueled asshole making him do pushups until he pukes."

Rox sympathized. Her own brain-chemistry-driven behavior as a teenager had gotten her into trouble too. The school counselor had been clueless about how to help her. But she couldn't convince herself that the boy was in serious danger. "I know you're worried, but Josh's life probably isn't at risk."

Isaac Lovejoy started to argue loudly, then stopped and calmed himself. "I disagree. Josh has been using opioids, and withdrawal can be painful and dangerous. He's also been depressed and anxious lately, and he even mentioned killing himself once. So I'm worried he's at risk for suicide." The man paused to collect himself. "My son is probably not going to cooperate, so they're probably beating or starving him as punishment."

Repulsive images popped into her head and Rox's stomach tightened. The reaction surprised her. She normally didn't visualize other people's pain. She glanced at Marty, and he nodded vigorously.

"How old is Josh and who has custody?" she asked, thinking she might be able to help this client.

"He's fifteen and we have joint custody. Josh lives with his mother but spends weekends and summers with me."

The father had equal legal rights. That was important. She wouldn't risk a possible kidnapping charge without a very compelling reason. "Let's meet in person to discuss more details, and I'll consider taking your case."

"Thank you. I can see you this afternoon."

"Are you aware of my fee?"

A pause. "I know it's expensive, but you might as well tell me."

"I require ten thousand in cash up front. Please bring it

with you this afternoon. If the case has additional expenses, we'll discuss them as we go along. If I conduct a successful extraction, I get another ten grand. Can you handle that?" She was occasionally willing to negotiate, but only one of her clients had stiffed her on the second payment. She'd also done an extraction practically for free.

Another slight hesitation. "Yes, I can get the cash today, but I'll have to liquidate some investments to make the final payment."

"You'll have time." She might not even be able to find the wilderness camp.

"Thank you!" Lovejoy sounded relieved.

"I have a few other conditions." Rox stood and headed for the fridge, taking the phone with her. "My privacy is critical. You can't share the location of my office or discuss the details of my services with anyone. If my business is compromised or I'm dragged into court, I'll be done helping other parents."

"I understand."

She pulled out a couple of beers. "Meet me at three, and bring photos of Josh. I'll text you the location and directions."

She ended the call and turned to Marty. "Join me on the back deck for a cold one? Maybe some pizza?" She hadn't had lunch yet.

"Sure." He walked over, still scowling.

She handed him a Rogue Dead Guy Ale, their new favorite microbrew. "What's your problem?"

"I'm still mad at you for doing that Idaho extraction without me." Marty shook his head. "Preppers are always armed to the teeth. Why would you take that risk?" He opened his beer, took a long pull, and headed out to the back deck.

Rox followed, grateful for the cool breeze. "Once I had the

location, I knew it would be easy. The group drinks heavy and sleeps hard."

Marty raised a bushy eyebrow. "No guard?"

"Nope. They're not true paranoids. Just a bunch of anti-social assholes who use the doomsday bullshit to live outside normal boundaries."

"Huh." Marty gave her one last dirty look. "Don't do that again. If we're partners, you have to treat me like one."

"That's fair." Technically, it was her business, and she only subcontracted with him for help. Or that's how they'd started. When she was searching for missing people or following cheating spouses, she didn't need a partner. But so much of her work now involved extractions that she relied on him more than either of them had expected.

Rox picked up her phone again and ordered a large pepperoni with added sausage on Marty's half.

"For MacFarlane, correct?" the clerk asked.

"Yes, thanks." They apparently ate pizza more often than she realized. Rox glanced down at her stomach. She hadn't gained any weight. Being tall had several advantages.

"What do you think about this new case?" Marty wanted to know.

"The challenge will be finding the camp. I don't expect the staff to be armed once we do though." Unless they worried about wild animals.

"That will be a nice change of pace." Marty lifted his glass in a sarcastic toast. He'd been shot during the last extraction he'd helped her with—another reason she'd gone to Idaho without him. That, and the heart disease that was trying to kill him.

Rox mulled over how they might search for the correction camp, realizing they didn't have enough information. But they had a meeting with the client scheduled soon. "We'll probably have to talk to the boy's mother and see if we can trick or intimidate her into telling us the name of the program."

"Good luck with that." Marty sipped his beer, then ran a critical eye around her back patio. "You need to powerwash those pavers, maybe replace a few." He got up for a closer look. "I could take care of it for you."

Rox laughed. "You gotta stop watching those home-improvement shows. You're supposed to be retired." Her stepdad had spent his whole life as a police officer and hadn't learned how to relax.

"If you stop moving, you die." Marty glanced her way. "Are you going to let me meet with the client this time?"

She almost relented, then stuck to her policy. "No, it's best to keep you as anonymous as possible."

He grunted his disapproval, then pulled out a pocketknife and dropped to his knees. "I'll scrape this moss while we wait for the pizza."

Rox laughed. "Suit yourself."

Chapter 4

Rox parked in the alley behind her office and headed inside, feeling a little sluggish from the warmth of the afternoon combined with a full stomach. The location in the Kerns area, just south of the freeway, was a little sleazy, but she hated to spend money on space she rarely used. She rented the small unmarked building under the name Karina Jones and tried to keep as low a profile as possible. Entering from the back kept her vehicle out of sight as well. The space was divided into two rooms, with the small foyer in front containing only two padded chairs and a table with a large monitor. Her personal area was somewhat larger but still minimalistic with only a desk and basic office equipment. She didn't spend much time here and needed to be able to clear out in a hurry. The exit door she'd just come in through served the same purpose— in case she ever needed to avoid a client or a police officer.

When she'd first set up her private investigator business, the idea of breaking the law had been jarring against her cop background. But after reuniting a young girl with a loving family member—and witnessing their joy—she'd gotten over her discomfort with the process. The work she did was essential. It also helped her make peace with her sister's death . . . most of the time.

At her standup desk, Rox activated the system she used to communicate with clients. The monitor in the front room showed only the top part of her body with her face pixilated.

The people who hired her typically never saw her face or knew her real name. The camera view on her side displayed most of the foyer, but she could zoom in on a client's face if she chose to. Only one person had walked out when he saw the setup. Most of her clients were so desperate for help they accepted her conditions.

Ten minutes later, Isaac Lovejoy knocked on the outer door, then walked into the foyer. A little shorter than her, he had a broad upper body that looked squeezed into his suit jacket. He'd made an effort to dress well for their meeting, and she liked that. Rox pressed the sound button and said, "Isaac Lovejoy?"

Unfazed, he sat down in front of the monitor with a zipped canvas moneybag on his lap. "Yes. I assume you're Karina Jones." Lovejoy glanced around the room, probably looking for the camera.

"I apologize for the impersonal nature of the meeting, but I have to protect myself. Some of my methods are less than legal, and if things go badly, you can't be forced to identify me in court if you don't know what I look like."

"That's smart." Lovejoy nodded. "What is your success rate?"

She smiled. He was a numbers guy, and she liked that too. "I've done six successful extractions with only one failure. And that's because I never found the girl. Her pimp ended up in jail though."

"You came highly recommended."

She didn't typically respond to flattery—another quirk of her strange brain. "What do you do for a living?" It only mattered if he worked for the government. Her own decade in the CIA was starting to seem like long ago.

"I'm head chef and co-owner of the Steelhead Bistro."

A restaurant she'd never heard of. Now that her neurons were firing differently, maybe she'd give it a try. She usually stuck with pizza, salads, and Thai food. And PBJs, Marty's favorite, of course. She googled the restaurant he'd mentioned as she mentally shifted gears. "Tell me about your son's situation. Start with how you learned he was taken to a wilderness camp."

A wave of pain flashed in Lovejoy's eyes. "I drove to my ex-wife's house Saturday morning to pick up Josh like I do every weekend. She answered the door but wouldn't open it. She just announced that Josh would be gone for the summer."

"She used the word *gone*?" Often, the small details were all she had to work with. *Gone* meant the camp probably wasn't local.

"I asked what the hell that meant and she said she'd sent him to a camp where he would learn to behave." Lovejoy shifted in his chair. "I was so mad that she'd done it without consulting me. After that, the conversation got pretty ugly and she threatened to call the cops."

"All of this was through the door?" Rox switched gears again and opened up a background-check website and entered the client's name.

"Yes. Why?"

"Is your ex-wife afraid of you?"

"No. Don't think that." Lovejoy shuddered. "We divorced because she cheated on me. I've never hurt her. And I didn't threaten her that morning. But I was on her front porch shouting, and she didn't want to deal with me."

Lovejoy's report came up on the screen. No arrests, but a restraining order filed by Carrie, his wife. "When did your ex file the complaint?"

"Right after that confrontation. But her fiancé probably

pushed her to do it." Lovejoy's jaw tightened. "The damn correctional program was probably his idea too. Carrie and Josh were getting ready to move in with the guy, and he's a control freak."

The ex-wife might simply be covering her own custody violations with legal paperwork. "Can't you go to court and file a petition to get Josh removed from the camp?"

The frustrated father closed his eyes for a moment. "I've consulted a lawyer, but he says it could take months and that a lot of judges actually send kids into the wilderness programs. So I can't expect to be successful. I sure as hell can't leave Josh out there all summer."

She didn't blame him. Rox looked at her notes. "Carrie never mentioned the name of the camp?"

"No."

"Where would she learn about the program? From a friend? Someone at work? Her mother?"

Lovejoy rolled his eyes. "It was probably someone from her fellowship."

A bolt of worry shot through her. Religious camps and cults were often the most secretive and therefore the hardest to find. "What church?"

"I think it's called Common Community Fellowship, and it's not really a church. Well, it is, but it's not that religious. That's where she met the guy she had the affair with." Lovejoy pulled a phone from his pocket, searched online, then added, "Yep. That's the name. There are two branches. Carrie goes to the one on Powellhurst."

As much as Rox disliked the idea of attending any kind of service, at least she had a place to start her search. Or maybe she'd ask Marty to go instead. "Tell me about Josh. What's he like?"

Lovejoy gave a tight smile. "He's a good kid, the kind of person who would give you the shirt off his back. But he struggles with depression, and his mother doesn't believe in taking medication for mental health." The man's shoulders sank. "So Josh started self-medicating with pot and pills, but lately he seems more distressed than ever. His mother just thinks he's got an attitude problem."

The addiction aspect made her nervous, and Rox had second thoughts about taking the case.

Her hesitation must have worried Lovejoy because he pleaded, "Please help me. Like I told you on the phone, Josh could be in withdrawal and suicidal." The client made a small noise in his throat. "They could be beating him daily. I've heard those camps can be brutal. And Carrie doesn't believe in sparing the rod. That was one of the things we fought about."

Rox was back on board. Physical and sexual abuse of kids was intolerable. She had no desire to ever be a parent, but she had no sympathy for people who made that choice, then messed it up. "What else can you tell me? Did Carrie ever talk about the wilderness program when you were still together?"

"No. She started with the Fellowship near the end of our marriage, then met Curtis Fletcher. He's an asshole." Lovejoy's face tightened. "I went to my lawyer about six months ago and asked about getting full custody of Josh, but he wasn't optimistic about that either."

"Did she mention anything about the logistics? Such as driving Josh to the camp? Or putting him on a bus?"

"No. She just kept shouting at me to do Josh a favor and let him get the help he needed." A catch in his breath. "I've never wanted so badly to hurt someone, but I kept it together."

"Would Josh cooperate with his mom if he knew she was taking him to a camp?" Rox was trying to assess the boy's state of mind and how he might respond to an extraction. Some people came to believe they deserved to be abused or oppressed. A young girl she'd rescued named Mia came to mind.

"I doubt that. Carrie can't control him. That's why she sent him away." Lovejoy sucked in a breath. "You think she drugged him to get him there?"

"Maybe. I know it happens." In the course of her business, she'd learned more than she wanted to about cults and methods of controlling people. And she'd started researching wilderness boot camps right before coming to the office. "Josh was most likely taken by force. If a parent grants temporary guardianship to a transportation service, or even to the program, they can literally kidnap the kid."

"Transportation service? What the hell is that?" Lovejoy's shock was palpable.

"Just like it sounds. It's for parents who can't deal with their kid's opposition or distress. Or they don't have time to make the trip, which can be across the country. So they hire professionals to pick up their child and take him or her to a behavior camp or military school or whatever they have in mind."

"I can't believe that's legal."

"Yep. It's all part of the tough-love industry." She decided to officially take the case. Josh Lovejoy was young and vulnerable and needed her help. "To be clear. You'd like me to locate the camp, extract your son Josh, and bring him to you?"

"Yes!"

"Show me the photo of him, then leave it, please."

Lovejoy complied. The boy was dark-haired like his father and shared his wide brown eyes, but his face was thin and unhappy.

She had sudden doubts about whether she could succeed. "If I can't find the camp, I'll refund half your money." She paused to let him process that.

He hesitated. "Okay."

"But since your ex is the one who knows where Josh is, I have to start with her. Give me Carrie's phone number and address, then tell me her full name, where she works, and anything else that seems important."

Rox mentally repeated the contact numbers as she heard them, and they were instantly embedded in her memory. But she would have to google the street name, not recognizing it. That surprised her. She'd lived in Portland most of her life, except for her stint in the CIA.

"Carrie Louise Lovejoy, and she works at the Columbia YMCA, mostly front desk stuff."

Easy access! "Anything else I should know?"

"She runs hot and cold and is completely unpredictable."

Her least favorite kind of person. "Good to know. I'll be in touch about my progress as I go along. Try to be available by phone in case I have questions."

Lovejoy breathed a sigh of relief. "Thank you." He glanced around. "Where should I leave this money?"

"On the table is fine. Just lock the door on your way out."

He stood, hesitated, then finally laid down the canvas bag. "Do I get some kind of contract or guarantee?"

"Nothing on paper. But I can put you in touch with a satisfied client if you'd like." She rarely had to follow through on that promise—but she could.

Lovejoy let out a small chuckle. "It's kind of late now. I

should have asked for a reference before I brought the money." He stepped back. "Work quickly, please. Josh's life could depend on it."

"I will."

Lovejoy turned and walked out.

Rox tapped the camera with the view of the front parking lot to see what her client drove. She also wanted to make sure he had left before she crossed into the foyer to pick up the cash. Lovejoy headed toward a white truck with a camper, not what she'd expected for a chef-business owner. Before her client could climb into his vehicle, a police car pulled into the lot and an officer jumped out, heading straight for Lovejoy.

What the hell?

Chapter 5

Rox watched the officer handcuff Lovejoy, put him in the back of the patrol car, and drive away. Had she made a mistake in taking his case? Her client's background check had come up clean, and the restaurant's website listed Lovejoy as the main owner, so he seemed decent on the surface. The arrest could be about anything, but most likely it involved his ex-wife and her restraining order. Had Lovejoy minimized the altercation with his ex-wife? Maybe he'd actually assaulted Carrie—or had a history of violence that wasn't documented in the system. She couldn't rescue Josh from the camp just to deliver him to an abuser. More information was needed.

Rox hurried into the foyer, grabbed the zippered bag, and stuck the cash into the floor safe in her office. She put the smaller photo of Josh into her shoulder bag and slipped out the back door. In her car, she pulled on her headset and called a friend in the Portland Police Bureau. Ernie Bowman had been Marty's squad partner for his last twelve years on the job, and she'd gotten to know him well over pizza dinners. She counted the rings as she waited for him to answer. Bowman picked up on seven. "Hey, Rox." A pause. "Is Marty okay?"

The old guys still played golf together, and Bowman was the only one on the force who knew about Marty's heart condition.

"He's fine. This is about a client who was just arrested in front of my office."

"What's his name and what do you want to know?"

"Isaac Lovejoy. I need to know why he was picked up."

"Give me a minute and I'll call you back. I'm on patrol and in the middle of something."

"Thanks." She hung up, then realized she should have apologized for bothering him at work. The fact that she understood that now was proof that the magnetic therapy was working. She started the car and headed home to discuss the case with Marty. Halfway there, she changed her mind and drove south to the Columbia YMCA on Barbur Boulevard. She'd only been inside the facility once to play basketball when she was younger, but she remembered how to find it. The humiliation of the game surfaced too. People had assumed that because she was tall, she could play, and she'd given in to peer pressure. So much physical contact with strangers! She'd hated every moment and never done it again.

At first glance, nothing about the building's exterior had changed except that the gray concrete had faded over the years. But as Rox strode into the building, she realized they'd added a sunroom-style foyer in the front. *Lipstick on a pig*, as Marty always said. Inside, she glanced around the main lobby. The same tall, curved counter and the same cluttered bulletin board on the opposite wall. A family stood in front of the reception area, blocking her view of the staff behind the desk. On the drive over, she'd considered several approaches, then decided to stick to observing Carrie in her work environment. Gathering real intel about the correctional camp would likely have to wait until the fellowship visit.

The smell of chlorine from the pool, mixed with sweat

from the gym, hit her hard. How could anyone work here? The family at the counter moved on, and Rox got her first view of the staff. A tall young man without an ounce of body fat and a petite, forty-something woman with strawberry-blonde hair and deep cleavage. Carrie Lovejoy?

Rox turned toward the bulletin board to look preoccupied while she watched the receptionist out of the corner of her eye. She needed just enough information about Carrie to pretend to know her when she visited the church to ask about the correctional program. What if she could find out with a phone call? The Common Community Fellowship probably had a secretary who answered the phones. Rox tried to recall if she'd ever been inside a church. Yes, once when she'd stayed the night with a friend when she was ten. The first and only time she'd done a childhood sleepover.

A burst of laughter from the front desk startled her. The receptionist's petite body produced an unnerving volume of noise. The young man beside her laughed politely, said "Good one, Carrie," then turned away to look busy. The phone at the counter rang, and Carrie answered in a deep, breathy voice. Overall, she seemed a little unsuited to working in an environment focused on children. More important, had someone at the YMCA recommended the wilderness program to her? Rox was tempted to walk up to the counter and ask, but she wasn't wearing one of her disguises.

Using her work phone, she called the front desk, then trotted up the steps and out of sight as it rang. Carrie's voice came on the line. "Columbia YMCA."

"Hello. I'm looking for help with my teenage son. Do you have any behavior-type programs?"

"Not specifically, no. We focus mostly on sports, and crafts, and summer camps."

"You mean like those wilderness camps for troubled kids?"

"No, we only offer fun activities, like swimming and hiking and campfire stories."

"Oh, right." Rox stopped climbing and turned back, wanting to watch Carrie's face now. "Do you know of any behavior-based wilderness camps? I'm at my wits' end with my son."

"I can relate to that." Carrie paused, then lowered her voice. "I do know of one, but it's exclusive, and I can't tell you much about it." She looked a little worried.

"Exclusive how?" Rox was genuinely puzzled.

"I'm probably not using the right word."

"Give me a name, please. My son needs help."

"Ridgeline, but you—"

An older man suddenly strode out of a nearby office and hurried up to Carrie. The receptionist looked flustered. "Thanks for calling," she mumbled, hung up, and turned her attention to the guy in the button-up shirt.

Damn. But at least she had a name for the program now. Rox hustled down the steps and out into the glass foyer. She didn't want to seem like a lurker. Carrie's use of the word *exclusive* was concerning. It probably meant secretive, and that didn't bode well. Still, Rox was encouraged that she would soon have the full name and contact information for the correctional program—which she needed to even start her specific research.

She headed back to her car, thinking the trip had been worthwhile. She could identify Carrie now and was pretty sure that Josh's mother didn't know the physical location of the camp. But Carrie might be able to provide the name of the transport service she'd used to have her son picked up.

Maybe one of the thugs could be bribed. Or seduced. If the program used its own carriers, that tactic wouldn't work, and finding the camp might be ridiculously time-consuming. Unless she could track down a previous client—either a teenager who'd graduated or the parent who'd sent him. What if the program required a nondisclosure agreement? Even if the parents signed them, the kids sure didn't.

As she started the engine, her personal phone rang and she glanced at the ID. *Bowman.* Rox answered quickly. "Hey, buddy. What did you find out?"

"Isaac Lovejoy was picked up for violating a restraining order. He'll probably be arraigned and released."

"Against Carrie, his ex-wife?"

"Yes. Is that it?" Bowman wasn't much of a phone talker and probably still on duty.

"For now. Thanks."

"Later."

They both hung up and Rox drove out of the parking lot. Even though she was relieved that her client hadn't assaulted his ex, she still had to consider whether she could trust him. She'd secured the first half of the fee, but he might be the type to cheat her on the extraction bonus. But she couldn't worry about that. If Josh was being physically abused or was suicidal, as his dad thought, she had to help him. Her biggest worry was that she wouldn't find the camp in time.

Chapter 6

Wednesday, July 5, 5:30 a.m., Central Oregon wilderness
Josh woke to someone shouting, "Get up, you lazy fucktards!"

He couldn't move. He'd had so little sleep, and his body hurt everywhere.

"Get up!" A boot slammed into his shoulder.

The pain jolted him to life. Josh sat up and pushed off the tarp. In the early light of dawn, the high-desert mountains surrounded him. He was in the middle of fucking nowhere, with practically nothing, and no one cared. His parents had sent him here to die a slow, torturous death.

"Move!" Ace kicked him again. The bearded man was a sadist, and Josh visualized stabbing him in the eye with a sharp stick. If he could only find one. Because he had no way to sharpen anything. All he had were the clothes on his back, a small shovel, and a tarp. He'd never been so dirty . . . or so tired . . . or in so much pain. Yet he pushed to his feet. He'd tried resisting the first week, but he'd been kicked, slapped, starved, and humiliated. The physical stress of the oxy withdrawal had been nothing compared to the everyday life as a Ridgeline "student." Now he just wanted to die, but he wanted it to be quick. Maybe today he would find a way. He hadn't been sure he deserved to live even before coming here.

"Get your morning duties done and be ready to go in five!" The camp counselor tossed a snack bag of granola and a pair of boots at him, then moved to the boy three tarps away and kicked him. "Let's roll!"

Counselor! Like hell he was. A bullshit title for a bullshit program. These people were getting shitloads of money to drag teenagers around the desert mountains and abuse them at every opportunity. Well, not everybody got abused. Just the kids like him, still wearing the brown *shit* T-shirts because they wouldn't cooperate with every little stupid rule. Josh pulled on the boots, which they took away every night so he couldn't run, then grabbed the tiny shovel and headed off to dig a hole to crap in. Without toilet paper. He'd been tearing off tiny pieces of his shirt to wipe with when he needed to. Other kids used leaves and rocks, but those had both left him too sore. Around him, a few campers had made little fires to heat milk to soak their granola in. They'd earned the privilege by kissing ass at every opportunity. So far, he hadn't even earned the right to carry a water bottle, and his throat was so dry and scratchy it hurt to swallow.

Back at his tarp, he wolfed down the gravel-like granola anyway. He would need it for the ten-hour daily hike that came next. But the food they gave him was never enough, and his body was starving.

"Dude, aren't you sick of taking his shit?" Another camper—*inmate!*—named Trevor walked up. Unlike him, the guy was small and blond, but still, another middle-class white kid. They all were. "Just try a little harder," Trevor said, "and you'll get some protein. You're wasting away."

They were all losing weight, but Josh had given up hope of earning any honey for his granola or salt for the beans they fed them every night—let alone beef jerky. "Ace hates me, so there's no point."

"No he doesn't. He's like that with everyone the first couple of weeks." Trevor had passed into phase two and wore a green T-shirt to show his *growth*.

The counselors all wore red. *Bloody bastards!* "I'm getting out of here the first chance I can," Josh whispered.

"Escape?" Trevor let out a harsh laugh. "Didn't they tell you on the first day that no one ever escapes, at least not for long?"

"Yeah, I heard that, but I'll die trying."

Trevor grabbed one side of Josh's tarp. "Come on. Don't be late."

Stunned by the gesture, it took Josh a moment to respond and grab a corner. A surge of gratitude washed over him as they folded the tarp. No one had done a kind thing for him in the ten days he'd been here. This was day eleven . . . of hell on earth. Josh pulled the tarp over his shoulders and pushed the shovel through the straps on his back. They carried the equipment everywhere, and most nights they made camp in a new place.

After a day of orientation at the base camp, his group had hiked thirty grueling miles, only stopping to eat and sleep when it got dark. He'd been in withdrawal and had puked all day. Ace hadn't stopped once for him. Ben, the other guide, had offered him water to rinse his mouth, but that was it. Every day since had been just as brutal. Josh hated his mother for doing this to him even more than he hated Ace. His dad might have signed the papers, but he knew this was his mother's boyfriend's idea. Curtis had been complaining about his behavior since the day they'd met.

"Let's go!" Ace shouted.

Josh jogged over to the line forming. They started every day by running for an hour. Could he do it again? It never got easier. But if he fell or tried to stop, Ace would kick him and humiliate him. Josh amazed himself every day with the things he could force himself to do. He suspected that was the point. But they weren't curing his addiction or making him a better person. If an opportunity to escape opened up before he got a chance to kill himself, he would take it. When he was free, he would head straight for the nearest oxy dealer to take away his pain. After that, he would confront his mom just long enough to spit in her face. She had let thugs kidnap him from her house!

Ace was suddenly shouting at him. "Your tarp is too damn sloppy!"

Oh hell. Another excuse to harass him. Josh pulled off the straps to start over with it.

"What do you say?" Ace demanded.

Josh ground his teeth, trying to decide what was harder—the words or the painful consequences of not saying them. He made himself choke them out. "Thank you for pointing that out to me. I'll take care of it." They called the forced response *radical acceptance*, some misguided behavior modification bullshit.

"Make it fast!"

Josh refolded the tarp as quickly as he could, knowing this effort would look even worse. But it didn't matter. Ace had already jogged back to the front of the hiker line.

From there, he shouted, "Let's have a good day, students! If no one falls or gets behind, you all get Vanilla Wafers with dinner."

No one responded vocally but Seth turned and stared at Josh.

Fuck! Peer pressure again. If Josh messed up and the group lost the privilege, Seth would punch him. Or throw feces under his tarp.

A minute later, Ace took off running and the ten boys

followed. Josh's bruised feet ached with every step and his stomach growled with an angry need. The sun came up behind the mountain, and a soft pink light filled the rocky landscape. Josh hated this place—with its endless red dirt, scrubby bushes, and dry pine trees—wherever the hell it actually was. He'd been blindfolded for the whole trip, and it had taken at least six hours.

When he'd arrived at the base camp, it had looked like a desolate outpost of tents, tarps, and plastic tubs. After ten days in the wilderness, it now seemed like a luxury spot he couldn't wait to get back to. But he would never see it again. Completing this phase of the program was impossible for him, so he had his eye out for a cliff to jump off today. Death would be a sweet escape.

Chapter 7

Wednesday, July 5, 8:05 a.m., Portland

Rox finished her dance workout—the only exercise she did, besides an occasional summer hike—then took a quick shower. In front of her closet, she hesitated. She now owned a purple dress and a dark-green sleeveless sweater but hadn't worn either yet. Neither seemed professional enough for a workday. She pulled on a cobalt-blue sleeveless blouse and black pants, then blow-dried her short wavy hair. The morning headache, a side effect of her treatment, started to subside.

As she shut off the noisy dryer, Marty's familiar knock echoed down the hall. Rox pulled on black sneakers, hurried toward the front of the house, and called out "Clear!" A law-enforcement term that meant *safe to enter.* She'd had to institute the policy after Marty walked in on her and Kyle one morning. A pang of longing hit her hard. Kyle had been a great guy—and one of the best sex partners she'd ever had.

The door burst open and her stepdad hustled in, carrying two plates. "I have bacon and cinnamon rolls."

There were also benefits to having him as a close neighbor. "Yum!" Rox started for the kitchen, then stopped. "What's going on? You're softening me up for something." Understanding—and using—manipulation was a new skill too. She hoped it would stay with her when the treatments were over.

"Nope. Just being nice."

He was saving the request or bad news for later.

"Good. Let's eat. I want to get rolling on this case."

Marty poured coffee for them both and they sat at the kitchen table. After Rox reached for a frosted roll, Marty asked, "What did you find out last night? I know you've got something." He'd been on a date the night before so they hadn't talked about the case since Lovejoy had first called.

"Tell me about your evening first." SiriKaren was a new girlfriend, his second in six months. Before that, he'd been alone for decades, most of it spent raising her and Jolene. Rox was happy that he was finally dating.

"We had dinner and went dancing, like always."

"That was your fifth date with her. Maybe you should invite her to stay over."

"Maybe you should mind your own business. Some of us think it's important to know each other before we take our clothes off." Marty shoved a bacon strip in his mouth and chewed loudly.

Rox laughed. "Life is short, old man." She immediately regretted saying it. His heart was damaged and he might only have six more months. Or he might have six years—if he took care of himself.

"I know. I like SiriKaren. We'll get there."

Rox grinned and bit back a comment about little blue pills. "Here's what I learned in my meeting with Lovejoy." She chewed a cinnamon roll as she ticked off the main details. "Isaac Lovejoy co-owns a restaurant where he works as a chef. His son Josh was probably picked up by a transportation service and escorted to a wilderness camp in northern Nevada or Utah. I got the name Ridgeline from the mother, who works at the YMCA." Rox washed her roll down with coffee. "And Lovejoy was arrested outside my office yesterday for violating a restraining order."

Marty scowled, his bushy eyebrows coming together. "Against his ex-wife?"

"Yes, but he has no history of violence. Or anything. He's clean."

"Still, not good."

"I know. I plan to check him out more thoroughly."

Marty rubbed his hand across the table. "This surface needs refinishing. Maybe with some bamboo. We could do your floor with it too. I love the bright look of that stuff."

Rox snapped her fingers. "Focus. We have an extraction to plan."

Marty rolled his eyes. "You're worse than your mother."

Ouch. "I'm not really anything like her." When Rox was thirteen, Georgia had left all three of them for a role on Broadway and had never come back. She'd visited, sent lovely gifts, and made promises, but never lived with them again. Marty had only come into Rox's life as a stepfather when she was six, but they'd bonded and he'd continued to raise her like his own daughter even after the divorce. But Jolene, her baby sister, had been his biological child, and Jo's death had knocked Marty's heart off-kilter for a long time.

"I know you're not. But Georgia used to tell me to focus, and you caught me off guard."

Rox didn't remember that. Had she picked it up subconsciously as a child? Why would it surface now? Because of the treatments? She let it go. "Back to work. I did some research last night and discovered that the program is called Ridgeline Wilderness Health." She scoffed out loud. "As though putting the word *health* in the title makes forced hiking and camping a positive thing."

Marty gave her a look. "Not all those programs are bad. Some kids come out with a new mindset and go on to live successful lives."

"But some are horrible and kids die from abuse or seizures or some other medical neglect." Anger surfaced in her throat. "More than eighty teenagers have died in those programs in the last twenty years. And no one is ever charged or convicted!"

"Eighty?" Her stepdad scowled. "That seems high."

"It's ridiculous. And no institution, except the media, actually keeps track. Or regulates the programs."

Marty reached over and patted her hand. "I like your new passion, but we can't save everybody."

Rox took a deep breath, surprised she'd gotten so worked up. "I know. But we are going to find and rescue Josh Lovejoy. If he's been abused, I hope his dad goes to the police."

Marty picked up their plates and put them in the dishwasher, talking as he worked. "What do we know about Ridgeline?"

"Not much. The website gives no information about where the office or the camps are located and offers only a phone number to call. I tried it last night and got a canned message. I'll try again in a few minutes. From what I read, most of these camps are mobile. The kids and counselors hike into the wilderness and stay out there for weeks or months."

"They must have a base camp that runs supplies out to them."

"Most likely. Still, finding Josh will be challenging. We'll have to pull off a major con to get him called back to the base camp. And then we have to find that."

Marty paced the kitchen, his face worried. "The transport

service, or whoever drives the kids out there, knows where it is. We should start there."

"Yes. And we may need to find the program's office building. I suspect it's based in Utah, where these camps seem to be concentrated."

He turned back. "That's a long drive. Paying a hacker would be easier."

Rox grinned. "You're getting pretty lawless for an old cop."

"Just because something is illegal doesn't mean it's immoral."

He'd never said that before. "And vice versa," Rox added. An idea popped into her head. "What if we can get the mother to drive out to the base camp? Convince her that Josh needs medical attention and she has to pick him up? We would follow her, of course."

"That could work." Marty rubbed his stubby gray hair. "I suppose the base camp will be an eight-hour drive."

"Probably." Rox's work phone rang across the room, and she hurried to her desk to pick it up. An unknown number. Another client? "Karina Jones."

"It's Isaac Lovejoy. I'm calling from the jail. I was arrested yesterday at your office."

"I saw." Rox put him on speaker and walked over to the kitchen table. "For violating a restraining order against your ex-wife."

"It's bullshit. She filed that as an intimidation tactic when we divorced." Her client was talking fast. "I've been to Carrie's home to pick up Josh dozens of times since then. She's just striking out because she's worried that I'll sue her for forging my signature on the correctional program application."

"You know for sure that she did?"

"I'm guessing. It seems like she would have to. But maybe those camps only need one parent to sign."

"Or she lied and told them she had full custody." Rox looked at Marty and he nodded. She'd asked him to check court records to ensure that their client had joint custody.

"Either way, I'm fighting her on this." Lovejoy's tone was tight with suppressed anger. "Once I get Josh back, he's not going to her house again."

Rox didn't blame him. "I hope your arrest doesn't work against your custody challenge."

"Oh shit." Despair made him plead, "You're still going to find Josh for me, aren't you?"

"I'll try." Rox glanced at Marty again. He'd taught her to never make promises she couldn't keep. "But the camp is mobile, so it will be challenging. How long will you be in jail?"

"That depends."

A moment of silence.

Then Lovejoy asked, "Will you use some of the cash I gave you to bail me out? I promise to pay it back."

This was a first. "I'll think about it."

Marty shook his head.

A loud voice in the background shouted, "Time's up!"

"I have to go. Please help me." Lovejoy hung up.

Marty took a moment to lecture her about the foolishness of wasting the advance payment on bail, but Rox didn't respond.

"Your silence tells me you plan to do it anyway."

Rox stood, ready to stretch her long legs. "That depends on how much the bail is. But for a few grand—of his money— I'm not going to let him stay in jail."

Marty cut in. "Let's at least check him out more thoroughly first!"

"I will."

"What's your plan?" Marty crossed his arms.

Rox suppressed her annoyance. "I can find people who knew Lovejoy and his wife when they were married and see what they thought of the relationship. I can also talk to his employees at the Steelhead Bistro." Rox changed her mind and grinned at her stepdad. "Better yet, you can do all that while I start looking for Josh."

"I was going to play golf today." His voice was deadpan.

"Suit yourself."

They both burst out laughing. As much as he liked golf, working a case was irresistible to him. He'd only retired from the department because the full-time pressure of the job had worn on him—and his body. Marty grabbed her grocery-list tablet and ripped off a sheet. "I'm ready."

Rox gave him the details she knew about Lovejoy, then stood. "I'll keep digging into Ridgeline and see what I can learn about it."

"I'll get Bowman to look at police logs and see if Lovejoy and his ex-wife have a history of altercations or 911 calls. Just because he was never convicted of assault doesn't mean it didn't happen."

"Thanks."

After Marty left, Rox called the county's pre-trial detention number and asked about Lovejoy's bail. The twenty grand surprised her, but she only needed to put down ten percent of that. She would give her stepdad an hour to get back to her before she picked up the cash from the office. Most of it would go into the bank before she bailed out her client.

While she waited to hear from Marty, she sat down with her laptop and opened the Ridgeline Wilderness Health site.

While looking for the phone number she'd stumbled on the night before, she scrolled through a marketing pitch with phrases such as *the therapeutic effect of nature* and *accountability through outdoor survival*. The website didn't even list a post office box to mail checks to. They probably didn't take them—just credit cards over the phone. After a minute of mental prep, Rox called the 800 number and got the message again, which thanked her for calling and asked her to leave contact information and the name of her referral.

Referral? Interesting. She hadn't listened long enough last night to hear that part. "This is Jolene McAdams, and I'm desperate to help my son. Please call me." She started to give her work phone, then switched to her personal number. She always answered her work phone with her Karina Jones business name, and when they called back, the inconsistency might trigger their suspicion. Without a referral, would they even call back? It seemed like they should be eager for her business. She considered calling back and listing Carrie Lovejoy as a reference, then changed her mind. The program administrator might actually call Carrie. Rox hung up. If they didn't get back to her, she would call again.

She did a quick search for the phone number and discovered that the prefix was based in Utah. No surprise. Now what? She really needed to find a parent who'd used the Ridgeline program or a kid who'd been through it. Facebook was no help. The only wilderness camps that came up in her search were for adult recreation. The only reference to a correctional camp had been posted by a newspaper that reported a male teenage camper charged with raping a female counselor. That surprised her. But it shouldn't have. Many of the kids in those camps were sent there by court order, so some had to be quite troubled, maybe even violent.

Josh, her extraction target, could be more problematic than his father was willing to admit. But beating and starving teenagers—like some programs did—wasn't a solution to delinquency.

The place to find a teenager was probably Instagram or SnapChat, or whatever the new online hangout was. But she didn't have an account for any of them. She used the Tracers' database whenever she searched for missing people, but in those cases, she had a name to work with. Frustrated, Rox opened Craigslist and created a personal ad asking for feedback to help her decide on a correctional camp, specifically mentioning Ridgeline as a strong contender. To help screen out the cranks and perverts, she didn't include her phone number, listing only a Yahoo email account she didn't care about as her contact point. She predicted that twenty-some people would email her but that only three or four would have real information. Maybe only one or two would message her to warn about the negative conditions of a particular camp. But those responders might also know the location. Rox repeated the process for the Craigslist site in Salt Lake City, Utah and Reno, Nevada.

After closing her laptop, she went in search of index cards or any kind of stiff paper. She finally settled on using the back side of old birthday cards and printed out her request in bold letters: *If you know anything about Ridgeline Wilderness Health, please contact me. I'm trying to locate a teenager who has a family emergency.* Rox listed the Yahoo email address again, then reluctantly added her personal phone number. She could change it with her service provider afterward if she needed to. The plan was to post the little signs at the YMCA and at Carrie's fellowship. Rox scooped up the cards and a roll of masking tape, then stuck them all in her shoulder bag. Marty hadn't checked back in yet, but Isaac Lovejoy was still sitting in jail. If she needed her client's help with information or even pulling off a con job, Lovejoy couldn't do it from a locked cell.

Before heading out, Rox googled Common Community Fellowship and found two locations in Portland, with one only a mile from Carrie's home. The simple website listed all their services on the home page—including a Wednesday night meeting that started at seven. Rox let out a laugh. Attending this service, church or not, would be the strangest thing she'd done yet for a client—besides bailing him out of jail.

Chapter 8

After picking up the ten grand from her office safe, Rox stopped at the bank to deposit the bulk of it, then drove downtown to the Justice Center Public Desk. The office was open 24/7, except for three intermittent hours when the clerks took breaks. Rox arrived during the afternoon closure and had to wait twenty annoying minutes. Even though it was probably too soon, she used her phone to check for messages from her Craigslist posting. A guy named Brad had already sent an email, asking if she was lonely and needed a new friend. Rox rolled her eyes. How bored or desperate did you have to be to spend time trolling for suckers?

She paid Lovejoy's bail without complications, then briefly considered driving to the jail to offer him a ride home. But it could take hours for the system to process the payment and even more time for the deputies to release him. Rox headed to the YMCA instead. Posting her notice on their bulletin board was probably a waste of time, but she had to start somewhere. As she stepped out of her vehicle, the warmth of the day surprised her. Summer had finally kicked off in the Northwest, where you could only plan an outdoor wedding between mid-July and mid-August. But she spent all winter complaining about the cold, so she never complained about summer heat. Inside the building, she glanced over at the reception counter but didn't see Carrie. Rox grabbed a pushpin from the corkboard, posted her notice over the top of a tattered *Roommate Wanted* poster, and hurried back out.

As she walked to her car, she thought about the articles she'd read detailing the abuse in the wilderness programs, and new research ideas came to her. She could call the reporters who'd written the stories, hoping to get location information, and possibly track down people who'd filed lawsuits. No criminal charges had been pursued by authorities, but maybe a few parents had tried to seek justice another way. Would the camp's location be listed in the legal documents? Not likely. But the teenagers who'd been through the program had to know, in general, where they'd been. Or did the escorts blindfold the kids on the drive out to keep the location a secret? *Damn.* This could prove to be her most difficult case.

At home she turned on the AC, kicked off her shoes, and sat down with her laptop. She opened the most in-depth news story she'd bookmarked, which had briefly mentioned Ridgeline, and searched for the reporter's information. She finally found *Western Life's* Contact page buried three layers deep in the website, accessible only by a small icon in a bottom corner. This magazine really didn't want to hear from the public. She scrolled through the writers and editors, called Amber Quan's number, and got her voicemail. Rox left what she hoped was a compelling message: "This is Karina Jones, a private investigator. I'm searching for a teenager who was abducted and taken to the Ridgeline wilderness program. His father didn't give permission and thinks his son may be suicidal. I need your help finding the camp. Please call me back."

While searching for another article by the *Salt Lake Tribune,* which she'd apparently forgotten to bookmark, Rox stumbled on a lengthy NBC story she'd missed. The graphic details were hard to take and she had to skim through. Its main focus was the Tierra Blanca Ranch in New Mexico, which had been a house of horrors for young kids. After nearly a decade of complaints, federal authorities had finally been called in to investigate—because the local police had kept shielding the business and the money it brought in. The owner had fled and was still missing. Rage and disgust forced Rox to her feet. She paced the room, talking herself down. Her client's son was not at Tierra Blanca, but if she discovered that the Ridgeline staff was physically abusive, she would make it her personal mission to shut it down.

When she felt calmer, she sat back down and called the information desk at NBC to ask about the three reporters listed on the story. The first one was no longer employed there, and neither of the other two answered the transferred calls. Rox left them both a message similar to her earlier plea to Amber Quan.

Stomach growling, Rox went to the fridge and opened it, staring at the emptiness. For someone who liked food as much as she did, there was often little to eat in her house. Because she went through it so fast? Or because she hated to shop—for anything?

Her work phone rang in the other room, and Rox hurried to answer it, expecting the call to be from Isaac Lovejoy, thanking her for the bail money. But the number was unfamiliar. She picked up. "Karina Jones."

"Hello. This is Scott Goodwin. Are you a private investigator?"

"Yes." Rox hesitated. Should she tell him she was too busy to even hear about his case? No, this might be something simple Marty could work on—and she liked this guy's voice.

"How can I help you?"

"My nephew is missing. The police won't look for him because he's been in trouble and they consider him to be a young adult who chose to leave home voluntarily."

Missing people cases could be very time-consuming. But she had to ask, "How old is he?"

"Sixteen. His dad, my brother, died a few years back, and Tommy took it hard." A little catch in the man's deep voice. "He's been bouncing back and forth between his mother's house and mine, but three weeks ago we noticed that neither of us had seen him recently."

Another kid on the streets, probably using drugs to mask his grief. Rox had compassion for both him and his family, but it wasn't her kind of case. "I'm not sure I can help you. Even if I locate your nephew, chances are that if he left voluntarily, he won't come home."

"I realize that. But I want a chance to talk to him and convince him. I know I'll never find him on my own." It wouldn't be easy for her either. But she hated to turn this guy away. His pain and compassion were palpable. Before she could respond, he blurted out, "I don't think Tommy left voluntarily."

"What do you mean?"

"I think my sister-in-law might have sent him to one of those outdoor camps."

A tingle ran up Rox's spine, an experience she'd never had before. Was a correctional program targeting women in the Portland area with troubled sons? "What's the name of the outfit?"

"I'm not sure. Donna, my dead brother's wife—or widow, I should say—denies sending Tommy. But she talked about it once when he first started to skip school and stay out late."

"She has custody, correct?"

"Yes, but I was Tommy's stand-in father while my brother was stationed in Afghanistan for years. We're very close."

She couldn't do an extraction for a non-custodial parent or guardian, but she might be able to help him anyway. "I'm working another similar case now, so I'll consider yours." She needed more information before she decided how to handle this. "Do you have time to come to my office tomorrow?"

"Maybe on my lunch hour. Where are you located?"

"I'll text you the address." Rox hesitated, not sure what to request for a fee. It was a missing-person case, but she might get lucky and find Tommy when she found Josh. "I'll need a two-thousand-dollar retainer, against an hourly rate of two hundred." She paused, but he didn't react, so she added, "You could waste a lot of money paying me to search the streets for him."

"Will you check those wilderness programs first? I really think that's where he is."

"They're pretty secretive. And since you don't have custody, you have to accept that all I can do is locate him for you."

"I understand."

"We can make decisions about how much you want to spend as I go along." Rox heard Marty's familiar knock. "I'll text you my address and see you tomorrow at noon. Bring photos of Tommy, please."

"Can I just send one to your phone?"

"Sure."

"Thanks. I'll see you soon."

Rox hung up and turned to the front door. "Clear!"

Marty hustled into her side of the duplex. "I hope you're

hungry. I ordered Thai food and it will be here any minute." Marty snickered, knowing she was always hungry.

They sat at the kitchen table, and she let Marty face the door and window. He'd been a cop longer than she had. Rox gave him a look. "You should have asked me about dinner before ordering. I might have had a date."

He laughed again and she finally joined him. Her social life had been pretty quiet since she and Kyle had broken up.

"What did you find out about our client, Isaac Lovejoy?"

"His wife made a few 911 calls when they were still married, but she never pressed charges."

Damn. Was her client an abuser? "What were the calls about?"

"Nothing too serious, or he would have been arrested. The wife mostly complained about him threatening her." Marty got up, looked in the fridge, and grabbed a beer. "I talked to the last officer to respond to their house, and he said nobody had been hurt and that the wife wasn't very sympathetic."

A troubled but non-violent marriage. And considering that Carrie had supposedly cheated, all that seemed within reason. Rox relaxed a little. "Hey, you gonna share that with me?"

"Sure." Her stepdad poured half the microbrew into a glass and handed it to her. "What are you thinking?"

"I'll be curious to see what Josh has to say about his parents. Even if Lovejoy isn't a great dad, he still has the good sense to realize that a forced wilderness camp isn't how you handle troubled teenagers."

"What's your solution?" Marty's tone held a challenge.

Rox shook her head. "I don't have to have answers. I'm not a parent. But the more I read about those camps, the more sadistic they seem. And if Josh is suicidal, we have to extract him."

"I'm with you." Marty raised his beer.

Rox touched her glass to his. "Thanks, partner."

The doorbell rang, and Marty jumped up to pay for their take-out meal. A few minutes later, as he sat back down to eat, Rox told him about the new-client call.

"What the hell?" Marty scowled. "Is one of those programs targeting this area with advertisements?"

"That was my thought." An idea popped into her head and Rox snapped her fingers. "What if someone in the police bureau or juvenile-justice system is recommending the program to women with delinquent minors?"

Marty stopped chewing. "I'll make those calls tomorrow. I know someone over at juvie."

"The person giving the recommendations might be getting a kickback for every kid they send over."

Marty nodded. "It wouldn't be a first."

After they finished eating, Rox stood and announced, "I have church to attend."

Marty got a big laugh out of that. "Good luck. You gonna wear a dress?"

"Maybe."

"Something besides blue?"

"Maybe." Rox waved him off with her hand. "Go home. There's nothing to see here."

"I want a full report when you get back." Her stepdad cleared the table, then walked toward the door. He turned back at the last minute. "Don't go all puritan on me if you get converted." Marty winked and scurried out.

Chapter 9

Rox pulled her box of disguises out of the closet and set it on the bed. She'd recently bought a mousy brown, shoulder-length wig that would be perfect for this mission. The long, sexy blonde and the curly red were both inappropriate for blending into a religious group, or even a spiritual group. She pinned on the phony locks, glad she kept her own hair short, then added a pair of big glasses with dark rims. She decided the black pants she was wearing were fine, but she traded the sleeveless cobalt blouse for something in the same color that covered her bare arms. In this situation, the less attention she drew the better. But her height was hard to change or hide. She hoped it wouldn't matter. Rox scanned through the Fellowship website again, looking for themes or guidance, and found a couple of repetitive phrases she could use to sound like she fit in.

On the drive over, she listened to Al Green's classic soul to help her feel calm. In-person reconnaissance with a fake identity was the most challenging aspect of her job. Her natural impulse was to be bluntly honest—or so she'd been told. But the treatments had softened her, and she could sometimes tell little white lies to keep from hurting Marty's feelings. She was better about reading people too. With any luck, none of that would matter this evening.

Rox pulled into the school parking lot next to the Community Fellowship, dismayed that the white-panel building was only a single level and smaller than she'd expected. She had hoped the meeting would have enough of an attendance that she would go mostly unnoticed except by the people she spoke directly to. But on a Wednesday night, if there were thirty attendees, she would be surprised.

Sucking in a breath for courage, Rox strode inside, practicing her persona on the way. The oak-panel foyer was crowded with people chatting before the service. Just what she'd hoped for. An older woman turned to her. "Hello and welcome." She smiled brightly and offered her hand. "Elsie Danes."

Rox gave her hand a limp squeeze, and said quietly, "Jolene McAdams." Her sister would have been amused by the use of her name.

"Is this your first time here?" Elsie asked.

Rox nodded at the older gal. "Yes. I'm looking for some friendship and guidance."

Another woman moved toward them, younger and heavier and wearing too much perfume. "Then you're in the right place. Welcome. I'm Regina."

"Hello. And thank you."

"You're alone?" Regina got right to the point.

This was where it got sticky. She had to be convincing. "My husband died recently, and I'm raising our son alone." Less was better, she'd learned.

"I'm so sorry for your loss." Both fellowship women spoke at once.

Rox swallowed hard and made herself think about her dead sister.

"What's his name?"

Who? Oh right, her son. "Martin." She stuck to familiar names because they felt more real—and were easier to remember.

"He's welcome here too." Regina gave another big smile.

Rox sighed, then channeled what she'd heard recently from her newest client. "Marty's sixteen and acting out. His father's death was really hard on him."

"Of course. We'll pray for him."

"Thank you."

The main door opened, and Carrie Lovejoy walked in with a man about her own age. Rox started to turn her face away, then remembered she didn't need to. She forced herself to reach out and quickly touch Regina's arm. "You're being kind. But I've been praying and it's not enough. I think I need to send Marty away." She pulled in a deep breath. "As much as it breaks my heart."

"You poor thing." Regina put her arm around Rox's shoulders and squeezed.

Rox stiffened and pulled away, feeling guilty. But she couldn't handle that much contact with strangers!

Elsie reached out a wrinkled, vein-lined hand. "What did you have in mind? A military school?"

"No, I'm considering one of those wilderness camps. I've heard they're effective, but I don't know where to even start looking."

"I know just the person to help you." Elsie turned and called out, "Carrie!"

The blonde woman from the YMCA had stopped to chat with an older man. But now she turned to face them.

"Can you come over?" Elsie gestured with a waving motion.

The doors to the inner church opened, and a petite Latino woman welcomed the foyer crowd.

Time to work fast. She didn't want to sit through a

sermon—or lecture, or whatever they did here.

Elsie introduced her and Carrie, and they shook hands. Carrie nodded, but her eyes weren't smiling.

Elsie repeated what Rox had said about her fake son, then asked, "Can you help her with that, Carrie? Curtis told me you sent Josh to one of those camps."

The man who'd come in with Carrie stepped over. "I heard my name." About her height, Curtis had thin hair, a pudgy belly, and mean eyes. He stared at Rox. "You're new."

"Yes." She knew she should offer her hand but couldn't make herself.

"Curtis Fletcher, Carrie's fiancé." He smiled and his eyes softened. He put his arm around Carrie and Rox noticed his wristwatch. It looked like a Cartier diver's watch, but she couldn't be sure. If it was, the price tag was over ten grand.

"I'm Jolene."

"You're pretty tall. Pretty pretty too." Fletcher chuckled.

Jackass. Rox gave a small smile.

Carrie stepped between them. "I have to use the restroom before the service starts. Come with me and I'll tell you what I can."

Yes! Rox followed her down a dark hallway, wondering if Carrie was trying to get her away from Fletcher because she was insecure, or if the blonde wanted to get out of earshot of her fiancé before she talked about the camp. The distinction wasn't something Rox would have thought about before the magnets had altered her brain.

In the damp tile bathroom, Carrie kept her voice low. "I can't talk much about the program because I'm not supposed to, but I can give you the name and you can use me as a reference."

"Thank you."

"It's Ridgeline Wilderness Health. The number is on their website."

Rox reached into her shoulder bag, pretending to look for a pen. "Why do I need a reference?"

"Oh, it's just a way of making sure they attract the right people. But I think they need all the business they can get." Carrie's cheeks flushed a little.

What was that about? "So what does the program cost?"

"Three hundred a day."

"Whoa."

"Yeah, I know." Carrie rolled her big blue eyes. "But it's worth it. Drug treatment is even more expensive."

"Where is the camp? Would I have to drive Marty up there?"

The blonde woman turned to the big mirror to check her lipstick. "They have programs in both central Oregon and northern Nevada. They started out in Utah, then had to relocate because the state passed a bunch of laws about how they could operate."

Running from regulation. Not a good sign. "How do I get there?" *Was that too direct?*

"You don't. They come pick up your kid. The camp moves around, and nobody is allowed to know the location."

Damn! "Why so secretive?"

"They've had some trouble." Carrie spun back. "You can't repeat any of this when you call Ridgeline. Let them tell you what you need to know."

Another woman entered the small space, and Carrie stepped toward one of the two stalls. "I really do have to pee. Good luck with your son." She stepped inside and the latch clicked.

Rox turned to walk out and spotted Carrie's purse sitting

on the counter. Her phone stuck out of an exterior pocket. The stranger moved toward the second stall, and Rox opened the door to exit the bathroom. *What if Carrie's phone held the information she needed?* She only had to borrow it for a few minutes, do a quick search, then return it. Or maybe leave it somewhere in the church. Rox's heart missed a beat. She'd never done anything quite like it before, and her years spent as a police officer tried to override the idea. But her time with the CIA had given her a more flexible view of legality and morality.

With two quiet steps, she reached the sink counter and grabbed the phone. Rox slipped it into her own bag and quickly left the bathroom. *What now?* As much as she wanted to exit the building, she feared it would look suspicious to ask questions about the correctional program, then disappear. Plus, she had to return Carrie's phone. Rox hurried down the hall, crossed the now-empty foyer, and opened a door on the other side. She planned to sit through the service just for show, but she wanted to be the last one inside.

In the smaller room, three young kids played with Legos in the middle of the floor while a teenage girl read something on her phone. *A daycare center.* The girl looked up. "Hey. Are you looking for someone?"

"No, I'm new here and wasn't sure where the prayer meeting was."

"That's in the main sanctuary."

"Oh, it looked like a service was starting." Rox was stalling.

"Yeah, it's like that. Labella talks about how to be a good person, then they do lots of praying. And hand-holding." The girl sounded bored.

"Do you know the topic for tonight?" *As if she cared.*

"No. But I'm sure it's about love and tolerance." She gave Rox an odd smile. "Or giving money."

"What's your name?" Still stalling.

"Rebecca." The girl's eyes narrowed. "The service is starting."

"You're right." Rox scrambled for something that might engage Rebecca. What were young girls interested in besides phones? *Oh right.* Rox remembered that she had a fake teenage boy. "I was going to bring my son to the fellowship, but he was worried he wouldn't know anyone. Now I can tell him I met a pretty young girl I can introduce him to."

Rebecca lowered her voice. "I'm not into guys, but don't tell anyone in the group or they'll send me to a conversion camp."

Was that a different program than the behavior correction? Was it part of Ridgeline? Carrie had mentioned several locations. "I'll keep your secret. I don't support those programs."

"No one should."

Rox wanted to ask more questions but didn't want to push her luck.

Rebecca glanced over at the kids. "You really should go. I'm not supposed to have anyone in here."

"All right. Nice meeting you." Rox stepped out and didn't see anyone in the foyer. She crossed it, pushed open one of the sanctuary's swinging doors, and slipped into the empty back pew. Elsie, who was seated on the inside aisle near the front, glanced back at her. Rox smiled, hoping she didn't have a guilty look on her face. She glanced around the high-ceiling room, which was bathed in an eerie glow from a row of stained-glass windows. The light reminded her that the summer sun was still bright out there. And that she would rather be anywhere else. Even home, mowing the lawn.

Focus! A quick count indicated thirty-three people were in attendance.

After searching the room, she finally spotted Carrie and her fiancé on the left, in a pew about halfway back from the podium. The blonde woman didn't seem agitated and wasn't searching her purse. Rox's shoulders relaxed and she pulled out the pilfered phone. She pressed the home key and the screen lit up. No password. More good news. Rox hit the Call Log icon and started scrolling through outgoing calls, checking for out-of-state area codes. With cell phones, locations were almost meaningless, so this could be a waste of time. But if she spotted a 700 number, it would likely be Northern Nevada. A 503 code could be Oregon. Carrie had indicated the program originated in Utah, and the office could still be there—even if the camps were conducted elsewhere. Technically, the Ridgeline administrative office could be anywhere. They didn't deal with walk-in customers, and their main business was conducted in the wild. They could even be operating out of someone's home. Rox made a mental note to call business offices in all three states, looking for registered owners.

Wanting to look attentive, Rox kept glancing up at the preacher, who seemed to be talking about jealousy. *Weird.* As she scanned back two weeks in Carrie's log, Rox noted two calls to an east coast number, and the digits locked into her memory, even though she didn't think they were important. After another five minutes, she came across an 801 area code. That was Salt Lake City. A very good possibility. Rox processed the phone number and continued scanning, glancing up every few seconds. She worried that someone—a deacon or usher or whatever—would notice her activity and ask her to stop . . . or leave.

An out-of-state incoming call caught her attention. A 775 area code. Reno, Nevada. That could be the camp director. Or the transport service. Rox committed the number to memory. Footsteps in the aisle made her look up. A white-haired man slid into the pew and sat a few feet from her. Rox slipped the stolen phone back into her shoulder bag. While she waited for the service to end, she worked through several options. She could walk up to Carrie to say goodbye, then attempt to slip the phone into her purse. Risky. Or she could come up behind the woman and be stealthy about putting it back. Also a little iffy. Rox's favorite choice was to put the phone on the floor, and when everyone got up to leave, kick it hard enough to slide all the way up to where Carrie sat.

Rox had never worked as a field operator when she was with the CIA—only as an analyst who rarely left her desk. She'd been exceptional at scanning data and recognizing patterns or inconsistencies. But her atypical brain had kept the CIA from giving her covert work. She was getting better at it now because the extractions required it. The treatments were helping too. But this fellowship crowd seemed fairly tuned into her, and she didn't think she could pull off a reverse pickpocket.

Suddenly, the attendees were on their feet and grabbing each other's hands. The old man next to her reached out and Rox was too stunned to resist. The Latina preacher started praying in a loud voice, and the congregation joined her in a recital. A few people eased out of the pews and headed for the exit. *Oh hell.* It was too late to kick the phone under the pews. Rox tried not to panic. She'd learned some solid intel, and now she just needed to keep from blowing her cover.

Get out! Rox gave into the impulse. She smiled at the old

guy, pulled her hand free, and bolted from the building. If it seemed safe, she would drop Carrie's cell phone in the parking lot as she jogged to her car.

Chapter 10

Thursday, July 6, 10:15 a.m.

After her morning routine, Rox poured a second cup of coffee and tried to decide which call to make first. Now that she had Carrie's permission to use her for a reference, it made sense to call the Ridgeline office again. If she could convince them she was a potential client, she might gain all the information she needed to extract Josh—without another effort like her nerve-wracking church visit the night before. She'd been able to drop Carrie's phone without anyone noticing—or at least not calling out to her—but the whole episode had been clumsy. Plus, Carrie might not have found her phone yet or had it returned, so she might suspect the church newcomer of being a thief. If that was the case, Rox couldn't use that ID again or do any follow-up. *Oh well.* She'd probably exhausted that line of information anyway.

Rox clicked on her laptop to find the Ridgeline website, then dialed the 800 number from memory. The same voicemail message played and Rox launched into her spiel. "This is Jolene McAdams again. I left a message yesterday, then realized I forgot to tell you about my referral. Carrie Lovejoy told me about your program at our fellowship. I'm eager to get my son Martin on the right track again. Please call me."

Rox worked through how her pretense might play out. She suspected they would want money up front and would only take a credit card. She could spend her client's money on the deposit, but what card to use? Her business card listed K.J. Investigations. That would be a red flag. If she used her personal credit card, the admin office might be suspicious that it didn't match the name she'd given. What if she used Marty's card? She could say her father-in-law or uncle was paying for the program. Relieved, Rox moved to the next step. Would they ask about her son and his problems? Or make her fill out a questionnaire? How the hell would she get them to divulge the location of the camp? Or even the office?

Rox walked out to the back patio, and while she watered the flowers Marty had planted, she called to cancel her treatment on Thursday. She had too much going on to spend the time this week. Her focus returned to Ridgeline. There had to be a way to trace the call back to their office location. If all else failed, she would call her buddy at the CIA and see if he could help. But without blatant criminal activity to report, she hated to waste his time. Then it hit her. When the payment processed against Marty's credit card, the Ridgeline name and phone number would be listed with his bank. Maybe even an address. Meanwhile, she still had a list of calls to make, including the business registries in Utah, Nevada, and possibly Oregon.

She hurried back inside and called the Nevada number she'd seen in Carrie's phone the night before. It went straight to voicemail: "This is RWH Transport. Leave your name and phone number."

Score! Rox said, "Sorry, wrong number" and hung up the phone.

RWH likely meant Ridgeline Wilderness Health, and this was their transport service. Unless they were using a ported cell phone number, the administrative office was likely in

Reno. But Carrie had said Ridgeline operated a camp in Central Oregon. It didn't make sense to send vans from Nevada to pick up kids for an Oregon camp, so they probably had service operations in both states. If she could find the local office, she could stake it out and follow a vehicle until it took her to the camping area. *In theory.* She had no idea how often they transported teenagers. Or how many camps they serviced. Or which one Josh had been taken to. But she felt encouraged. Piece by piece, she would figure this out and bring the poor boy home. The hardest part for her would be leaving all the other teenagers to tough it out. But if the situation was obviously abusive, she could send authorities back to the camp to make arrests and rescue the detainees. Because that's what they were. Young adults held captive and forced to participate in activities they probably despised.

A glance at the time made Rox jump up. She had a meeting with Scott Goodwin, the new client who had a missing nephew. *Potential new client.* She wouldn't make up her mind until she'd met with him. The only reason she considered helping him while she was already working a difficult case was the possible connection to the same wilderness program. Rox dropped both of her cell phones into her shoulder bag and headed out.

On the drive to her office, she wondered again about the possibility that Ridgeline was targeting the Portland area. That seemed like a broad marketing approach, but maybe they only focused on certain groups, like churches and other social communities, where people influenced each other. She would ask Goodwin about his connections when she saw him. Or more accurately, she wanted to know about his nephew's mother, the person who might have sent him to the program.

Impulsively, Rox called Bowman again and had to leave

another message: "Hey, it's Rox. Do you know anything about Ridgeline Wilderness Health? It's a correctional camp for teenagers. They operate out of Nevada but they have a camp in Central Oregon, and I think they're targeting Portland for clients. Let me know."

Eager to get the information, she called a more familiar number. She and her ex-boyfriend hadn't spoken since their breakup—right after she started the treatments. He hadn't liked the changes in her personality, but she hadn't wanted to give up the therapy. The magnets were her one chance to experience emotions and perceptions the way other people did. Even if the effect didn't last, she still wanted the insight—both as a person and as an investigator.

Kyle, who worked as a homicide detective for the Portland Police Bureau, answered quickly. "Rox, so good to hear from you."

She was obviously still in his Contact list. "How have you been?"

"Busy, as always, but good."

"Are you dating?" *Shit.* She hadn't meant to ask that, but the question had come into her mind, then popped out of her mouth. Were the treatments wearing off already?

"I've been out with a few women, but nothing serious. What about you?"

"Still tall and awkward, so not many dates here either." Rox laughed, suddenly nervous. "I'm busy too. The cases just keep coming. When I started this business, I thought the extractions would be more occasional." She had dated Detective Kyle Wilson long enough to trust him with incriminating information about herself. She still trusted him.

"It's a great gig for you and a much-needed service." He paused. "Just stay safe, please."

"I try." Rox took the 213 exit and headed north. "Speaking of cases . . . I'm working one that involves a correctional program called Ridgeline Wilderness Health. I think they operate out of Nevada, but they seem to be pulling clients from Portland right now. Have you heard anything about the business? Any public complaints?"

"No, but those issues wouldn't come to my department. I can ask around though."

"Thanks." Rox wanted to keep the conversation going. She'd missed him. "It's been eye-opening researching these programs. Many of them are horribly abusive."

"That's what your case is about? You're planning to extract a kid out of a wilderness camp?" Kyle sounded skeptical.

Rox hesitated, resenting his tone a little. "Maybe."

"Take Marty with you and be prepared for anything."

Yes, sir. Rox smiled to herself. Kyle still cared about her. "I will. But I highly doubt any of the employees carry weapons. Some of them may be sadists, but since they deal with minors, if they were armed, they would have been shut down already."

A long pause, then finally Kyle asked, "Would you like to have dinner with me sometime?"

Startled, Rox took a moment to respond. "That sounds nice, but I should think about it. I still have a few treatments left."

"Okay. But the offer stands."

"Thanks. We'll talk again soon." She hoped he would call back with information about her case—and another dinner offer. She really wanted to see him. A little sex would help take the edge off her stress too.

At her office, she turned on her computer and googled the phrase *Scott Goodwin Portland*. She found a profile on LinkedIn and a brief news article in the business section of the *Oregonian*. Goodwin's photo surprised her. A stunningly good-looking man. Thick dark hair, a classic nose, and a strong jaw. Rox tried to guess his nationality. Greek maybe? Was he single? He hadn't mentioned a wife or girlfriend when they'd talked the day before. Rox checked his LinkedIn status. Yes, indeed, he was single. She wondered if his body was as nice as his face.

She tapped her own cheek. "Focus!"

The news brief referred to Goodwin as an *entrepreneur with holdings in real estate, restaurants, and entertainment.* Rox checked the clock. Did she have time to run a background check before he arrived? No, but she would do it soon, maybe as they talked. She heard a car engine and spun toward the monitor for the parking lot. A new silver BMW rolled into the front space and a tall man climbed out. Six-five, she guessed. Nice. Not many men were her size. Kyle was six-two, but if she wore heels they were the same height.

Scott Goodwin walked to the front door, and Rox shifted her eyes to the lobby monitor. "Hello, this is Karina Jones." A strange worry surfaced. If they dated, she would have to tell him her real name.

"Hi. Scott Goodwin here." He glanced at the monitor on the outer desk with an amused expression. "This is a little more cloak-and-dagger than I expected."

"I'm sorry, but I protect myself when I take extraction cases—for good reasons."

"I understand." He took a seat, and she noticed the tight fit of his sports pullover.

"But since I won't be doing an extraction for you, we

might be able to dispense with this process."

"I hope so." Goodwin smiled, and he was beautiful.

Rox checked herself. "But I haven't decided about your case yet. I need to know why you think your nephew might be in a correctional program."

"Donna, my ex-sister-in-law, talked about it one time when I picked up Tommy. She was really upset about his behavior and ranting about solutions. She mentioned military camp and wilderness camp."

"When was this?"

He scrunched his forehead, hesitating. "About six weeks ago."

"Did she mention a specific program?"

"I've been thinking about that, and I believe she said something about Rockridge."

"Could it have been Ridgeline?"

He nodded. "Yeah, that sounds right."

A good reason to take the case. "Did she mention where or how she'd heard of the program?"

"No, but it was probably her church. Donna is pretty focused on it. That's part of why Tommy keeps coming to stay with me."

Another tingle, this one on the back of her neck. "What church?"

"Common Community Fellowship. She says it's not really a church, but it is. She attends the one on Centennial."

So Ridgeline was targeting at least one social organization. A thought struck her. Maybe the fellowship owned or sponsored the program. That would mesh with what the girl in the daycare had said about the gay-conversion camp. Those programs were always religious. Yet wilderness camps weren't. Rox shook off the idea for now.

She needed to be open-minded and keep researching, especially the business' background.

"What's wrong?" Goodwin asked.

"Nothing." She shifted gears. This was a missing-person case and she needed to think like a cop. "When did you last see your nephew?"

"It was a Sunday. Tommy had spent the weekend with me, and I dropped him at his mother's after dinner. I was supposed to see him again the next week, but he stopped taking my calls, and his mom eventually told me he'd run away."

Something about this was off. "Why would his mother not want you to know she'd sent him to a behavior camp? She has custody, correct?"

"Donna knew I hated the idea. I expressed that when she mentioned it." Goodwin's lovely face flashed with pain. "I think she's been drinking heavy since Greg was killed in action. She's not herself. I've tried to help her, including paying for a lot of my nephew's expenses, so Donna doesn't want to alienate me." Goodwin pulled his shoulders back, and his eyes pinched with grief. "I think she also resents me. Just because I'm alive and Greg is dead."

Weird. But it also made sense in a stage-of-grief process. "Would you give me Donna's number? I'd like to talk to her." Rox waited while he looked in his phone. She would also speak with someone in the police department who handled missing-persons cases and see what territory had been covered. Tommy might simply be a runaway.

Scott Goodwin kept staring at his phone, his shoulders slumped. When he looked up, his eyes were blurred with tears and he seemed devastated. "I miss my brother so much. And now I feel like I've failed Tommy."

Rox's heart ached for him. Impulsively, she hurried into the foyer and put a hand on his shoulder. "I'm sorry for your loss. I'll find your nephew if I can."

Goodwin patted her hand, still on his shoulder. "Thank you."

After a moment, he straightened his posture. "You mentioned a retainer, so I brought the two thousand." He reached for his wallet.

"I can't promise to find him. And since you don't have custody, I can't physically bring him to you if I do. But I'll do my best to reunite the two of you." Rox reluctantly reached for the cash he offered, then tried to reassure him. "I'm pretty good at this kind of thing."

"I believe you." Goodwin gave her another of his beautiful smiles. "Do we sign any paperwork?"

"Only if you want to." Some non-extraction clients insisted on it, but many preferred not to document their own actions, which were often about spying on someone else.

"No, I trust you." Her client stood. "I should get back to the office."

"Text me Donna's number when you have a moment."

"Okay." He reached out with both hands and squeezed one of hers. "Thank you."

After Goodwin left, Rox hurried into her office and stuck the money into the safe. She might need it later to bribe a few people. Once she'd found his nephew, or given up trying, she would ask Goodwin out to dinner. Kyle didn't seem to like her new personality and she was tired of being lonely.

Chapter 11

Thursday, July 6, 11:55 a.m.

Marty walked into the restaurant and instantly felt uncomfortable. High ceilings with exposed ducting and minimalistic decor were trendy now, but he preferred a cozier dining space with a landscape painting or two. He glanced around. No vinyl-and-formica booths either. Just plain black tables with hard metal chairs. *Sheesh.* Why was austerity the cool thing now?

A young hostess with bright-pink hair greeted him. "Just one for lunch?"

Did he look too grumpy to have a friend? Marty tried to smile. "Someone is joining me. An old guy in uniform."

The girl looked perplexed but led him to a table in the interior. Every seat by the windows was taken except one near the door to the kitchen. Marty asked to sit there. The hostess gave a polite smile and led him over without a word. No points to her for friendliness. Still, he needed information. "Do you like working here?" he asked as he took his seat.

"Sure. Why?" Another confused look on her pretty face.

"I'm just wondering what you think of your boss, Isaac Lovejoy. I'm considering him for a partnership."

"I don't know. I just started last week." She walked away.

Well, hell. This could be a waste of time. There'd better be something decent on the menu. He opened it, relieved to see a list of tasty sandwiches and microbrews. The stack of huge round drums against the rear wall indicated they made beer on the premises.

The front door opened, and he looked up to see Bowman enter and head straight for him, duck-walking like always. His old partner was short and muscular but did the uniform proud by not carrying much of a gut. They were alike that way. But Bowman was bald—except for a wedge of salt-and-pepper hair at the base of his skull.

He plunked down in the chair facing the window. "What's up with this place? It's not really our style." As beat cops, they'd eaten a lot of pastrami sandwiches at Sam's Deli and even more burgers at Heavy Chevy's.

"It's research for a case Rox and I are working," Marty explained with an apology. "Our new client is the chef and co-owner. It seemed wise to check it out. I want to see what his employees think of him."

Bowman grabbed his menu. "They'd better have a cheeseburger or pattymelt."

Marty laughed. His ex-partner was even more of an old crank than he was. "The sandwich list looks good. Beer too."

Bowman grunted. "I'm on duty."

Marty decided not to drink in front of him and planned to buy a six-pack of microbrews to take home. He and Rox were both out, and it was too damn hot to go without beer. "I'm having the Volcano burger." The description included horseradish-cheddar cheese and jalapenos.

"Not me. My ulcer is getting worse."

Marty shook his head. "See a doctor. Get that test for bacteria. It could be an easy fix."

"Yeah, soon." Bowman gave an exaggerated wink.

Marty laughed. If he hadn't had a mild heart attack—which Rox still didn't know about—he wouldn't have been to a doctor lately either. Or discovered the heart disease. But the incident had happened during sex with his previous girlfriend, and he couldn't bring himself to tell his daughter the specifics. He was also afraid to try getting naked again. The new woman he was dating was being patient, but he had to face the situation eventually. Or stay home and be lonely. He'd done that for decades while he raised his girls and nursed his wounds. Georgia's abandonment had broken him. He'd never really faced it until he'd retired and didn't have his job to keep him occupied. He'd also never told Rox that her mother had left partly because she couldn't relate to her quirky daughter.

"How's your heart?" Bowman knew about his diagnosis, but not the heart attack.

Marty had never told anyone. "I'm fine . . . for a dying man."

A server walked up. The skinny young guy wore pants that fit like a glove. "Hi. Do you have questions or are you ready?"

They gave their orders, both adding black coffee, and the waiter started to walk away. "Hey," Marty called out. "I have a question."

The server turned back. "What's that?"

"What do you think of the owner, Isaac Lovejoy?"

The kid smiled. "He's great. Why?"

"I'm considering him for a business venture, and I need to know how he treats his employees."

"He's respectful and fair. We don't get benefits, but that's typical for restaurant work."

Marty signaled for the server to step closer and lowered his voice. "What do you know about his ex-wife? Is she going to be a problem? I've heard rumors." Marty needed to find out if the restraining order she'd filed had good cause. He and Rox couldn't deliver a kid from one abusive situation to another.

"Carrie used to work here as a manager, and I never liked her." The server didn't bother to be discreet with his voice. "But I don't think she's involved in Isaac's life anymore."

"What was their relationship like? Did they fight?"

"Not here at the restaurant. Except at the end when they were splitting up."

Marty pushed his luck. "Did he get physical with her?"

The waiter's eyes narrowed. "Why do you ask? I thought this was about a business deal."

"It is. I need to know who I'm dealing with."

The skinny server stared at him for a long moment. "What's your name? I'll tell Isaac you're here." He obviously felt protective of his employer.

"Please don't. I need to be able to conduct due diligence."

"Okay." The guy walked away.

Bowman gave Marty a peculiar look. "What's the deal with this case? Rox called me too. She wants to know about a wilderness program called Ridgeline."

"Our client's ex-wife sent their kid to one of those correctional camps. The dad thinks his son might be suicidal and wants to get him out."

Bowman lowered his voice. "You're going to assist her?"

Marty nodded. "If we can find it."

"I wish I could help, but I've never heard of it, and the few officers I've talked to don't know anything either."

"The program seems to be secretive, which is not a good sign."

A waitress walking by suddenly spun toward the center of the room.

Marty heard fast-moving footsteps and turned in the same direction. Two men in dark suits hustled through the restaurant toward the back. One was Kyle Wilson, a homicide detective and Rox's ex-boyfriend. *What the hell?*

Marty jumped up. "I have to check this out."

Bowman stood too, and they followed the detectives into the kitchen. The noise and chaos of prep cooks and servers putting out lunch didn't deter the cops. They strode up to a tall man in a white chef's hat.

"Isaac Lovejoy?"

"Yes. What's going on?" The guy looked alarmed, and everyone in the kitchen had stopped to stare.

Detective Wilson stepped toward Lovejoy and grabbed his arm. "We need to ask you some questions about the murder of your ex-wife."

Chapter 12

After meeting with Goodwin, Rox headed home and ate a PBJ for lunch, feeling too busy to make anything else. She checked her task list to see where she'd left off, then called the Salt Lake City number she'd memorized from Carrie's phone. After a few rings, she heard the same canned message that had played when she called the number from Ridgeline's website. *Odd!* She hung up without leaving another message. Maybe the business used an office system that allowed outgoing calls on several numbers, yet when you redialed them, the call routed to a central receptionist or message line. She hated those.

The lunch carbs had made her sleepy so she headed for the couch to lie down for a moment. Her phone rang and she glanced at the screen. No caller ID appeared but the digits seemed familiar. Part of it matched the 800 number on the Ridgeline website! They were finally calling her back. Time to get real. She took a moment to practice her background spiel. *Jolene McAdams. A troubled son named Martin with a dead father.* She could do this. "Hello."

"Is this Jolene McAdams?"

"Yes."

"This is Ruth from Ridgeline Wilderness Health, returning your call. Are you still interested in our wilderness therapy program for your son?" The woman sounded middle-aged and professional.

"Yes, thank you for calling back."

"The first step is to fill out an application. We have some essay-type questions, so it will take some time. Are you comfortable with that?"

"Uh, sure." Rox didn't enjoy writing essays, but it was probably better than trying to get through an interview.

"Don't worry. It's worth your time. This is a great program."

"Where do I get the application?"

"I'll send you a link. What's your email address?"

Rox gave her the Yahoo account. "I'd like to get going on this right away. Martin has started skipping school, and half the time I don't know where he is."

"I'm sending the link right now." Ruth made a clicking noise with her tongue. "Before I collect a deposit, I need to read you our policy statement."

They wanted money before she even applied? "How much is the fee? And what happens if my application is rejected?"

The administrator chuckled softly. "Since you have a referral, you're not likely to be rejected. We want to help people. But if for some reason that happens, you'll get the money back."

"How much?" Rox needed details.

"Three thousand. That covers the first ten days of the program."

Rox hesitated—like any sane parent would. "Okay."

"This is our policy." Ruth sounded less sure of herself. "Ridgeline transports its students from their homes to the base. Let us know in the questionnaire if your child will come willingly. If not, we'll plan for a strong-arm pickup. Your child is allowed to bring the clothes on his or her back. Nothing else. You will not be given information about the location of the base camp or the routes of the hiking trips. If there's a family emergency, you can call this number and we'll get word to the camp. Your child will be escorted back to you, at your expense."

Damn. They were secretive!

Ruth continued, "Students aren't allowed to quit unless they have a serious medical condition. Your child will not be returned to you until he or she graduates the program or you stop paying."

Students? What a euphemism. "That seems a little excessive."

"We've discovered what works best, and we know that parents can sometimes be enablers." Ruth sounded confident again.

"Will I be able to visit Martin?"

"After your child passes Phase Two, visitations can be arranged at the base camp, but we don't encourage them.

"But you said I couldn't know the location."

"For the first few months, it's important that you aren't able to pick up your son and help him quit—should he find a way to contact you. Once he passes important milestones, he may be ready for a visit, but again, we don't encourage them."

"I understand." Rox needed to find a parent who'd been to the base camp. But the program might have changed locations. It had moved its camps out of Utah, so maybe that was a pattern. Rox's laptop made a dinging sound, so she opened the new email and clicked the top link. A PDF application opened in a new tab. "Should I start filling out this form?"

"Yes. Then upload it to the second link in the email."

"How soon does all this happen?"

"As quickly as you would like it to. So get started on the

questionnaire."

Rox had a dozen more questions, but Ruth wasn't likely to answer any. "Can I call you if I'm not sure about something in the form?"

"Just dial the main number, and I'll get back to you."

No direct contact. What a racket. "Thanks for your help."

"Do you have a credit card handy? We prefer to take the deposit up front."

Rox reached for Marty's card, which she'd borrowed the day before, soon after realizing she would need it. "Here's the number." She read it out loud, wondering if Marty's name would come up in their system. If they asked, he was her father-in-law and had agreed to pay for his grandson's therapy.

"I'll email you a receipt. Get the application uploaded, and we'll proceed." Ruth chuckled softly again. "Assuming there are no red flags."

"Like what?"

"Serious mental illness is the big one. Our counselors are not trained to deal with that."

"No. Martin is just grieving and angry and acting out."

"We can help him. Thanks for trusting Ridgeline." Ruth hung up.

What a bullshit line. Rox clenched her fists. She'd just spent three grand of Marty's money and had learned almost nothing. Still, her communication with the program's office was the most direct line to real information. She just had to devise a way to get Ruth to let location details slip.

Rox grabbed a diet soda from the fridge and started the application. After filling in the standard demographic and contact information, she listed *self-employed bookkeeper* as her occupation. It seemed innocuous yet difficult to check out.

For religious affiliation, she named the Common Community Fellowship. But the essay questions about her child's behavior and her parenting style stumped her, and she had to search online for ideas. She pasted in copied phrases about *loss of privileges*, *accountability*, and *open communication*.

Forty minutes and much irritation later, she uploaded the document. Apprehension immediately set in. What if they accepted it, as Ruth had implied they would? The next step was for the transport people to pick up her son. Which would be an ideal way to find the camp—if she actually had a teenager named Martin. Could she hire someone to play the part and let himself be abducted and driven into the woods? Maybe an eager young actor would take the job as an experience to draw from.

Rox's phone rang, and she saw that she'd missed two calls from her stepdad. She grabbed it and headed for the kitchen. "Hey, Marty, what's up?"

"Kyle just picked up Isaac Lovejoy for questioning in his ex-wife's murder."

What the hell? "Carrie Lovejoy is dead? When?"

"I don't know about the time, but the department obviously thinks Lovejoy is the perp. I was having lunch at his restaurant and watched them cuff him." A horn started honking in the background, and Marty shouted over it. "I'm headed home now, but I should be able to get more information after he's been questioned."

This was bizarre. She'd never had a client arrested before, let alone twice . . . and for murder. She wanted to believe Lovejoy hadn't done it, but she could see why he looked guilty. He was plenty mad at his ex. "What have they got on him?"

"I don't know. Kyle brushed me off at the restaurant.

Bowman is going to see what he can dig up."

"Any details about Carrie's death?"

"Not yet."

"Stop over when you get home. We need to brainstorm."

While Rox waited for Marty, she called Kyle, knowing he wouldn't answer. He was probably in a small windowless room conducting an interrogation with Lovejoy. She left a message asking for a return courtesy call about her client. If Kyle wanted them to start dating again, he would get back to her. She might as well work that angle. Did Isaac Lovejoy have a defense lawyer to protect him from aggressive questioning? None of it was really her concern, but she felt strangely responsible. Especially for poor Josh. His mother was dead and his father was suspected of murder. She had to get the boy out of the camp one way or another. If Carrie had paid in advance, Josh could be stuck there for months.

Rox was standing in the kitchen eating a mouthful of leftover lasagna when she heard Marty knock. Without waiting for her to respond, he walked in carrying a six-pack. Marty hustled into the kitchen, sweat shining on his brow. "Beer? It's damn hot out there."

"Of course." She had the air conditioning on, so she skipped her usual offer to head out to the back deck. Rox reached for the brew her stepdad held out and sat down at the small table. "Tell me exactly what happened."

"There's not much to tell. I saw Kyle and another detective, Crider, I think, walk into the kitchen at the Steelhead Bistro. I followed them and heard Kyle say he wanted to ask Lovejoy questions about his ex-wife's murder. They cuffed him and walked him out—right in the middle of lunch hour." Marty took a long drink of dark ale, then let out a loud "Ahhh!"

Another of his annoying habits she ignored. "You said Kyle brushed you off. What does that mean?"

"Just like it sounds. I tried to get him to step aside and give me some information, and he waved me off."

She could see Marty's disappointment. Or was that hurt feelings? She still wasn't an expert at facial expressions. "I'm sure it's because the arrest was in a public place."

"I know. Hopefully Bowman will call soon with a few details." Marty leaned forward. "How did it go at the church last night? Did you actually see Carrie?"

"I talked to her and learned a few things."

"Like what?" Marty cut in.

"She confirmed that she'd sent Josh to Ridgeline and said it had camps in northern Nevada and Oregon. Apparently, they used to operate out of Utah, but they had to move because the state cracked down on those programs."

"A sign that they're probably not ethical." Marty made a face.

Disgust?

Her stepdad continued, "I was doing some reading online and discovered that a lot of those programs have closed because of problems that led to bad publicity and reduced demand."

"It's surprising that anyone still sends their kids." Rox needed to tell him about finding the Nevada transport office number, but she was a little worried about his reaction to her cell phone caper.

"What are you not telling me?"

Marty was good at reading people—and she was still terrible at masking her emotions.

Rox plunged in. "I had an opportunity to take Carrie's

phone so I did. I scanned it for out-of-state calls, then gave it back. Sort of." Rox gave a don't-be-mad grin. "I found the number to a transport office in Reno. If we can con them into telling us where the local vans are, we can follow a driver to the camp."

Marty rolled his eyes. "I don't even want to know what *sort of returned it* means." He suddenly looked worried. "Please tell me you masked your identity."

"Of course."

He took another long drink of beer, then swore. "Now that Carrie's dead, the missing phone could become a big deal in the homicide investigation."

Rox swallowed hard. She hadn't thought of that. "Let's just be glad Kyle is handling it."

"You got lucky there." Marty stood and put his empty bottle in the recycling. "As bad as this is for the kid, having his mother die will get him sprung from the camp. We shouldn't have to do an extraction."

Rox was less sure. "They don't let kids quit. And if the police hold our client in jail, who's going to contact the camp and tell them Carrie's dead?"

"Lovejoy's lawyer?"

"He may not have one." Rox got up and paced the small dining room. "Ridgeline is secretive and hard to contact, but I talked to an office person this morning. Then I filled out an application for my son Martin." She turned to her stepdad with another grin. "I can't call the office about Carrie's death because the administrator might recognize my voice. So you'll have to."

Marty shrugged. "Let's wait and see what happens with Lovejoy. He may be released and be able to handle this himself."

"Call Bowman. We need to know what they have on our client."

"He said he would get back to me."

Rox had another dark thought. "What if the camp won't release Josh because he has no custodial parents to release him to?"

Marty heaved a sigh. "What a mess."

Rox finished her ale, processing several possibilities. "Ridgeline is in the business to make money, and it's unlikely Carrie paid much in advance. They won't keep Josh if no one is footing the bill."

"What about the fiancé? He might have some say in all of this."

An image of him flashed in her mind. "I met Curtis Fletcher last night. He gave me the creeps."

"I'll check him out." Marty's phone rang in his shirt pocket and he grabbed it. "Bowman." He set the cell on the table and put it on speaker. "Hey, partner. What have you got for us?"

"Rox is there?"

She leaned in. "Yes. Thanks for helping."

"Don't get your expectations too high. Here's all I know. Carrie Lovejoy left a prayer meeting last night to go home and pick up some stuff before going to stay with her boyfriend. Instead, she ended up strangled in her SUV, which was parked behind a tavern. A bartender noticed the vehicle and found her dead around two in the morning."

"They questioned Fletcher, her fiancé?" Rox asked.

"Extensively. Fletcher said he left the same meeting and stopped to see his mom on the way home. His mother claims he stayed several hours to help with a computer problem. And Fletcher texted his girlfriend several times to let her know he would be late, but she didn't respond." Bowman's volume faded, as though he had moved his phone. "They won't have an exact time of death until the autopsy is completed, but Crider says the victim had been dead for a couple of hours when they arrived at the scene. Fletcher also pushed the detectives to question Isaac Lovejoy, because of some recent altercation."

"Thanks." Rox glanced over at Marty.

Her stepdad picked up the phone. "What do they have on her ex?"

"I'm not sure," Bowman said, sounding impatient.

"Let me know if you find out." Marty hung up and slipped the phone back in his pocket.

Rox felt a tightness in her lungs. "I wish I'd never bailed out Lovejoy. I don't think he did this, but I worry that he'll get blamed."

"Don't jump to defend him. He could be guilty."

She knew that. "Or Carrie could have been killed by a stranger after stopping for a drink." Rox had never worked homicide cases but she knew that scenario was unlikely. Sixty-two percent of all homicide victims were killed by someone they knew. "I contacted Kyle about the murder, so he may get back to me with more information."

Marty blinked and rubbed his head. "I shouldn't have had a second beer. I need to lay down for a minute."

"As long as you're in that mode, I might as well tell you. I put three grand on your credit card with Ridgeline." Rox gave a sheepish grin.

His mouth dropped open. "For the deposit? That's crazy."

"I know. They wanted ten days up front. But we can always dispute the charge after we get the transport service information."

"I notice you didn't use your card."

"I couldn't." Rox started to explain then realized he was teasing her. *What was a good comeback?* "Better you than me."

Marty laughed. "I'll just lay on your couch instead of going home—in case you need me to call Ridgeline about Josh and his mother's death." Marty shuffled into the living room and lay down. "Mind if I turn on the news?" He could only fall asleep with the TV on.

"Go ahead." While Marty tuned into the early edition of the local news, Rox called Kyle. No answer. She left another message, then sat down in the armchair to watch the TV. The anchorwoman opened with a report about Carrie Lovejoy's murder. She had even less information than they did.

"I'm surprised the media got hold of this one so quickly." Marty didn't sound sleepy now.

"I'm not. Our society has become all news, all day."

"Shhh!" Her stepdad was on full alert.

Rox focused on the news anchor's words: "A few hours before she was killed, the victim's cell phone was stolen in a prayer service. Witnesses say the thief was likely a newcomer named Jolene McAdams. She's described as very tall with shoulder-length light-brown hair. If you know Jolene McAdams, please call the number on the screen. The police would like to talk to her."

Marty bolted upright and snapped his head to stare at Rox. "If that's the name you used with your Ridgeline application, we're screwed."

Chapter 13

Friday, July 7, 9:25 a.m., Central Oregon wilderness
Josh kept climbing the rocky path, one foot in front of the other. *Don't stop. Don't think. Just function.* His feet were bruised and blistered, his throat ached from the red dust and lack of water, and his stomach heaved with a sickness he'd never felt before. It couldn't be food poisoning. They didn't give him any fresh produce or real protein. But he worried about bugs and worms. They were living like animals out here. None of the kids had showered or changed their clothes in over a week. The counselors rotated out every few days, and Josh suspected they hiked back to where they'd left a jeep, then made trips to the base camp to shower and pick up food and water.

What kind of sick fuck would take a job like this? They had to be well paid, unless they were sadistic . . . or masochistic . . . or both. A desire to kill his tormentor burned in every fiber of Josh's body. Ace had singled him out and made his life hell. Other campers were allowed to carry water bottles and sometimes got beef jerky after a tough hiking day, but not him. Maybe Ace abused him as an example—to show the others how bad it could be for them if they got out of line.

Josh looked up the steep trail. *Oh fuck.* He'd fallen behind again. He pushed himself to pick up his pace, but he had nothing left. What would happen if he just stopped? Just sat down and didn't move. Without making a conscious choice, he dropped to his knees.

Up ahead, Trevor called out, "Man down."

Heavy footsteps pounded down the rocky trail. Ace was coming! Josh tried to push to his feet but felt dizzy.

"Get up, you maggot!"

A boot landed in his ribcage. Pain radiated through his chest, but he didn't cry out. Not anymore. *Get up*, he told himself. He wanted to die, but he had a faster way in mind. A kick to his back blasted adrenaline through him, and Josh forced his weary legs to straighten. He visualized himself beating Ace to death with a heavy piece of wood, and that got him moving again. Maybe later, as they neared the top of the mountain, he would hike past a jump-off point. Death would be a sweet relief. For now he had to keep moving.

They stopped an hour later for lunch, and Levi, the other counselor, handed each camper a plastic sandwich bag with a handful of peanuts and dried apricots. Josh got his last, as always. "Please give me some water."

Levi pulled a small bottle out of his own pack and handed it to him. "Make it last."

Josh dropped to the ground, too tired to find a big rock to sit on like most of the others had done. He shoved some of the dried fruit into his mouth and forced himself to chew. His throat was so raw he worried about making it bleed. He feared choking to death too. The peanuts hurt going down, but they had protein and he was grateful. Today was the day. He would either kill himself or kill Ace. If he stabbed a counselor, they would have to take him to jail. In juvie lockup, he could sit down all day. They would feed him real food. And not hurt him. He probably deserved to be punished for what he'd done, but not like this. The way he'd treated that girl had been selfish and shameful, but not evil. He'd been loaded out of his mind. Maybe he would plead insanity and be sent to a clean, pleasant mental institution.

But that was all fantasy. He didn't have the strength to assault the big man—even at his best. Now he was at his worst. The sun beat down on his back and sweat dripped from his face, but he was too weak and tired to even move into the shade.

"Move out!" Ace yelled. The bearded bastard started back down the mountain the way they'd come. Thank god. The campers struggled to their feet and shuffled to the narrow path.

An hour later, they branched off, taking a different route to the bottom. After a while, Josh heard the familiar sound of water rushing downstream over rocks. A creek! He longed to wade into the cool water and rinse off everywhere. And guzzle a gallon of it! That would be so delicious!

As they thundered down the steep hill, the sound grew louder, more like a river. His anticipation wavered. Rivers were deep, and he didn't swim well. But Ace probably wouldn't let anyone get in, especially if it seemed like fun to the other campers.

A few minutes later, they descended through a cluster of giant red boulders, and the water came into view. Twenty feet across and moving fast. Not a gentle swimming hole. Dread filled his belly. They were going to cross here and keep hiking.

"Josh, you're first!" Ace grinned, his face more evil than usual. "You can show the others what not to do."

Fear and hatred locked his legs and he couldn't move. The other boys stepped aside as Ace came at him and grabbed his arm. "Get moving. It's not as deep as it looks."

"What about a safety line?" Josh cried out.

Ace laughed. "This is wilderness school. Do you see any ropes out here?" The jackass dragged him to the river's edge, and Josh had no strength to resist. "Go!" Ace pushed him into the stream.

Josh stepped forward, and the pull of the water startled him. He shoved his arms out to catch his balance. How deep was it? Would the water surround him up to his chest? Trembling, he took another step, wider this time, and didn't fall. The cold penetrated his jeans below his knees. As long as the water stayed below his waist, he could do this.

Behind him, the campers chanted, "Go, Josh, go!"

He took a few more steps, and the pull of the water circled his thighs. What if he lost his balance and got sucked downstream? He would drown, and that terrified him. He wanted to die, but not slowly in a freezing river. They might never find his body. He wanted his mother to see him dead. To see the scrapes and bruises and know what she'd done to him.

The other boys' chanting grew louder and more insistent. Josh pushed forward until the river reached his belly. *Halfway there,* he told himself. It would start to get shallower and easier again. He took another step, and the bottom gave away. The water swept him sideways and pulled him under. Josh fought to surface, but he kept tumbling. The freezing temperature sent him into shock, and he couldn't even think straight. Still, he struggled to get his head out of the water. When he finally surfaced, he sucked in a huge breath.

When his eyes cleared, he spotted a downed tree jutting out into the stream. If he could just get over a few feet. Josh swam wildly, desperate to reach the log. The cold was unbearable. He frantically kicked his legs and his fingers caught a branch. He pulled hard and got his head and shoulders up onto the dead tree. Crawling along the wood, he heard cheering in the distance. He hadn't drifted far. Josh didn't know whether to laugh or cry.

When he reached the muddy bank, all he could do was lie there, shaking. Disgust filled his belly, and he vomited into the red dirt. He was worthless. He couldn't wade across a river without nearly drowning. And when he'd had a chance to escape through death, fear had taken over and he'd wasted it. Now he was too exhausted to even move away from his own vomit.

Time passed, and he faded in and out of consciousness, with no idea of how long he'd been there. Eventually, the hateful sound of Ace yelling made him open his eyes. "Get up! We've still got ten miles to go before we reach our new bed-and-breakfast."

Josh pushed to his knees, hunger driving him. When they made camp, he would get to eat. If he made it to the day's destination. Ending this misery was still his priority. He would be braver next time.

Soon he was on an uphill trail again, near the back of the group, putting one foot in front of the other. *Don't stop. Don't think. Just function.* Behind him, Trevor said, "You're pretty tough, Josh. You just don't know it."

Josh didn't feel tough. He felt hollow, except for the hatred. For Ace, for his mother, for himself.

Trevor was still talking. "Seth got washed downstream after three steps, and Levi had to rescue him. After that, they let the rest of us use a rope."

None of that meant anything to him. But Trevor was trying to be nice. "I'm glad everyone is safe," Josh finally said. Trevor passed him on the trail and slapped his shoulder.

"We'll make it through this."

Later, as the climb steepened, Ace called out to the group, "Careful! If you break a leg, you still have to walk."

Josh looked up the trail again. It rounded a curve with a tall rock formation. On the other side, the terrain dropped off. From here he couldn't see how steep the slope was, but his heart surged anyway. Maybe if he ran and threw himself off the edge, he'd land hard enough to die. Or at least break a leg and get carried out. They wouldn't really make him walk back with a broken leg, would they? They had to give a shit about being sued, didn't they? He almost laughed. They'd nearly let two kids drown, so no, they weren't worried.

He was closer to the curve now and couldn't see anything to the right of the trail. That meant the terrain was steep. Or maybe not there at all. This was his chance, and he had to get it right. He couldn't take another day of this, let alone three months. Josh slowed, creating some distance between him and Trevor. He didn't want to hurt his only friend in this hellhole by slamming into him.

Seven more steps along the rocky path, then he would start to run. If he could muster the extra energy. The peak of the cliff was only thirty feet beyond that. Then he would be free of this pain and misery.

Three, two, one.

Josh charged forward, his legs feeling like stacked mush. Near the edge, he stumbled. But the momentum carried him forward even faster. A foot from the edge, he closed his eyes and leapt into space.

Chapter 14

Friday, July 7, 7:25 a.m., Portland

Rox skipped her dance workout, took a quick shower, and sucked down some coffee. Her task list felt overwhelming, especially now that she'd taken a second case. But first she felt compelled to check the inmate-search website for Isaac Lovejoy. He wasn't answering his phone, so he was either still at the Police Bureau being questioned or he'd been booked into jail. She found him in the county facility, where he'd been processed at five that morning with a charge of possession of a Schedule II drug.

On the surface, that seemed odd, but Rox knew how the department worked. Kyle or Detective Crider—whoever was leading Carrie's murder investigation—had decided to keep her client detained but didn't have enough to prosecute him for murder. So they'd charged him with some minor bullshit thing. Maybe Lovejoy had drugs on him when he was arrested, or maybe the detectives had taken a blood sample and found intoxicants in his system. They might have even fabricated the charge. It happened sometimes when police officers needed leverage.

Rox scanned the fine-print details and discovered that her client's bail had been set at half a million—a fifty-thousand-dollar bond. He would be locked up until they found a better suspect or the case went to trial. Unless Lovejoy could afford a powerful defense lawyer. She rather doubted it. But there was nothing she could do to help him. Except to find Josh.

Her next call was to Kyle, and he surprised her by picking up. "Hey, Rox. I'm glad you called." He sounded chipper for someone who'd probably been working most of the night.

Damn. He probably hadn't listened to her voicemail and thought she was calling to accept his dinner invitation. Feeling guilty, she searched for something nice to say. "I've been thinking about you a lot." True, but not in the way he thought. "Did you get my message?"

"No, sorry. I was in the interrogation room most of the night. Are we going out soon?"

Just tell him no. Rox vacillated. If she played along, she would get more information. But that was deceptive. Still, if she hadn't met a sexy new client the day before, she probably would say yes. She decided to aim for the middle ground. "You said just dinner, as friends. I'd like that."

An awkward pause. "It's a start. When? I'm busy for a few days with a new homicide, but Sunday night should work."

She needed to pump him for details right now. "What about lunch today?"

He hesitated again. "Can you meet me near the department? I have witnesses to question this morning, but I hope to be back here by noon."

"Where? Heavy Chevy's?" It was a cop favorite.

"Great. See you at noon."

Rox hung up and paced the room. She needed Kyle's help, but she didn't want to use him or make him feel used. Still, the date had been his idea. The complexity of her interactions with him surprised her. This was new, post-treatment territory, and she didn't think she liked it. Bluntness was so much simpler.

She went to the kitchen for another cup of coffee and a breakfast bar, then sat down at her desk and looked over her task list again. She started with the easiest and checked Marty's credit card statement online. After his heart-disease diagnosis, he'd given her access to all his accounts, plus a list of post-death instructions. But she wouldn't think about those now. She scanned a short list of charges for the last week, surprised by how much he spent on golf. The Ridgeline payment hadn't processed yet. Rox logged out, feeling as if she'd invaded Marty's privacy.

Next on her list was calling the NBC reporters again. They hadn't gotten back to her, no surprise, but she would try again before writing off that lead. No one answered, and she left another pleading message. The rest of her list focused on tracking down the back-end details of the business and its owners, who might be operating in three states. Carrie had said the company no longer operated in Utah because of regulations, but Rox checked the state's database anyway— and didn't find anything named Ridgeline. She googled the Nevada business registry and keyed *Ridgeline Wilderness Health* into its search bar. The website's engine was slow, and Rox counted while she waited. At thirty-two seconds, she got a hit. The company's page loaded and she scanned the details. An S-corporation with a Reno address that had done business in the state for four years and listed its function as *individual and family services*. The program's website claimed they'd been *successfully transforming teenagers* since 1994, so the move to Nevada had been recent. On a whim, she keyed Ridgeline into the search bar by itself and got a second hit on the Get Straight program, which was also listed as an S-corp. The separate listings made her wonder if a parent corporation owned both businesses.

She clicked back to the Wilderness Health page and scanned farther down, hoping to find ownership details. Rox spotted a name that made her catch her breath. Curtis Fletcher was the registered agent.

Rox slumped back against her chair, too surprised to think clearly for a moment. Carrie's fiancé was, at the very least, connected to Ridgeline. He might even be an owner. Registered agents in business listings were sometimes a company's legal counsel, but usually only for big corporations. Her brain finally kicked into gear. Fletcher's connection to the program explained where Carrie had heard of it and how Josh ended up there. Fletcher may have even pushed for Josh to go. Lovejoy had suggested that his ex was moving in with her fiancé. Maybe Fletcher had insisted that she get her son straightened out before the move. A wild thought jumped into her head. Had Fletcher also murdered Carrie? What motive would he have? Just because the guy had given her the creeps didn't make him a killer.

Rox bolted from her chair, ready to get moving. She needed to question Curtis Fletcher. But guilty or not, he was dealing with the death of his girlfriend and wouldn't likely take her calls. This angle of the investigation seemed like a good fit for Marty. He could even tail the fiancé if that's what was needed. Rox decided to walk over and chat with her stepdad. She hadn't been to his side of the duplex in weeks, and she had only one other significant task: Pack for a trip into the wilderness, whether it was central Oregon or northern Nevada. If they learned any real information about the camp's location, she wanted to get on the road ASAP. Or if they figured out where the transport vans were parked, she wanted to be ready to keep watch and tail one to the camp.

Outside, the morning air was already warm, and she

decided to change into the sleeveless green sweater before her lunch with Kyle. He would be happy to see her in something besides blue. She crossed the connecting sidewalk to Marty's front door, gave three loud raps, and waited. It took him a full minute to yell "Clear!"

Rox walked in, noticing the smell of sawdust. Marty stepped out of the hallway into view, wearing a tool belt and safety glasses—like some kind of building maintenance guy.

"What the hell are you remodeling now?"

"Just adding some shelves." He grinned and pulled off his glasses.

He'd always been this way, but to a kid it had seemed normal for a single dad, working full time and raising two daughters. Later she'd been on her own and employed full-time too, so she hadn't seen much of him. His true hyperactivity had surfaced after he retired and they'd bought the duplex together.

"I've got something more interesting for you." Rox slid into his built-in kitchen booth. "I checked out Ridgeline on the Nevada business registry. Curtis Fletcher is listed as the registered agent. That's Carrie's fiancé, Josh's soon-to-be stepfather."

"What the hell?" Marty dropped his tools and slid in across from her. "Maybe the camp's not that bad. The mother must have known how the kids are treated."

"Maybe not. I'm sure no one does except the kids and counselors who are out there experiencing it." She wondered why more teenagers didn't complain. Or maybe they did, and no one really listened. A dark thought crossed her mind. "Maybe Carrie realized too late what the correctional program was like. Or discovered too much about the Ridgeline business model. Curtis Fletcher might have killed her to silence her."

Marty cleared his throat. "Let me check the guy out before you run with this idea. Remember, the detectives arrested Isaac Lovejoy, Carrie's ex."

"I know. Fletcher might just be an investor who doesn't really know much about how the business operates. He might have just been tired of dealing with an obnoxious teenager and suggested sending him to Ridgeline to straighten him out before they got married."

"Now that Carrie is dead, the camp is likely to send Josh home." Marty nodded vigorously, as though wishful thinking would make it true.

Rox shook her head. "The woman I talked to in the Ridgeline office said no student goes home until they graduate—and that can take months."

"You need to notify the office right now that Josh's mother is dead and that he needs to come home." Marty leaned forward. "Pretend to be his grandmother or something."

"No, you have to call. I've left messages. They know my voice."

"Fine. I'll do it." Marty got up to find his phone.

Rox stood too and checked the time. She didn't want to be late for her lunch. Marty came back with his cell, and she reached out for it. He let her have it, and she keyed in the number from the Ridgeline website before giving it back.

"Here goes." Marty pressed the dial icon.

"Wait!"

He hung up.

Rox processed several jumbled thoughts, then finally said, "What if Curtis Fletcher already notified the camp about Carrie's death? You calling and making up a grandfather that might not exist could make them suspicious and paranoid."

"So what's the harm? Especially if Josh is already on his way home?"

"If Fletcher hasn't told them, and you make them suspicious, it could tip our hand and make it harder to get Josh out." She paced the kitchen as other possibilities came to her. "Carrie's fiancé may not like Josh, especially since he has drug and behavior problems. Sending Josh to the camp was probably Fletcher's idea."

"Good point." Marty rubbed his hair. "He could be happy to leave him there."

"Where would they escort Josh home to? Unless he has another relative, like a grandmother in the area. I have to talk this over with our client." Rox pulled out her own phone. "Lovejoy was booked early this morning and may not be fully processed yet, but I'll try."

Her call to the jail was a waste of time. Only his lawyer could see Lovejoy. Her client wouldn't have general visiting privileges until next week. She glanced at Marty's kitchen clock again. "I have to go get ready for my lunch with Kyle."

"I'll bet he can get you in to see Lovejoy."

"Maybe." She already had several favors to ask him. "When I get back, I plan to pack for a trip to Nevada. It's time to find the transport office and the camp. I'm sure Josh would like to attend his mother's funeral."

"I'll see what I can learn about Curtis Fletcher." Marty grabbed a small paper tablet from a kitchen drawer. "Give me his address if you have it, and I'll drive over there and see if he's home. I might even come up with a ruse to chat him up."

Rox smiled. Marty liked the undercover work as much as she did. She recalled the address from the business registry and recited the information from memory. "I also have a boy named Tommy to find. Do you know who's working missing-person cases now?"

"No. Sorry." Marty bounced on his toes, ready to get to work.

"I'll ask Kyle." Rox started for the door. "Good luck." Her dark thoughts about Fletcher surfaced again, and she abruptly turned back. "Be safe, please."

Chapter 15

Forty minutes later Rox entered the Heavy Chevy Grill on Salmon Street, about two blocks from the Portland Police Bureau. A wave of memories flooded her, and she paused to absorb them. She'd eaten many lunches here with friends from the bureau, but she'd also dined alone more times than she'd cared for. She looked around to see that nothing had changed in the decade she'd been gone. The fifties theme still included classic-car photos and black-and-white checkered tablecloths. She'd never liked the decor, but the food was excellent. She passed two officers she knew on her way to a table and said hello but didn't stop to chat.

Kyle was late, as usual, but the sight of him walking in made her heart happy. He was classically tall, dark-haired, and handsome—and wore a gun under his charcoal-gray suit. Always a bonus! Just because she didn't like to carry one herself didn't mean a weapon wasn't sexy on a man. On the surface, he was perfect for her. For the nine months they'd dated, he'd seemed great under the surface too—liking most of her quirks.

"Hey, Rox. You look nice. That's a great color for you." Kyle sat across from her, facing the window.

"Thanks. I have a purple dress too, but I haven't worn it yet." She smiled shyly. Her ex-boyfriend knew her better than anyone, except maybe Marty. Still, she felt nervous, as though it were a first date. But it wasn't. She was here to gather information, and he thought she wanted to get back together. This would be a delicate balance—even for someone with social skills.

"How are you?" Kyle patted her hand but didn't linger. He didn't care for public displays of affection.

"I'm good. Keeping busy with interesting cases." Rox picked up the menu but didn't look at it. She had to be honest. "I still have a few treatments left, but I'm skipping them this week."

"How are the side effects?"

"I'm past the bad migraines, but I still have a minor headache every morning."

"So you're feeling better?" Kyle looked confused. Or concerned. She couldn't tell.

"Somewhat." She had other side effects too, like the hearing loss and an occasional memory slip, but they would pass. Or so her doctor said.

"How's Marty?"

"The same. He put up new shelves this morning."

Kyle laughed.

A server stopped, poured coffee, and took their order. They both knew the menu and what they wanted. When the waitress left, Rox said, "This was a good idea. I haven't had a pastrami sandwich since we ate at that deli on the coast."

"I've missed you."

She wasn't sure what to say. *Keep it simple.* "I've missed you too." The few Match.com dates she'd gone on hadn't worked out, but at least she was trying now. She'd been alone during her career at the CIA, and it had been unhealthy. She'd spent too many extra hours at work, and her social life had consisted of Skype chats with her family members. She smiled at Kyle. "How's your work? You mentioned a new homicide."

"Yeah. It's ugly. A woman was beaten and strangled, most likely by her ex-husband."

Carrie had been beaten?

Kyle downed half his cup of java, then added, "The suspect has no alibi, and we interrogated him for hours, but we just started collecting evidence."

The assault was new information, and she had to be sure they were talking about the same person. "Who's the victim?"

"Carrie Lovejoy. It was on the news last night." Kyle stared into Rox's eyes. "Marty was at the restaurant when we arrested her ex-husband. Do you know anything about that?"

Was Kyle pumping her for intel? Rox almost laughed, but this was too serious. "Can I still trust you to protect what I do?"

Kyle hesitated for a split-second. "As far as I can . . . without ruining my career."

She decided to tell him everything. Almost. "Isaac Lovejoy hired me to extract his son Josh from a wilderness camp. He thinks the boy might be suicidal. I can't really vouch for my client, but my instinct tells me he didn't kill his ex-wife."

"She had a restraining order against him."

"So? They'd had an argument about the correctional camp, because she sent their son without his consent. Maybe even forged Isaac Lovejoy's signature." She now realized that with Fletcher's connection to Ridgeline, the father's consent probably hadn't been necessary. "According to my client, his ex was trying to make him look bad—in case he took her to court over the whole thing."

Kyle nodded. "You're helping my case. Killing his ex is an easy way to get full custody without the hassle and expense of lawyers."

Rox couldn't argue. But she'd met both of the men in

Carrie's life, and she liked and trusted her client more. Rox had to bite her tongue to keep from saying that. Bringing up her visit to the church wasn't a good idea. "Do you know anything about Ridgeline Wilderness Health?"

"Never heard of it." Kyle looked down at his empty cup. "You know I don't work juvenile cases."

Rox started to ask another question, but Kyle cut in. "A few hours before her death, Carrie attended a prayer service, during which her phone was taken from her purse." He looked up and locked eyes with her. "Most likely by a very tall woman who was new to the service that evening. Do you know anything about that?"

Oh hell. If she admitted to interacting with the victim, someone on the task force would have to officially question her. Rox couldn't afford to get sucked into a homicide investigation. With his mother dead and his father in jail, Josh needed someone to step in and protect him. Curtis Fletcher— with his cold eyes and ownership in a tough-love correctional camp—wasn't likely to be that kind of person.

"You're not answering me. Not a good sign." Kyle's expression was deadpan.

Relieved that he didn't look angry, Rox tried to explain. "This case is complicated, and a young life is in danger." She remembered Tommy, the missing boy. "Maybe several young lives. I have to put them first. And I don't know anything that can help your investigation."

After a long moment, Kyle said, "You'll tell me if you learn something?"

"Of course."

The server came back with their sandwiches. "Anything else?"

"More coffee, please." Kyle's eyes were puffy from lack of

sleep.

The server hurried off, and Rox stared at her meal, not as hungry as she'd been a minute ago. "Will you tell me what you have on my client?"

Kyle already had a bite in his mouth. "Motive and opportunity."

"What's the drug possession charge about?"

"He had pain pills in his pocket and no prescription."

A bullshit charge! She'd known it. But they obviously didn't have any trace or blood evidence yet. She was even more certain that Lovejoy was innocent. "You said Carrie was beaten. What exactly does that mean?"

"Complete confidence?"

"Always."

Kyle leaned forward and kept his voice low. "Broken nose, cracked ribs, and bruises on her wrists as if someone had restrained her."

Who would beat Carrie and why? It almost had to be one of the men in her life. "What about Lovejoy's hands? Any injuries or signs that he was involved?"

Kyle shrugged. "Not yet."

They didn't have a case. She remembered her chat with Marty about Curtis Fletcher and why he might want his girlfriend dead. "You should look closer at Carrie's fiancé."

"You shouldn't tell me how to do my job."

Ouch. Her blunt old-self surfaced without warning. "That was rude."

"Sorry." Kyle gave her a half-smile. "That's more like the Rox I used to know."

She was quiet for a minute. "The treatment's effects may not last. But even if they don't, I have new knowledge that's a permanent part of me."

"I'm happy for you." He met her eyes with sincerity—then took another bite.

Rox picked up her sandwich. She might as well eat too. She still had a busy day ahead and possibly a long drive to Nevada.

Chapter 16

Friday, July 7, 12:45 p.m., Reno, Nevada

Ruth Hammond read through the application again, chewing her nails. Something about the language wasn't right, but she couldn't put her finger on the problem. The payment concerned her too. The name on the card didn't match the mother's name on the application. Jolene McAdams had said her father-in-law was paying for the program, and that was pretty common. Grandparents often had the money when the parents didn't. The teenager's name was Martin, the same as the grandfather on the credit card, which made sense too. But she'd googled the name Martin MacFarlane anyway, because it was her job to screen applicants. Her instructions were to deny any parent who was a lawyer and to carefully screen applicants with law enforcement careers. She also ran credit checks and refused anyone with a credit score under seven hundred.

The name Martin MacFarlane—in association with Portland, Oregon, where the applicant was located—had come up in a news article about a retirement banquet for lifetime police officers. If he was the same man, that was a mild strike against the application. Also, when they talked on the phone, the woman had seemed a little off, with a tone that was rather unemotional. Most people were pretty desperate by the time they considered a wilderness boot camp for their child.

On the other hand, the business needed students and cash flow, so they were less picky now. Ruth decided to call Mr. Fletcher and run it by him. Her boss had moved to Portland and started running the boot camps out of Central Oregon—after all the trouble with his brother and the lawsuit from the Metzler family. But Mr. Fletcher didn't need to be in Reno to run the business. They shared files on a virtual private network and held meetings by video conferencing. Normally, she would contact the operations manager first if she had important questions, but he was in the hospital with a burst appendix. Ruth found Mr. Fletcher's number in the laminated directory she kept on her desk and called him.

Her boss answered right away. "Ruth, what's going on?" His voice sounded strange.

"I'm sorry to bother you, but Mark isn't available. His appendix burst, and he's in the hospital." Ruth laughed nervously. "But you probably knew that."

"Yes. Get to the point, please. I'm having a rough time right now."

"Sorry, but I have an application I'm not sure about. The person paying is the boy's grandfather and a retired cop."

Mr. Fletcher gave a small sigh. "I'm sure it's fine. Unless the parents have other issues."

"Nothing specific. The mother is a recent widow and a bookkeeper. But I've been doing this a long time, and something feels off about her."

"What's her name?" His tone was sharp and worried now.

"Jolene McAdams."

"Fuck!"

Oh no. Not more trouble. "What's wrong? Do you know her?"

"She came to the fellowship the other evening and asked Carrie about Ridgeline. Then Carrie's phone went missing, and we think the strange woman took it."

"That's weird."

"When did she apply?"

Ruth thought back through the sequence. "Jolene McAdams first called and left a message Wednesday morning."

Mr. Fletcher cursed again. "That was before she talked to Carrie." Her boss suddenly let out a small sob. "Carrie was murdered Wednesday night after the phone incident at the fellowship."

Ruth sucked in a startled breath. She didn't know the boss' fiancé, but still, the woman had been killed! "I'm so sorry. You must be devastated. I feel horrible about calling you with this."

"I'm glad you did. The police think Carrie's ex-husband did it, but now I'm wondering who the hell this Jolene McAdams really is and why she's targeting Ridgeline."

Someone seeking revenge? Not everyone left boot camp happy with their experience. "Do you think this Jolene woman killed Carrie?"

"I don't know. She's big enough." He sobbed again.

Ruth felt so bad for him. "Is there anything I can do to help?"

"Deny her application and refund her money. If she calls again, record her voice, but don't tell her anything."

"Yes, sir." Ruth remembered that his fiancé's son was currently in the program. "What about Josh Lovejoy? Should we send him home?"

"Hell no. I don't want to deal with him. Besides, the kid needs this program. He's a pain in the ass."

"What about his dad?"

"He's in jail. The police think he's the killer. So Josh has nowhere to go, and I'm not taking him to my place."

The counselors would have to let the kid go at some point. One boy had been in the program for six months before he finally graduated, but this was different. "I'm not sure—"

Her boss cut in. "Just leave him in the program until we hear from his dad, or a lawyer, or state authorities."

Ruth didn't argue. "I'm so sorry about Carrie. Are you gonna take some time off? Should I tell the staff so they don't bother you?"

"No and no. I'll be fine as long as Ridgeline keeps making money. My other businesses are borderline."

Ruth worried about her job now. The boot camps were still profitable, although not as busy, but the gay-conversion therapy camp they ran out of Nevada was struggling. "I'm doing my part."

"I know you are," Fletcher said. "Please find out anything you can about the new applicant's grandfather. What's his name, by the way?"

"Martin MacFarlane." Ruth wasn't optimistic but she would try.

"Call me if you hit any red flags." The boss hung up.

Chapter 17

After an awkward goodbye with Kyle, Rox headed for her car, parked several blocks away. She cut through the beautiful parks across from the Police Bureau and was reminded how lovely downtown Portland was in the warm months. Halfway to her vehicle, she changed her mind and turned toward the huge concrete building that also housed the county court. She hoped Kyle wouldn't see her in the bureau and think she'd purposely avoided walking over with him.

Inside the building, she paused and took a moment to appreciate the cold beauty of the stone walls and circular stairs in the lobby—which contrasted sharply with the kinetic energy behind the security barriers. She'd loved her time in the bureau, but too much of it had been spent inside these walls instead of out on the streets. Once her bosses had realized how good she was with data, she'd gotten stuck behind a desk. The CIA had treated her the same way. If Jolene hadn't been murdered, she might still be in D.C., staring at numbers and patterns all day. Rox pushed away the guilt. Although her life now was significantly better, she would trade it in a heartbeat to have her sister back. Jolene was the only real female friend she'd ever had.

Rox strode up to the counter and smiled at the woman behind the safety glass. "Hi, I'm Rox MacFarlane. I was an officer here for six years, and now I'm a private investigator. I'd like to speak with a detective who handles missing persons."

The woman, about her age, nodded but didn't smile back. "I think Sam Kushing is the only one in the building at the moment. I'll see if he has time."

She'd worked with Kushing once on a custody case. After a brief phone conversation, the desk officer let Rox through the security door and walked her back to the specialized unit. When she entered, Detective Kushing stood, a thin older man with blond-gray hair and a sweet smile. "Good to see you again, MacFarlane." He shook her hand. "How's your dad?"

Everyone knew Marty, who'd been with the bureau for thirty-five years. "He's good. As long as I keep him busy."

Kushing chuckled. "Have a seat and tell me how I can help you."

"I'm looking into a missing teenager. Tommy Goodwin. He disappeared about three weeks ago."

The detective cocked his head. "Who hired you? That's still an active case for us."

"His uncle, Scott Goodwin."

"Yeah, the mother mentioned him." Kushing turned to a nearby file cabinet. "Let me get out my notes." He probably had electronic documents too, but old-school cops liked handwritten memos.

"Donna Goodwin reported him missing?"

"Yes." Kushing's eyes narrowed. "I'm not sure how much I should tell you, but since you're trying to find the kid too, I don't see a downside."

"His case may overlap with another teenager I'm searching for." Rox wondered if Kushing had any experience with correctional programs. "Have you ever heard of Ridgeline Wilderness Health?"

"It's one of those boot camps. We worked a case a few years ago that involved a teenage boy who wasn't really missing but in the program instead."

"That's what my client thinks might be going on with his nephew—that Tommy's mother sent him to a wilderness camp or military school but doesn't want to admit it."

"So why would she report her son missing?" Kushing stroked his chin. "I remember thinking that she seemed kind of detached. Or at least not hysterical the way a lot of parents are when their kid disappears."

"What's your take?" Rox asked, frustrated with the uncertainty of the case. "Did Tommy run away or did his mother ship him out and not want to tell anyone? Particularly Tommy's uncle, who's like a father to him."

Kushing looked up from his notes. "I honestly don't know. We checked hospitals, homeless camps, and youth facilities. We also posted flyers with Tommy's image at all the places teenagers hang out downtown and tried to question the transients at Dirty Kid Corner. But they won't talk to police." The old man shrugged. "We only had one call about a sighting that seemed legit, but nothing came of it. Tommy Goodwin is still missing."

Rox decided to step up her effort to find him. "What's your take on the mother?"

"She seemed pretty marginal. Like she wasn't taking care of herself. You know, dirty hair and physically shaky, the way a drunk or addict is before they get their daily feel-good."

Everyone handled grief differently. Rox's compassion for the family deepened. "Donna lost her husband in Afghanistan recently, so she may not be in her right mind."

Anger flashed in the detective's eyes. "Still, if she knowingly wasted our time and effort . . ." He let the thought go.

"Anything else I should know before I waste my time too?"

"You need to accept that the kid might have left the area. Or overdosed somewhere and hasn't been found yet."

She'd considered all of that. This wasn't her first missing-person case. "Can you give me specifics about the day he disappeared?"

"The mother last talked to Tommy on a Friday morning before school. He went to his uncle's over the weekend, then Scott Goodwin dropped the kid off Sunday night. Tommy apparently took off right after that." Kushing glanced at his notes again. "June twenty-third."

"Did Tommy get a call from a friend or say anything about where he was going?"

"Ms. Goodwin wasn't very clear about the details. She admitted she'd been drinking heavily over the weekend."

Maybe Tommy had run away. Alcoholic parents could be hard to take. Rox asked Kushing for Donna Goodwin's phone number, and after a slight hesitation, he gave it to her. "Don't tell her you got it from me. Your client could have given it to you, right?"

"Yes." Rox stood. "Do you want me to update you if I find Tommy?"

"Please." Kushing shook her hand again, and Rox left, eager to meet with Donna and decide for herself if the woman was mentally ill or just playing everyone. Rox knew she had to stay focused on her first client, but instinct told her the cases could be related. If she could convince—or con—Donna Goodwin into telling her the truth about where Tommy was, she might learn Josh's location too.

As she drove down Second Avenue, Rox recalled Kushing's mention of Dirty Kid Corner. At Third and Oak, it was only about eight blocks away, not far from the downtown homeless camp. The transients who hadn't been willing to talk to a police officer might open up to her. Since she was already in the area, it couldn't hurt to show Tommy's picture to a few people.

She found a parking spot in a coffee roaster's lot and climbed out, remembering her last visit to the area. She'd chatted with a young girl working in a soup kitchen run by a cult leader. The mission had closed and an oyster bar was now open in its place. But the nearby homeless camp and Voodoo Doughnuts were still operating. Rox walked back to Third Avenue and scanned the intersection. Scruffy travelers with bandana-wearing dogs occupied the sidewalk in front of the Church of Scientology. Across the street, a group of teenagers huddled around a shelter made of cardboard. She headed for the kids, not feeling optimistic.

She told the runaways she was a youth counselor who wanted to help Tommy, but they all shook their heads when she showed his photo.

"Are you with the Rainbow Coalition?" an older boy asked.

"No, his uncle asked me to find Tommy."

"You might try the park," a girl suggested. "We panhandle over there sometimes."

"Thanks." Rox started to leave, then turned back. "Hey, have you ever heard of Ridgeline Wilderness Health?"

The boy gave an exaggerated shudder. "I've heard some bad things."

"Like what?"

"Walking all day, not enough food, sleeping outside without blankets." He gave her a weird smile. "Kind of like being homeless."

Interesting perspective. "Anything else?"

A young girl spoke up. "I was staying in a teen shelter and

one girl said she'd been sexually abused by a staff member at one of those camps, but I don't remember the name."

A troubling new element. "Thanks again." Rox headed back to her car. The Waterfront Park was massive, and searching it would probably be a waste of time.

On the drive home, she called Donna. When she didn't answer, Rox hung up. She wanted to think this through. She might only have one chance to get information from Tommy's mother, and she didn't want to blow it. A face-to-face talk would be better. For that, she needed to know where Donna lived or worked. She called Scott Goodwin and left him a message, remembering at the last moment to give her investigative name. "Hey, this is Karina Jones. I still need to chat with Tommy's mother, and I'd like to do it in person. Call or text me with her address, please."

Rox pulled into her own driveway and noticed that Marty's car was gone. She hoped he was checking into Curtis Fletcher, who might be the key to finding both teenage boys. In the house, Rox checked her email. She scanned through a bunch of troll-type Craigslist responses to her personal ad, then came across a message from Ridgeline. She clicked it open, eager to see if they would give her information about the transport service for her fake son.

The content was brief: *Your application has been rejected and your deposit will be refunded. Please don't contact us again.*

What the hell? For a business that was hurting for clients, the rejection made no sense. Unless they'd somehow become suspicious of her. Maybe it was the use of Marty's credit card. *Damn.* Rox told herself it didn't matter. They would find the local transport office another way. It would just take longer. Now she didn't have to hire an actor and worry about his safety during the abduction-style pickup.

She called Marty, but he didn't answer so she texted him: *BTW, Ridgeline denied my application.* Would he understand the abbreviation for *by the way*? She usually had to spell out everything for him. But at least he was finally reading and responding to texts. Sort of.

Her work phone rang, and she looked at the ID. Scott Goodwin returning her call. Rox picked up and said, "Hello."

"Hey, it's Scott Goodwin. I'd love to buy you dinner and get an update on the case."

Chapter 18

Marty drove up Miller Road into the new Northwest Heights development, surprised by the size of the houses. As soon as he'd started the climb, his expectations had altered, but now he realized the neighborhood was definitely upper middle class. Maybe even rich. Many of the homes had views of the city skyline and the coastal range beyond it. He didn't envy them. Money always created its own problems. He'd had a good life without a need for frills.

Near the top, he turned on Skyline and drove slowly, watching for house numbers. He didn't want to park directly in front of Fletcher's residence. Bowman had found the address in the bureau's database—because Fletcher had once reported a vehicle vandalized. But it probably hadn't happened in this area. The only other thing Bowman had found was that Fletcher had been arrested in Portland for indecent exposure when he was twenty-one. After that, he'd let his Oregon driver's license expire, then renewed it fifteen years later—most likely after moving out of state for a while. Now the Ridgeline owner was forty and lived in a million-dollar home. According to Rox, the teen-correctional business was in decline because people were turning away from the harsh programs, but Fletcher was still doing just fine—at least on the surface.

Marty spotted a close-enough address and parked behind a delivery truck on the right side of the street, giving him a diagonal view of Fletcher's home. The charcoal-and-burgundy-brick structure featured two round turrets flanking the front, with a wide, sweeping set of matching steps leading up to the front door. *Classy.* Marty reached under his seat for his binoculars. He would have to be careful in this neighborhood and move his car a few times or someone would report him.

Was anyone home? No vehicles sat in the driveway, but the massive three-door garage could easily house several cars. Marty reminded himself that Curtis Fletcher's girlfriend had just been murdered, and the man was likely grieving—even if he had done it himself. As a cop, he'd seen that a few times. What did people normally do the day after such a tragedy?

When he'd learned that his daughter Jo had been shot by her crazy, polygamous husband, he'd been too shocked to do anything for days. He'd cried and slept and talked to both Rox and Georgia, his ex-wife, on the phone. After Jo's service, he'd become enraged and energized enough to drive to the remote house where his baby girl had died. But he'd lost his courage at the sight of it and hadn't gone inside. Everyone in the home had died that fatal day, leaving no one to help him understand why Jolene had married into the weird little cult. He still didn't know. And thinking about her still hurt his heart.

Movement in a window caught his attention, and Marty pulled the binoculars to his eyes again. Through open blinds, he could see parts of a large, likely-male figure moving around. Marty called the number Bowman had provided, not optimistic that it was current or even connected to Fletcher anymore. The call went straight to voicemail: "This is Curtis Fletcher. You can leave a message, and I'll try to get back to you."

No hint of warmth and no promises. Marty hung up. He needed to see the man's face and look into his eyes before making any judgments. He'd never worked as a homicide detective, but after thirty years as a police officer, he knew when people were lying. He climbed out of his sedan and crossed the quiet street. He'd worn a suit and tie for the occasion, figuring he might have to play this out. Still, the prospect of the encounter made him nervous. But if Rox, with her blunt compulsions, could do tradecraft fieldwork, so could he. Her treatments had given her more flexibility, more intuition, and he was proud of her.

As he walked up the long, curved driveway, the sun blazed in a blue sky, making him sweat in his long-sleeved layers. *Not good.* He rang the doorbell and rehearsed his lines. This would be no problem. He'd already made some con-based phone calls in his partnership with Rox, as well as played out a few phony-security-guy gigs. Whatever it took to rescue young people from their messed-up situations. It beat the hell out of playing golf or working on the damn house.

No one came to the door. Marty rang again. Finally, a voice came over an intercom somewhere. "Go away. The sign says *no solicitors.*"

Marty looked up, scanning for the camera. "I'm Bill Parsons, a grief counselor, sent out by the Community Fellowship."

Silence for a long moment, then footsteps sounded and the front door opened. Five-eleven with a big belly and not much hair, the man looked worried but dry-eyed. "I appreciate your concern, but I don't really need any help."

"You're Curtis Fletcher?" A force of habit to confirm.

"Yes. But God—or the collective human spirit, whatever you believe—can't help me with this." A note of pain in his voice.

"I'd like to try. We can at least pray together." Marty really hoped the man wouldn't take him up on that.

"I'm fine, really. Just because I go to the fellowship doesn't mean I'm religious."

Marty didn't understand, but also didn't care. "What about Carrie's son? I'm sure he needs counseling."

"He's getting that where he is right now."

"He's not here with you?" Marty tried to look surprised.

"No. He's not my responsibility." Fletcher gave a strange, tight smile. "You have to go, because I'm leaving soon."

"God bless you. Take care." Marty turned and left, puzzled by the man's demeanor. Fletcher wasn't grieving the same way Marty would if his wife had died, but the man did seem distressed. And it was clear he had no intention of bringing Josh home from the wilderness camp. They would have to extract him as planned. If the boy learned of his mother's death and felt trapped in the program, his suicidal thoughts might be overwhelming.

On the sidewalk, Marty moved past where his car was parked on the other side—in case Fletcher was watching him. When he was out of eyesight, he crossed over, hurried back to his sedan, and climbed in from the passenger's side, where he had less exposure. Slumped down, he waited, wondering if Fletcher really planned to leave or if he'd just wanted to get rid of him.

A few minutes later, he heard a vehicle rolling down a driveway, the only sound on the quiet street. Marty eased over to get behind the wheel, keeping himself low in the seat. The other vehicle cruised by, moving rapidly. Marty started his car, waited for a count of twenty, then pulled a U-turn. Near the curve below, he spotted a red BMW speeding downhill. Keeping a safe distance back, Marty followed, hoping for some traffic to blend into.

At the bottom of the winding road, the BMW turned left and headed south. Marty sped up, not wanting to lose sight. At the highway, Fletcher went east, heading into Portland. Marty followed for twenty minutes, until the red sedan pulled into a parking garage under an office building downtown. Three stories tall, it housed multiple businesses. Marty followed the vehicle underground, then passed it as Fletcher parked near the entrance. After finding an empty space on the far side of the structure, Marty climbed out and hurried through the dark parking area to the building's entrance. Fletcher was nowhere in sight.

Inside, Marty stopped near the elevator and noticed the button for the second floor was lit. Rather than follow his target into a confined space, he scanned the directory board, starting with the second floor. He stopped at Fletcher & Sons Investments. *The father's business?* Marty jotted the name in his notepad and headed back to his car to wait. Twenty minutes later, Fletcher exited. Marty decided to stay with him for a while. He didn't have anything pressing to do. His dinner date with SiriKaren wasn't until eight, when she got off work.

Fletcher's next stop was Swanson's Funeral Home, not surprising considering the man's girlfriend had just died. If Fletcher was making final arrangements, it might take hours. *Did Carrie have other family here?* Marty considered heading home and letting Fletcher go for the day, then changed his mind. He circled around the block, then parked across the street from the white-brick mortuary. Expecting the visit to take a while, he leaned back in the seat and rested for a minute.

A while later, he blinked his eyes and shook himself

awake. *Sleeping on the job. Great private eye he was.* Marty glanced across the busy street, relieved that the BMW was still at the funeral home. After a short five minutes, Fletcher hurried out and climbed back in his car. Marty stayed on his tail until they ended up at a strip club called Wild Girls Galore.

That was one way to deal with grief!

Chapter 19

Rox arrived at the restaurant early and waited in the tacky lobby. She'd chosen a funky but tasty Chinese diner to keep the meal casual. Yet she'd changed into a silky blouse. *Just a meeting with a client, not a real date,* she reminded herself again. Still, if it went well, she intended to pursue the relationship after she closed out the case. Tonight would be strictly professional. The black-and-red walls with gold-dragon images were annoying enough to keep the encounter naturally short. She caught sight of herself in a gold-rimmed mirror and scowled. When had she started looking forty? Maybe it was time to invest in some good skin-care products. At least her sky-blue blouse was flattering.

Her client walked in a few minutes later, and his attractiveness made her heart flutter. Scott was probably out of her league. *Goodwin,* she corrected herself. Law enforcement people called everyone by their surnames, and she'd retained the habit with her clients—except when she worked with couples who had the same last name.

Goodwin came toward her smiling. "Hi, Karina."

Damn, he was tall. She forced herself to smile politely, instead of grinning like she wanted to. "Hello."

"Thanks for meeting me on such short notice." He had fresh breath too.

"No problem. I had to eat anyway." Rox gestured toward the hostess. "Let's get a booth."

When they were seated, Goodwin reached over and touched her shoulder. "That's a lovely color on you."

Her heart surged. "Thanks. Blue is the only color I wear." *Damn.* She had not intended to say that.

He blinked hard, then gave her a sweet smile. "If it looks good, why not stick with it?" He picked up his menu, still smiling.

She hoped he meant it. Because that was her real self. "I know you want an update on your missing nephew, but I don't have much to report."

"It's okay. It's only been twenty-four hours." He touched her hand this time. "I mostly wanted to see you."

Yes!

A waitress walked up and offered them hot tea. Rox nodded. "I'm ready to order." She looked at her client. "Do you need more time?"

"Nope. I always have spicy pork."

His consistency made her smile. Maybe this could work. Rox ordered her usual crispy chicken with cashews.

While they waited for their meals—which tended to arrive in five minutes—she told him about her trip to the missing-person unit at the bureau. "I wanted to get the investigator's take on Tommy's disappearance."

"What did he say?"

"He's uncertain. He sensed that Donna didn't seem as worried as he would have expected, but that she also seemed shaky, like an alcoholic."

"I knew she'd been drinking heavily. That's why she's avoiding me." Goodwin sighed. "I don't know how to help her."

His concern was touching. "We'll focus on finding Tommy first."

"At this point, I hope you do find him in one of those

programs. At least I'll know he's alive."

Rox had tried not to go there. "Even if we don't locate him, that doesn't mean he's dead." She wanted to comfort the poor man, but she wasn't good at it. She squeezed his hand, then quickly sat back. "Sometimes teenagers run away from their parents and move across the country. They may stay out of touch for years, but they usually come back." Her sister had been well beyond her teenage years when she chose to separate from her family, but the effect had been just as painful.

"You're right. I'll stay optimistic."

The food arrived a few minutes later, and Rox's stomach growled audibly.

Goodwin laughed. "That was fast! And I'm glad you're hungry. I like a woman with an appetite."

Better and better.

While they ate, they talked about families, and she learned that he had been married for a few years when he was younger but had never had children. "I like kids," he added. "I do a lot of volunteer work with them. But there are so many who need attention I don't feel right about bringing more into the world."

"I feel the same. Only I've never actually volunteered to hang out with children. You must be a saint."

"No, just a kid at heart." He laughed, then changed the subject. "Tell me about your work as an investigator. It must be fascinating."

"The extractions can be intense, with high adrenaline pumping." Rox put down her fork, determined not to eat and talk like the slob she usually was. "But most of what I do involves reading through files and checking a lot of websites that don't pan out."

"Do you ever tail people?" His amber eyes sparked with interest.

"Sometimes. But I don't really like doing the divorce cases. They're tedious and depressing."

"How do you pull it off? Following someone and not getting caught?"

"I'm still new at it, but most people don't expect to be followed, so they don't really pay attention."

While they ate, she asked about his work.

Goodwin laughed. "Tedious and depressing." He waved it off with his hand. "Owning businesses that you're not directly involved in is easy, but boring. That's why I volunteer with kids."

He asked about her time in the CIA and she chuckled. "Tedious, but only depressing when we failed our objectives." She couldn't speak freely about what she'd actually done there so she changed the subject to politics, and they had a long lively discussion.

As they finished their meals, he asked, "Did you find out anything about Ridgeline? That wilderness camp you mentioned?"

"A few details, but I still haven't located where they actually take the kids." She was still hoping to hear from someone who'd read one of her flyers or seen her social media posts. "I'm probably going out tomorrow to do some of the tailing we just talked about."

"Good luck." He grabbed both her hands. "If you find Tommy, call me right away."

"I will." Rox pulled her hands back. He was still a client. "I need to get going. I have to pack and do more research tonight."

As she stood, her personal phone rang in her purse.

"Excuse me." She turned and pulled it out. *Marty.* "I have to take this." Rox walked toward the cashier at the front, intending to pay for both meals. She'd taken a considerable retainer from Goodwin. But for the moment, she stepped into the lobby for privacy and answered the call. "What's up?"

"I've been tailing Curtis Fletcher all day, and you're not going to believe where he is right now."

"Surprise me."

"A strip club called Wild Girls Galore."

Huh? "That's a little weird for a guy who's supposedly grieving. Unless he killed Carrie and is out celebrating his freedom."

A pause, then her stepdad said, "I went inside to check it out."

Rox smiled. "Of course you did. Like any good investigator would."

"Exactly. But here's the thing. Half of the girls in there look thirteen. I really think they're underage."

Her instinctual dislike of Fletcher deepened. "I'm sure the place was full of guys who like 'em young. That still doesn't prove he killed his wife." Rox wanted her client released from jail, so she hoped Fletcher would turn out to be guilty.

"Here's another thing," Marty added. "Fletcher didn't act like a customer. He went into the back, then talked to employees like an owner."

More disgust made her tense. "That's just creepy. He runs abusive boot camps for troubled teenage boys while paying teenage girls to shake their breasts for dirty old men." Rox started to wonder if Fletcher was a sociopath. Four percent of all humans were, and the mental condition was often genetic, passed down through generations. "We need to dig up more info on his business dealings."

"I followed him to an office as well," Marty offered. "Fletcher & Sons Investments."

"Well done. I'll check the business registry for it." Rox glanced over and watched Scott Goodwin pay for their meals. She needed to be polite and get back to her date. "I have to go." She hung up, hurried over, and thanked him for dinner. "It was very nice."

Scott walked her to her car. "I enjoyed getting to know you."

"I liked it too." She wanted him to kiss her, but it was too soon. She gave him a shoulder hug. "I'll talk to you later. Goodnight."

At home, Rox checked her Yahoo account and found four more messages. Three were in response to her Craigslist ad and none were helpful. One pervert offered to *make her Ridge Rock*, whatever the hell that meant. The fourth email came from someone who'd seen her flyer at the YMCA. She read the long note from PartyBoyHunter:

My friend saw your message on the board and told me to contact you. The Ridgeline camps are hell on earth, and you SHOULD NOT send your kid there. My cousin got shipped to the camp in Nevada that was supposed to make him not gay, and he killed himself while he was there. By drinking poison!!! Last summer, my dad forced me into the wildernesses bullshit program near Sun Ridge. I escaped twice, but the first time a local cop picked me up and took me back. By the time I got out again, I'd lost 20 pounds and now my lower back is fucked up from carrying heavy shit uphill all day. They treated me like a pack mule. Not all the kids had it that bad, but I'm only 17 and I have nightmares all the time. I'm somewhere safe now and my dad can't find me. DO NOT send your son to Ridgeline or he will hate you forever.

Her body had tensed while reading the email, so Rox tried to make herself relax. But her fists were still clenched, and she had to push back from the desk. Why were these places even legal? Why didn't they get sued out of business? Because parents signed airtight contracts and felt guilty for their part in the whole thing. Local law enforcement obviously protected the camps. Rox hurried to the kitchen for a beer, then sat down to read the message again. Where the hell was Sun Ridge? She googled *Sun Ridge Nevada* first, but no valid links came up. She tried *Sun Ridge Oregon* and landed on the town's website. The map showed a location south of Bend. A five- or six-hour drive but still a hell of a lot closer than Nevada.

Rox sat back in her chair and took a long, cold drink of beer. The good news was that Josh was likely still in the state, somewhere around Sun Ridge. But finding and extracting him would be challenging. Central Oregon had thousands of acres of wilderness, and the base could be anywhere.

She hit reply and sent Hunter a message: *Thank you for contacting me! I'm not planning to send my kid to Ridgeline. In fact, I'm a P.I. and I'm trying to rescue a young man who doesn't want to be there. So I need to know exactly where the camp is. Please get back to me as soon as possible with as much information as you can. Or call instead, if that's easier.* She signed it *Karina* and left her work phone number.

She gave herself a fifty-fifty chance of hearing back from him. Assuming HunterBoy really was male. Girls were sent to the camps too. On Ridgeline's website, they featured a photo of several young girls, with a caption labeled *Bobcats,* as if they were a Girl Scout group. Her research had uncovered other programs that were co-ed, but most separated the genders.

Rox sipped her beer, wishing she could call Isaac Lovejoy and give him an update. But inmates were inaccessible and could only call out—if they were lucky. All she could do for now was write him a note and snail-mail it to the jail. The fact that Josh still had to be rescued from the camp even though his mother had died frustrated the hell out of her. She considered calling the Sun Ridge police, hoping they might even know where the camp operated. But after reading Hunter's message about the cops picking him up and taking him back, she hesitated. Law enforcement people hated custody issues and tried to stay out. Still, with a dead mother and a father in jail, they might cooperate this time.

Rox found the Sun Ridge Police Department's number in a sub-level of the city's website and made the call.

Chapter 20

Saturday, July 8, 6:45 a.m., Ridgeline base camp
Suddenly awake, Josh opened his eyes. Oh god, he was alive, and his suffering was real. He'd been dreaming about his body being broken into pieces, but now the excruciating pain was everywhere. He felt like he'd been hit by a train. His left ribs and lower left leg were the worst. He tried to feel his chest but could hardly move. Where was he? He blinked his eyes to bring the surroundings into focus. Despite the dark, he realized he was inside a sleeping bag. That was unexpected. And this was a tent, not just a tarp. Was he at the base camp?

Images crashed together in his mind. Leaping off the cliff into the air, then landing hard on the rocky ground and blacking out. That was his most vivid memory. He also had flashes of being carried off the mountain on a stretcher. Some woman had given him pills and taped his ankle. Josh pulled his arms free of the sleeping bag and winced at the pain in his left shoulder. *Fuck!* He had planned to die and be free of the pain and pointlessness. Now he could be crippled. And these fuckers might still make him hike.

Tears rolled down his face into his ears. He needed to be in a hospital—with a morphine drip. Why wasn't his mother stepping in and taking him home? Had they not told her about his accident? It didn't matter. He couldn't count on her anymore. He was on his own. Wherever the hell he was. Josh unzipped the bag halfway and sat up, moaning like a baby. To hell with dying. If he was back at the base, this was his chance to escape. He tried to stand, but his ankle screamed in pain and he collapsed back to the hard tent floor. Maybe he wouldn't leave today, but he would get free.

A fat guy in a red counselor T-shirt stepped into the tent and shouted, "Time to move."

"I can't. My ankle is broken."

"No, it's just badly sprained." The counselor tossed a walking stick at him. "Use this to get into the van. But roll your bag up first. I'll take care of the tent."

"Am I going home?"

The fat man laughed. "Not until you graduate."

Chapter 21

Saturday, July 8, 6:55 a.m., Portland

Rox opened her eyes and looked at the clock. She had five minutes before the alarm went off. *Perfect.* She hated waking to the noisy blast and almost never did it anymore, but today she would make a long trip to Sun Ridge. If things went well, she'd be driving home later tomorrow with a teenage boy. Then what? She sat up in bed, suddenly worried. Josh had no parents to go home to at the moment. Would the boy end up in foster care? According to Marty's surveillance report, Curtis Fletcher felt no responsibility for the kid. Maybe Josh had other family, a grandmother or aunt who would take him in. She really needed Lovejoy to call her from jail. She had tried—and failed—to get permission to see him.

Rox climbed out of bed, hoping for the kid's sake that his dad wasn't a killer and would be released soon. She clicked off the alarm and stood, wondering if she should drop the case, give her client his money back, and let the authorities handle the situation. She thought it through. If social workers bothered to get involved at all, they would put Josh into foster care, which could be brutal. Once kids were in the system, getting them out could be difficult, even for family members.

She padded into the kitchen to make coffee, haunted by the email from Hunter, whose cousin had killed himself. Lovejoy was worried that his son was suicidal too. How often did that happen in these programs? She couldn't leave Josh—even for a few more days. The risk was too great. Not to mention the physical abuse and captivity factor. Teenagers were young adults with free will, and forcing them to hike and camp for months at a time was inhuman. Her client would want her to follow through and bring Josh back to society. If Tommy Goodwin happened to be in the program too, she could at least let his uncle know where to find him.

With a new sense of urgency, Rox decided to skip her workout again, promising that she would do some hiking of her own when she wrapped up the case. While the coffee brewed, she took a quick shower, expecting Marty to show up any moment. He had wanted to leave by seven, but she'd vetoed the idea. They still needed location details. No one had answered the phone at the Sun Ridge Police Department the night before, but a friendly voicemail had invited her to leave a message. She'd briefly explained that her client had a family emergency and she needed to locate the Ridgeline camp.

Rox dressed for possible hiking, then checked her phone messages. No return call. She booted up her laptop and logged into her Yahoo account. A new email from Hunter. *Yes!* Rox opened it, surprised by the length. She skimmed through quickly: *You may not be able to find that boy. The program makes kids hike to a new place every day and sleep on the ground with just a tarp. Kids who pass several levels get to go back to the base camp for short stays. But I never made it out of the first level so I eventually escaped and hiked into Sun Ridge. I might be able to help you find the base camp, but it won't do you any good if the kid is out hiking. Sorry.*

Damn. Why didn't he just give her the information? Rox read through the message again, more worried than ever about Josh and more determined to find him. If she could locate the base camp, she could convince a staff member to take her out to Josh, or maybe just hike out on her own and bring him back in. Surely they didn't walk more than ten or twenty miles away from the camp. She hadn't ruled out help from the police department yet, but she wasn't counting on them either.

Rox heard Marty's knock and called out "Clear!" Frustrated, she hit reply and keyed in: *Please call me with specific directions to the base camp. The boy I'm trying to find might be suicidal!*

She sent the email and turned to Marty, who'd walked up behind her. "The camp in Oregon is near Sun Ridge, and I'm messaging with a kid who's been there."

"About time we caught a break. That's south of Bend, about a five-and-a-half-hour drive—if we only stop once." Marty tried to see over her shoulder. "What else did he say? There's a lot of wilderness out there."

Rox moved out of her chair. "Read the whole thing. I'm hoping Hunter will call with real directions."

While Marty sat down to get the details, Rox went to the kitchen for more coffee. She put a couple of waffles in the toaster too. A few minutes later, her stepdad came in and poured himself a cup. "I think we should get on the road. You can check your email on the way, right?"

"If I can find some wi-fi hot spots. But I'll have service in Bend, at least." Rox pulled out butter and syrup. "I hope Hunter will call me."

"Don't count on it. He's only seventeen and might be scared to trust you." Marty pulled out plates. "You got any bacon?"

She shook her head. "Someone in the town of Sun Ridge

knows where the base camp is. If Hunter doesn't follow up, we just have to find that local person and bribe them if necessary."

"Don't count on that." Marty sat down at the table. "Ridgeline probably hires a lot of locals and buys most of its supplies from Sun Ridge retailers. They won't do anything to shut down the flow of money."

So that was how those programs survived. "Hopefully, we'll have directions before we get there." She popped out the waffles and looked in the fridge for some protein to go with them.

"Let's hit the road as soon as we finish breakfast," Marty urged.

"I did most of my packing last night, but I want to go through a checklist with you." Rox put their waffles on the table with some leftover rotisserie chicken.

Marty rolled his eyes. "I always feed you bacon."

"That's why you have heart disease."

"No, it's not. The damage is from stress." He twisted his mouth into a smirk. "You know, from dealing with you."

Rox laughed. "Seriously, old man, are you packed for hiking? And camping? We might be out overnight." She dreaded the thought. Hiking was lovely, or at least the scenery was. But huddling around a fire and peeing in the bushes was outside her comfort zone. Still, she would do whatever was necessary. Her worry about Josh intensified with every new program detail.

"Uh, no. I didn't think about sleeping in the woods." Marty took a big bite and talked with his mouth full. "But I can be ready for that in ten minutes."

It had taken almost an hour to get the truck loaded with food, tents, and tarps—and another hour to drive south to the Santiam Pass turnoff—but the trip over the mountain went quickly. A blue sky, lush green hillsides, and occasional glimpses of rivers and lakes kept them both calm. She'd let Marty drive so she could check for messages. Her phone had stayed silent, and when she tried to call the Sun Ridge Police again, her call hadn't connected. Most of the drive was wilderness, so she wasn't surprised by the lack of cell service. Rox tried not to worry. On the other side of the Cascades, the landscape morphed into a sparse pine forest, with little growing between the trees, except some scrubby sage. Along the road, the dirt turned red, except for patches of black volcanic rock. The farther east they traveled, the dryer and more desert-like the scenery became. She realized why they hosted a wilderness camp out here: it didn't rain.

When they reached Bend—a big skiing town at the base of Mt. Bachelor—they stopped at a mini-mart for gas. After stretching her legs, Rox booted up her laptop while Marty ran into the store for coffee. She plugged her phone into the computer, searched for an unlocked wi-fi connection, then checked her email. Hunter had responded!

She opened the message: *Take Briggs to the top. When it splits, go right for about 3 miles. Turn on the logging road after the crazy curve. The base camp is somewhere out there. In a flat spot near a creek. You can text me if you get lost but don't call. And I may not be much help. My escape was a year ago.*

Marty climbed into the truck. "You hear from the kid?"

"With directions. I think we can find the base camp now. It's right off a road, so we shouldn't have to hike." She worried about Marty's heart. If a long climb to reach Josh was necessary, she'd leave the old man at the base whether he liked it or not.

"Too bad. I was looking forward to stretching my legs." Marty started the engine and pulled back onto the road.

An hour later, they reached the town of Sun Ridge, population: 22,652. The downtown buildings were all single-level and ancient, with only one bank that looked new. Marty stopped at a small city park a block off the main road. Rox pulled sandwiches from the cooler in the jumpseat and passed one to Marty. "Should I try calling the local police again? We know where we're going now."

"Skip it. We might just be making trouble for ourselves." He gave her a sheepish look. "Us cops tend to overreact and want to take control of situations."

"I know. And I called last night, so I'm on record as notifying them."

"Good enough." He bit into his PBJ. "Thanks for making my favorite."

"They pack well and don't need refrigeration, so it's all I brought." Rox winked, even though it was true.

Marty finished his meal quickly and started the truck. "Let's do this."

Rox was still eating, but she grabbed her phone and got online. A Google map of the area showed Briggs Road as south and east. First they had to find Troutdale at the end of town. Rox gave the directions out loud, then finished her sandwich. Worry about what they would find at the base camp, combined with her sense of urgency, made her stomach uneasy. So much about this case felt off-center. She'd never rescued someone who wouldn't have a family member waiting with open arms. Plus, the timing of Carrie's brutal death was unnerving. What if Curtis Fletcher had killed her? Did he have a reason to want Carrie's son dead too? Rox shook it off. She had to stay focused on finding Josh.

At the town's last stoplight, Marty made the turn onto Troutdale Road. "What's our strategy?"

"Find the camp and bring Josh out."

He raised one eyebrow. "No recon, no disguises, no cover story?"

"We don't need a cover story. The truth is reason enough to let him go." Rox tried to be optimistic. "This could turn out to be our easiest extraction yet."

Marty grunted. "I just spent five hours driving, so it better be."

"I think we still have another twenty miles or so." She thought about poor Hunter hiking all that way to escape the program.

The road sloped gently uphill, passing a massive red-rock outcropping in the distance. *Was that ridge the basis for the town's name? And the program's?* After a few more miles, scrubby pines dotted the rolling landscape and the climb got steeper. When they finally made the turn on Briggs Road, a high-mountain wilderness surrounded them.

Marty cut into her thoughts. "What if Josh doesn't want to leave? I mean, when he hears what's going on with his parents?"

Rox let out a harsh scoff. "I don't think it will be a problem. In fact, we might have other teenagers begging us to take them too."

"Are we going to look for Tommy, the missing boy?" Marty's tone was wary.

Rox nodded. "Yes, but only if it doesn't complicate getting Josh out." She remembered Hunter's warning about not finding Josh because of the long overnight hikes away from the base camp. "If Josh isn't at the base, I'll hike out to where he is. You can stay at the camp with the truck and make sure nothing weird goes down."

Marty snapped his head in her direction. "Like what?"

"I don't know. I just don't trust this business or its employees."

"I hear that."

They were quiet as they traveled up the steep, winding road. Tall pine trees, jagged red rocks, and scrubby sage lined the sides. Rox was glad she'd brought hiking boots.

After seven miles of twists and S-curves, the road finally leveled out, indicating they'd reached the summit. Rox checked Hunter's email for directions. "After the split, turn right. After three miles, we watch for a curve and a logging road."

"It's the middle of damn nowhere!" Marty whistled. "We'll need gas again soon."

Twenty minutes later, they found the turnoff Hunter had described. Dirt and gravel, with deep chuckholes, the last few miles of road would be slow and bumpy. That's why they'd driven the truck. "We're watching for the base camp now."

"What are you expecting? A cabin? Or just some big tents and canopies?"

"I don't really know."

After bumping along for fifteen minutes, the road abruptly ended at the base of a rocky cliff.

"Well, hell!" Marty looked over at her. "Did we miss something?"

"We must have." Or Hunter had given them bad directions. "The camp might not be right next to the road. Let's look more deeply on the way back. Maybe there's a trail."

Five minutes later, Rox spotted a worn dirt path that led

to an opening behind a cluster of pine trees. "Stop!"

Her stepdad shut down the vehicle and they climbed out. Rox glanced over at Marty, noting that he wasn't wearing his Glock. She almost asked him to grab the weapon—more worried about bears than armed counselors—but decided against it. Teenagers could be nearby. She moved quickly down the dirt path and into the opening, scanning the area. Empty, brushed flat spots where tents had stood surrounded a charred fire pit in the middle.

"Shit! They're gone." Rox kicked the ground.

Marty stepped sideways, bent down, and touched a dark spot in the dirt. "Someone left a trail of blood."

Chapter 22

Rox knelt down next to her stepdad and stared at the wet area. "Are you sure?" She hadn't seen much blood in her law enforcement career.

"Yes. It looks fresh."

"Damn. What if Josh is hurt? Or any of the kids?" Her head felt tight, as though it was being squeezed.

"It's not a lot of blood. And shit happens when you're in the woods. A staff member could have cut himself whittling." Marty stood. "That fire is still smoldering. The base camp was here this morning."

Rox clenched her fists. "Someone must have told them we were headed here." She rubbed her temples, striving to mitigate the headache coming on. "Why else would they leave right fricking now? After being in this spot since last summer?"

"Who would know?" Marty's forehead puckered like a Shar Pei.

"I left a message with the Sun Ridge police last night. I didn't specifically mention coming here, but I asked for their help in locating a Ridgeline camper."

"I hate to think that an officer tipped them off, but I've lost faith in many of my brothers in blue." Marty rubbed his stubby hair. "Did you tell anyone else? Maybe Isaac Lovejoy?"

"I have no way to talk to him in jail. And why would he sabotage us?"

"The kid who gave us directions?" Marty made a skeptical face, not believing his own suggestion.

"Not likely." Rox glanced around. "Let's check the area. Maybe they left trash or something that will give us a clue."

Marty grunted and began to search. Rox headed across the campsite, not seeing anything but a pile of coffee grounds dumped near the fire pit. Past the edge of the clearing, she spotted dozens of small, mounded dirt clumps, scattered across the pine needles of the forest floor. *What the hell?* After a moment, she realized what they were. Miniature latrines. If the base camp had been here for a year, why hadn't they dug a bigger pit, farther away? And what did they do with their garbage? Haul it out or bury it?

She stepped carefully among the pine needles, searching for bigger mounds, indicating a trash pile. Digging through garbage was an old-school but effective way to gain information. Disgusting, but it paid off sometimes.

"What are you looking for?" Marty called out behind her.

"Buried trash, a dropped notepad, or a hiking map." Rox kept moving, her eyes scanning both directions. A creek rippled in the distance. "At least they had a water source."

"I think we're wasting time," her stepdad shouted. "Let's backtrack and try one of the other dirt roads."

As they neared the small stream, Rox noticed a long, raised lump in the carpet of brownish-red needles. She moved toward it, mentally measuring the disrupted area. About five and a half feet long. When she reached the mound, she stopped, and a cold shiver ran up her spine.

"What the hell?" Marty moved up beside her.

Rox knelt down. "I hope it's a trash pile." She had left her work gloves in the truck so she used her bare hands to brush off the mound of needles and sage branches. A red piece of cloth appeared under the layers of brown debris. "No!" Her pulse accelerated and she brushed faster.

The red cloth covered an arm.

Marty dropped down and started clearing the other end of the mound. A moment later, a young girl's body emerged.

"Oh no!" Marty sounded as distressed as she felt.

Rox stared at the girl. She looked fourteen and deathly pale under a pink sunburn. "Goddamnit. This is so wrong."

Marty grabbed her arm. "Try calling the local police again."

"I don't have service here."

"I'm taking pictures." Marty pulled his phone from his pants pocket. "We have to carry her out of here."

"Okay." Typically, moving a dead body wasn't a good option, but the poor kid had been abandoned once already. They couldn't leave her to wild animals while they rounded up authorities—who might not give a shit. "What the hell do you suppose happened to her?"

"I don't know, but she doesn't look beaten." Marty moved in for a close-up of the girl's face. "Or broken. I don't think she fell."

"Maybe she had a seizure." The thought came to mind because her treatments could trigger seizures, so she'd researched them.

Her stepdad gasped, a sound that startled her.

"What?"

"She's not dead." Marty jumped to his feet. "We need to get her to a hospital."

The staff had just left her? Stunned, Rox helped Marty carry the girl to the truck and load her into the cab. Heart still pounding, she grabbed a blanket from their camping supplies and covered the unconscious camper, then nodded at Marty.

"Drive. I'll keep her breathing."

"The bastards! I've never witnessed anything like this." Marty's voice shook with rage. Rox had never seen him so upset.

On the long trip into town, she rubbed the girl's face and thumped her chest when her breath became faint. Rox wished she knew the teenager's name, but she talked to her anyway, pleading with the girl to hang in there. Her long-ago training for emergency scenarios kept her emotions in check. She just had to stay calm and keep the girl alive. Rox took a moment to pull out her phone and attempt a 911 call, but she couldn't connect.

Where would the call go anyway? To the Sun Ridge Police, which probably employed only a few people—none of whom she trusted. The tiny town probably didn't have a hospital either, and if they had a clinic, it was likely closed on Saturday. Where did local folks go when they had medical emergencies? The hospital in Bend!

Rox turned to Marty. "Just keep driving to Bend. Even if they have urgent care here, the docs are going to transport her anyway. This will be faster."

He gave her a thumbs-up. Rox suspected he was still too upset to speak.

The St. Charles ER moved quickly into action, getting the girl onto a gurney and cutting the clothes off her body as they wheeled her into the trauma center. "Check for stings or bites!" one of the doctors shouted. Rox wanted to follow and ask questions but knew they would brush her off. Her explanation—that they had found the girl while looking for another teenager—had already earned raised eyebrows.

When Rox mentioned the wilderness camp to the charge

nurse, the woman's lips tightened. "I hate those programs."

Marty bounced on his feet beside her. They were both anxious to get out of the hospital before cops arrived and slowed them down. "We need to go back and look for the base again," Rox said. "Here's my number if anyone wants to talk to me." She gave her work phone, just as she'd given her investigative name. She hoped the girl would soon be able to tell her own story, leaving them mostly out of the situation.

The nurse jotted the number on a notepad, then looked up again. "No idea who she is?" Frustration in her voice.

"Call Ridgeline Wilderness Health and ask them who they left for dead." Rox tasted the bitterness of her words.

"Thanks for saving her." The nurse turned to give instructions to another caregiver.

"Let's go." Marty grabbed her arm and they hurried out.

At the truck, Rox asked, "Want me to drive for a while?"

"No. I'm too pissed off to just sit as a passenger."

She felt the same. "Are we going back to search again?"

"Not right now."

She wanted to argue but didn't. They both climbed in and Marty explained. "A blind search could take days or weeks. That's a big wilderness. Meanwhile, we might get lucky and have the authorities shut down the camp."

"If they can find it." Rox shook her head. "Or if they even care. I'm calling the locals again." Rox found the number in her call log and pressed it.

After several rings, a woman's voice said, "Police Department."

"I need to speak to the person in charge."

"Just a moment."

A minute later, a male voice came on the line. "Chief Manford. What can I do for you?"

"This is Karina Jones again. I left a message last night about a teenager in the Ridgeline program."

"And?"

She wanted to know if he'd tipped off the camp, but asking was pointless. "I'm a family friend of Josh Lovejoy, and I have to find him and bring him home."

"You'll have to take that up with Ridgeline. We don't interfere with their program. They're doing a great thing for those kids."

Oh no. "The boy's mother is dead, but the Ridgeline office won't return my calls."

"I'm sorry to hear that, but I don't know how I can help you."

A brick wall, as she'd suspected. "They left a kid for dead up there and moved their camp in a hurry."

A long pause. "I find that hard to believe. It's a good program."

"A girl went into a coma, and they walked away from her like she was trash!" Rox shouted, unable to control her fury.

Marty patted her arm and gestured for her to calm down.

The Sun Ridge police chief snapped, "Don't be such a drama queen! I'm sure they intended to come back for her. You have no idea what it's like to keep a group of troubled teenagers in line."

Drama queen? What an asshole. "They covered her with pine needles and left her."

"I'm sure whatever happened was an accident." His tone softened. "They probably thought she was dead and covered her to keep the coyotes and bugs off until they could bring her down. I'll look into it."

"I want to know where the camp moved to."

"I have no idea."

Rox didn't believe him, but she was too upset to continue, so she hung up.

She and Marty were both quiet for a minute. Finally, Rox said, "We have another option."

"What's that?"

"Find the transport office and follow the van when it goes out."

"Let's give it twenty-four hours and see what happens. If Josh doesn't surface, we'll go back for him."

Chapter 23

Sunday, July 9, 8:45 a.m., Portland

After sleeping late and sitting around with coffee and the newspaper for an hour, Rox finally got dressed. Twelve hours of riding in the truck the day before had been strangely exhausting. Her head was eager to get back to work but her body was not. She still had leads to explore, but other than the location of the transport office, none seemed that critical. Her concerns for now were simple: Would Ridgeline send Josh home so he could attend his mother's funeral service? And would they drop him off where they picked him up—at his mother's now-empty home? That seemed irresponsible. More important, how would she learn any of this? Curtis Fletcher hadn't returned her phone calls. Marty had volunteered to sit in front of the man's house this afternoon, but that seemed iffy. He'd made it clear he had no interest in Josh.

She also needed to know when Carrie's service would be held. Rox planned to be there as part of her investigative process. Homicide detectives attended murder victims' services to see if anyone unexpected, such as the killer, showed up—so she would do the same. She might even run into Kyle at the memorial for the same reason, which could be weird. But she would let the detectives solve Carrie's murder. Her purpose was to ask attendees about Ridgeline and the Oregon-based transport to its camps.

Rox opened her laptop, loaded the Fellowship website, and checked its events section. Carrie's service was scheduled for that evening at six. Rox added it to her task list for the day, then checked her email and groaned. Another flood of Craigslist-based messages had come in. She clicked each one open with a quick scan. Most were bizarre spam messages, some sexual in nature. She made a mental note to delete the Yahoo account after this case was over. Buried in the spam were two messages that focused on Ridgeline.

One was from a young girl named Rosa who couldn't spell or use complete sentences. The message was so truncated it was almost meaningless: *Rdline last sumer hated ok now.* Rox tried to extrapolate. Rosa had participated in a Ridgeline camp last summer and hated it, but now her life was fine?

Rox opened the last email, from the address *sharonlee876,* and scanned the message. Her mouth dropped open, and she read through it again more slowly: *A Ridgeline camp targeted me. The one called Get Straight that's meant to convert kids who think they're gay back into being normal. When I say targeted, I mean they blackmailed me. They sent pics of my son kissing another boy and threatened to tell my church, plus upload them online if I didn't send Luke to the camp. So I borrowed ten thousand against my house to pay for it. And Luke is still gay. I never told anyone about the blackmail because I'm ashamed. But I thought someone should know. It's not a very Christian way to operate a business. Especially one that doesn't work. Please don't reply. I don't want to think about this again. S.L.*

Stunned, Rox got up and walked to the back deck to process the information. The morning sun was warm and lovely, but her plants needed watering again so she went back inside. Even if participation in both behavior-based boot camps and gay-conversion therapies was declining, blackmailing churchgoers to drum up clients was disgusting. Ridgeline was getting away with it because of the stigma attached to homosexual children in religious groups—and apparently the shame of giving in to blackmail.

Maybe that was why Donna Goodwin pretended Tommy had run away—because she was too ashamed to admit she'd sent him to conversion therapy. Had she been blackmailed too?

Shock escalated into outrage, and Rox desperately wanted to call and report the incident. But to what agency? She had no idea where the gay-conversion camp was located and no real proof of anything. Her source didn't want to be contacted and wouldn't likely back her up. Still, this seemed like a scam the feds would be interested in. She added *Call FBI about blackmail* to her list. But it could wait until after they extracted Josh.

Her conversation with the teenage girl in the fellowship daycare came back to her. What was her name? Something religious? Oh right, Rebecca. Rox added a chat with the girl to her list, but that would have to wait until later as well. She had to stay focused on Josh. *And Tommy*, she reminded herself. The possible link between the cases could be important. Tommy's mother might know where Ridgeline's base camp had moved to. They might have several sites that they rotated. Rox recalled the conversation she'd had with the missing-person detective and the moment she'd asked for Donna Goodwin's contact information. The number Kushing had given popped into her head, and Rox punched it into her phone.

A woman answered, sounding a little tipsy. "This is Donna."

"I'm Karina Jones, a private investigator. Scott Goodwin hired me to find his nephew Tommy."

"Oh. I didn't know."

Maybe the woman was just sleepy. "Can we meet? I'd like to talk about the case."

"There's no case. Tommy ran away."

"But you want to find him, don't you?"

"Of course. But I can't make him come home even if I do." Donna sobbed and hiccupped at the same time.

Rox wanted to ask about the possibility of a correctional camp but decided to wait for a face-to-face conversation. Donna might not lie to her in person. Especially if she was drunk at ten in the morning. "Are you home?" Rox asked. "Can I stop over? Or buy you lunch?"

"I'm not hungry, and I'm not going out." The woman took a slurp of something.

Rox talked over the sloshing sound. "I'll come over. You're still on Prescott?"

"Yes." A wary tone. "How do you know where I live?"

"I'm an investigator. And I'm trying to help your family."

"No one can help me. Brett is dead, and Tommy is gone. My life is pointless." Donna hung up.

Rox felt bad for the woman and started to wonder if Goodwin was wrong about Donna sending her son to Ridgeline. Rox wanted to drive over and ask anyway, just to see the mother's reaction. She texted Marty to let him know her plans, then grabbed her shoulder bag and headed out. Her office was on the way, sort of, and she decided to stop by and pick up the cash she'd left in the safe. She might need it to bribe a transport driver or a store clerk in Sun Ridge when they went back. She had no faith that Ridgeline would release Josh. Curtis Fletcher was connected to Ridgeline, possibly an owner, and leaving Josh at the camp would be the easiest course of action. The boy needed someone to intervene.

Rox called the county jail again and tried to convince the desk deputy to take a message for her client.

"I can't do that. I'm not the inmates' secretary. If you need to reach him, have his lawyer call or come in."

"I'm not sure he has one."

"Everyone has a court-appointed public defender."

"Can you tell me who that is?"

"I'll transfer you to the records office." The line went quiet for a moment, then a canned message recited the office's hours of operation—which didn't include Sunday. Rox cursed and slammed down her phone. Inmates were so isolated! She took some deep breaths, found the number for the Bend hospital, and gathered up her stuff. On the way out, she put in her earbud and made another call.

As Rox climbed in her car, a receptionist answered, "St. Charles Hospital."

"Hi. I'm the woman who brought in the unidentified teenage girl yesterday. Can you tell me how she's doing?"

"You don't know the patient's name?" The woman was a little condescending.

"No. I found her in the woods and brought her in. She was unconscious and had no ID. But I'd like to know if she's okay."

"I wasn't here yesterday and don't know anything about her. I'll see what I can find out."

"Thanks."

Rox drove halfway to her office before the receptionist came back on the line. "She was transferred to the children's hospital in Portland. She's in the ICU, but she's stable and likely to recover."

"Great news. What happened to her? Why was she left for

dead?"

"Uh. Her chart says hypothermia and a high level of benzodiazepines."

Where had the kid gotten sedatives in a wilderness camp? "No identification yet?"

"No, but our admin office is working on it."

"Thanks." Rox hung up and took the exit to her office. Maybe the girl had stolen the meds from a counselor and taken an overdose. Then hypothermia had set in, making her look dead. Knowing the camper probably hadn't been assaulted by Ridgeline employees, a level of tension left Rox's body. Still, the bastards had left her! What had they intended to tell her parents? The police chief seemed confident the staff would have come back for the body. Had something like this happened before?

A few minutes later, Rox stared at her office building's front door. Someone had drilled out the lock and left it ajar! *What the hell?* She'd never even worried about a break-in. Rox pushed the top of the door with one finger, not wanting to smudge any prints the intruder may have left. The front room seemed fine, but there was nothing to steal except the monitor on the desk, and it was still there. The interior door lock had been drilled out too. Dreading what she would see, Rox pushed it open. Her file cabinet drawers had been yanked out, and her papers had been rifled. She spun toward her desk. Her laptop was gone, and the big monitor that had been attached to it was askew. *Shit!* A thousand bucks out the door. Her slim backup hard drive was still on the desk. Thank goodness! She still had copies of all her files, plus her home laptop. Also, the thief wasn't likely to get past her security to access the software. Rox glanced at the corner floor. The square that held the safe was still tightly in place.

Rox pried it up, accessed the steel box, and pulled out the cash. She slipped it into her shoulder bag, then scanned through her printed files, which were scattered around the cabinets. Nothing seemed to be missing, yet it was obvious someone had been looking for information. But who and why? Her current clients were both concerned with protecting teenage boys, so it probably wasn't either of them. A wild thought hit her. Had Curtis Fletcher come here looking for information related to Carrie or Josh? That seemed unlikely too.

It had to be about another case. She'd worked a divorce situation a few weeks earlier, and the cheating husband might have come looking to destroy the incriminating information against him. Rox checked that file. The paperwork was still there, and the digital photos were on her computer. She'd given her client a thumb drive and hadn't bothered to make any prints. A worried thought came to her. The cheating husband may have been looking for information about his estranged wife—such as her new address. *Damn!*

She would call the woman to alert her and upgrade the building's security, maybe even put an iron-grid exterior door on the front. Fortunately, most of her clients didn't know about the back door. She gave it a quick check. Still intact. Should she call the police? It was most likely a waste of time. Unless the intruder had left prints and was already in the system, property-crime detectives would never make an arrest. Maybe she was reading too much into the break-in. It could have simply been a meth addict with a drill and a crowbar, looking to steal a computer he could sell. He'd probably searched the file cabinets looking for drugs, watches, or jewelry.

She pulled out her phone and took photos of the drilled-out doors and ransacked files, then texted them to both Bowman and Marty with the message: *Seen any MOs like this before?* Bowman would check the bureau's database for similar crimes. Rox called Marty, reported the incident, and asked him to find a locksmith.

"I just looked at your text, and I think you'll need a whole new front door. I'll take care of it for you. But for now, I'll rig something to keep it secure."

Damn, she loved him. "Thanks, Marty! You're the best." She'd never called him *Dad*. But she'd also called her mother Georgia from an early age—at her mom's request.

"Where are you going now?" Marty asked.

"To see Donna Goodwin. She's the mother of the missing boy."

"Shouldn't we be focused on Josh?"

Rox bristled a little. "I took a retainer from Scott Goodwin so I have to make an effort. Plus, he thinks Donna sent her son to a correctional camp, so this could help us find Josh."

Marty was silent for a moment. "We need to locate a transport office in Oregon. I'm sure Ridgeline either has one or contracts with one."

"I know. Maybe Hunter, the kid who gave us directions, can help with that." Rox was skeptical, but she would email him and ask. She recalled the message from Sharon Lee and told Marty about Ridgeline's blackmail scheme for its other program.

"What a dirty business. I hope we can shut them down." He started to hang up, then said, "Hey, email the woman who was blackmailed and ask her about the transport office."

"I will." Probably another waste of time. "I'll be in touch." Rox closed the call and headed out to her vehicle. She wasn't looking forward to her chat with Donna, a woman with nothing left but despair.

In the parking lot, she noticed a tiny piece of something white and picked it up. Part of a breath mint? Had the intruder dropped it?

Chapter 24

Donna Goodwin lived in a modest home a few miles south of their duplex. Rox parked next to the Honda CRV in the driveway, which was probably ten years old. As she walked up to the door, she had serious doubts about whether Tommy's mother could help her locate Josh. Ridgeline was too expensive for the owner of this house—unless she had help paying for it. But Rox had to honor her promise to search for Tommy too, so she might as well learn what she could from the person who'd last seen him.

Donna took a full three minutes to respond to her knock. With the summer sun directly overhead, Rox broke into a sweat while she waited. Finally, the faded-green door opened slightly, and a disheveled woman peered out the gap. "Who are you?" Mascara was smudged under her eyes.

"Karina Jones." Rox had almost said her real name. "I called you earlier about coming here to discuss Tommy's disappearance."

"I'm not dressed." She glanced down at her orange-floral bathrobe and flip-flops.

"It's all right. I know it's Sunday, and this won't take long." Rox tried to give a charming smile, but knew she'd failed. The sight of Donna distressed her. The woman was obviously not doing well. Rox couldn't focus on that—she was on a mission.

The grieving woman led her into a dark, cluttered house with all the drapes pulled tightly closed. Food-crusted bowls covered the coffee table in the living room, and a faint smell of rotting garbage drifted in from the kitchen. Donna gestured at the couch. "Have a seat. I'm sorry about the mess."

Rox nodded. She couldn't make herself lie and say it was fine. "I'm sorry for what you're going through. I assume you haven't heard from Tommy."

"No." Donna picked up a glass from the table that looked like it contained orange juice.

With a little splash of vodka? "When did you see him last?"

"Friday morning before school. He came home Sunday evening for a minute before he took off again, but I was in the bathtub and didn't actually see him."

"Did he say where he was going?"

Donna shook her head. "Tommy had stopped talking to me."

"Tell me about his friends and hobbies. I'd like to start my search next week."

Donna waved her hand in a dismissive gesture. "I went through all this with the police." She spoke slowly, as if trying to be careful not to slur. "They talked to Tommy's friends, and no one knows anything."

"Where does your son normally hang out? Any clubs or sports?"

"He plays basketball at the Y. Or at least he used to."

"The YMCA? Which one?"

"On Powellhurst Street. The youth group had a lot of activities there."

Another odd sensation she'd never experienced—in her chest this time. "Kids from the Community Fellowship?"

"Yeah, but I stopped going. I'm not sure I believe in a higher power anymore—unless he's a sadist." Her mouth twisted into a bitter scowl.

Rox wasn't in a mood to discuss theology. She had too many questions and not enough patience to be anything but direct. "Did you send Tommy to a gay-conversion camp?"

"No!" Donna's expression suggested that Rox might be crazy. "Tommy's not gay."
No hint of deceit or shame.

"What about a corrective wilderness program like Ridgeline?"

"I don't know what you're talking about. Tommy's a good kid." Donna gulped her drink. "Yeah, he had started staying out for days at a time and not telling me where he was. His grades had slipped too, but he wasn't in any kind of real trouble." It took the mother a minute to enunciate all that.

Rox believed her. At least the part about not sending Tommy away. She had one more long-shot question. "Does Tommy know Josh Lovejoy?"

Donna shrugged. "I think I heard him mention a Josh once, but I don't know that last name."

A hard knock on the door startled them both. Donna pulled her robe together. "I can't handle more company right now."

Rox stood. "Should I see who it is?"

"Please."

As Rox moved toward the door, another knock sounded. "Portland Police! We need to talk to you."

A wave of dread flooded her as Rox hurried to the door. She heard Donna get up and follow.

Two uniformed officers stood outside looking solemn. The older one asked, "Are you Donna Goodwin?"

"No, but she's right here."

Donna stepped into the doorway beside her.

"Can we come in?" the same officer asked.

"No." Donna shook her head. "Just tell me."

The cop wiped his sweaty brow. "Ma'am, we have news about your son Tommy."

"What? Where is he?" A note of hope in the mother's voice.

The officer reached out and touched Donna's arm. "A hiker found him in a shallow grave. I'm sorry, but we think he's been dead for a few weeks."

Chapter 25

Rox paced her house, dreading making the call. Or maybe she didn't have to contact Scott Goodwin. Surely Donna would let him know Tommy was dead. Still, Goodwin was her client, so she felt obligated to reach out. She had wanted to see him again personally—just not under these circumstances.

Still stalling, she took a moment to change into black pants and a navy-blue blouse. A dress would have been more appropriate for a funeral service, but she didn't have a black one. She hadn't known Carrie Lovejoy—except for their brief encounter a few nights ago—so attending her service wasn't about paying respects. She wanted to see who attended, how they acted, and who knew each other. Curtis Fletcher, in particular, was a person of interest. A wild speculation popped into her head. Had Fletcher killed both Carrie and Tommy? But why? What was the victims' connection? Other than the Fellowship, where she was soon headed.

Rox checked herself in the mirror and abruptly realized she couldn't attend. Fletcher had seen her Wednesday at the prayer service. Although she'd been wearing a wig and glasses at the time, he'd commented on her height. For sure, her six-foot frame would attract his attention at the memorial. *Damn!* She would have to send Marty instead and rely on his feedback. Or she could go along and stay in the car, watching people in the parking lot. She texted her stepdad: *Lots going on. I need your help.* She'd been trying to reach him for an hour. Sometimes when he was golfing he turned off his phone.

Before she could change her mind, she switched to her work phone and called Scott Goodwin. He answered quickly and sounded upbeat. "Hey, Karina."

Scott had recognized her number, which meant he'd created a contact listing for her and must be interested. Rox shook off the thought. It didn't matter now. "Hello."

Before she could continue, he cut in eagerly. "What have you found out?"

Damn. Donna hadn't told him. The grieving mother had probably been too drunk or too devastated. "I'm sorry, but I have some bad news."

"What? Tommy's in the wilderness program?"

"No. He's dead." Rox mentally kicked herself. That had been too abrupt. "I'm sorry."

"Dead? How? What are you saying?" His voice pitched up a notch.

"The police think Tommy was murdered. His body was found in a shallow grave in Forest Park." Five thousand acres of trees—right in the middle of Portland's upscale neighborhoods.

"Oh god. No!"

"I'm sorry for your loss." Rox didn't know what else to say. She didn't have any other details yet. She'd made calls to both Kyle and the missing-person unit but had only been able to leave messages.

"I have to call Donna."

"She knows." Rox had offered to go to the morgue with Donna to identify her son, but the distressed woman had lashed out at her. Now Rox hesitated to offer Goodwin comfort. "Can I do anything? Of course, I'll refund your deposit."

"Thank you. I'll call you tomorrow. I can't think straight right now." Goodwin abruptly hung up.

Rox sat down, her body still fatigued from yesterday's traveling. Today had been rough too. First her office had been broken into, then the news of Tommy's murder had hit her hard. Not because she grieved for a boy she didn't know, but because it forced her to rethink her whole investigation. On the surface, both cases involved a troubled teenage boy. Yet the fact that Josh and Tommy had attended the same fellowship meant there might be something bigger at stake. Instinct told her to keep digging. If Tommy had been killed, Josh might be in mortal danger as well. And she was no closer to extracting him than when she'd started the case.

Marty's knock snapped her out of the funk, and she called out, "Clear!"

Her stepdad bounded in, looking chipper for an old guy who'd driven hundreds of miles the day before. "What's going on?"

Rox gestured for him to have a seat. He was making *her* feel old. "Our second client, the missing boy? He turned up dead in Forest Park, bludgeoned and buried in a shallow grave." She shook her head, knowing what Marty would ask. "I don't know how or when. I just happened to be at his mother's home when officers came to break the news."

"That's damn sad." Marty worked his eyebrows. "So is Tommy a runaway who fell in with drug dealers or maybe a gang?"

"I've considered that." Rox stood. "I need more coffee."

Marty followed her to the kitchen so she kept talking. "But the fact that Tommy and Josh both attended the Community Fellowship makes me think the boys knew each other, and that Carrie and Tommy's deaths are connected.

With Tommy murdered, I'm more worried than ever about Josh."

"Other than the church, what have you got?" Marty challenged.

He was forcing her to think it through. "Maybe nothing. Josh was sent to a wildness camp by a mother who wanted to correct his behavior so she could move in with her fiancé." Rox poured coffee, now a little stale, and took a sip. "Tommy ran away from home because he was grieving and angry and using drugs. On the streets, you can get killed for a lot of reasons." Rox visualized the people she'd seen on Dirty Kid Corner and the surrounding blocks. Some were mentally ill and might strike out in a schizophrenic psychosis. But that didn't explain where the body ended up.

"So the only connection is the fellowship." Marty nodded. "But I trust your instinct. Let's look into it. Maybe both boys were involved in the same activity."

"A youth group," Rox said. "Tommy played basketball at the YMCA where Josh's mother worked." Rox gulped more coffee. "Speaking of Carrie, her memorial service is at the Community Fellowship in forty minutes." She grinned at Marty. "I need you to attend."

He groaned and made a face. "Why?"

"Because I went there already, remember? And I took Carrie's phone. I can't hide my tallness. Someone will make the connection and look at me very closely."

"All right. But you have to be available to help me keep everyone straight."

"Don't worry. I'll be in the car." She gave him a mock-shock look. "You mean you're going to text me with questions while you're in the church?"

"Yep."

This would be interesting. Rox's work phone rang again. A vaguely familiar number. She nodded at Marty and took the call. A canned voice announced: "You have a collect call from the Multnomah County Jail. To accept these charges, press one. To deny the call—"

Rox hit the button, and the voicemail switched to another message. Moments later, Lovejoy came on the line. "Thanks for talking to me. I hope you believe I'm innocent."

"For now, yes." Rox paused. "I have some good news and bad news about Josh."

"What?" He sounded alarmed.

"We found the area where Ridgeline conducts its wilderness programs, but the base camp had just moved. I think the local police tipped them off that I was looking for it."

"I'm not surprised. But please don't give up. I'm worried sick about Josh. Especially if they told him his mother was dead." Noise in the background, mostly loud male voices, made it hard to hear her client. "The poor boy was already depressed."

She knew Lovejoy didn't have much time on the phone, so Rox got right to the point. "I have no idea what Ridgeline plans to do with Josh, and Curtis Fletcher won't return my calls. But I'm still on the case. We're going back out to Sun Ridge as soon as we have more information."

"Thank you."

"You need to contact Ridgeline and demand they release Josh. If you can get permission." Rox spelled out the number.

"I have nothing to write that down with."

He couldn't remember a phone number? She gave it to him again, and he recited it back, sounding uncertain.

"What's your public defender's name? That's the only way I can get information to you."

"Amy Borden, but she hasn't even been to see me."

That reminded her to ask, "If I successfully extract Josh and you're still in jail, what do I do with him?"

"I have a sister in Seattle. Lynn Severs. Josh knows how to contact his aunt."

Relieved that the boy had somewhere to go, Rox felt her energy kick in. She asked the long-shot question again. "Do you know a boy named Tommy Goodwin?"

"No. Why?"

"He went missing and turned up dead."

"What does he have to do with Josh?" Tightness in his voice again. "You're freaking me out."

"It's probably nothing. I'm sorry."

Someone shouted loudly in the background, and her client said a quick goodbye and hung up.

Rox looked at Marty. "Time for church, old man."

Chapter 26

Marty put on a black suit with a white shirt, then selected a dark-red tie. He glanced in the mirror and smiled. He looked darn spiffy and wished SiriKaren could see him right now. His girlfriend liked him to wear nice clothes, especially when they went dancing. They'd finally consummated their relationship the night before, and it had been great. Well, mostly. The first time was always a little awkward, but at least his body hadn't betrayed him.

He caught himself whistling as he walked over to Rox's and put a stop to it. Besides the fact that she hated the habit, he didn't want to talk about why he felt so chipper. Not yet. Eventually Rox would meet SiriKaren, who was Pakistani and ten years younger than him. *They'll get along just fine,* he told himself.

Rox stood outside her place, looking fierce and beautiful at the same time. "Let's take your sedan."

"Excellent idea. That eyesore of yours doesn't blend in anywhere." He hated boxy vehicles and didn't understand the appeal. But he loved Rox more than he'd ever expected to. She'd been such a peculiar child. So unlike his sweet and predictable Jolene. But Roxanne had been special in her own way—and fascinated with his police officer job—so they had bonded easily.

Rox nodded and surprised him. "I've been thinking about that. I'll probably trade in the Cube for something that looks just like every other new car on the road." They climbed into his sedan, and Rox asked, "What's your cover for being there?"

He was still worried about that. "I have to stick with the line I gave Curtis Fletcher when I knocked on his door the other day." Marty gave Rox a quick grin. "A grief counselor, sent by the fellowship to comfort him."

"Oh boy." Rox shook her head. "If Fletcher asks someone from the group about you, your cover may be blown."

"Maybe not. There's another Community Fellowship, and I'm from that congregation." He shrugged, hoping to ease her mind. "It'll be fine. I'll avoid Fletcher and limit who I engage with." Marty backed out of the driveway and headed east.

"We still need to find the Oregon transport office." His daughter sounded worried. A new emotion for her.

"We will." Marty reached over and touched Rox's shoulder. "What's bothering you most?"

"Our client's son. If Josh is suicidal, he might already be dead after a couple of weeks in an abusive camp." Rox let out a sigh. "The counselors already left one kid for dead, so they might have left Josh too. He could be out there, being eaten by coyotes."

Marty was still stunned about the girl they'd found—and the lack of concern displayed by the Sun Ridge brothers in blue. But he'd done some reading, and the program had been around for twenty years, with only one camper dying from a seizure. "Ridgeline can't make a habit of that behavior or they would have been shut down. Even tough-love parents don't put up with that." He made a left and drove toward the freeway entrance.

"Maybe they buy off the parents who complain."

"Josh is probably all right. But we'll find him and get him out." Marty was glad to still have a meaningful purpose. Even with SiriKaren in his life, he needed to feel useful. Especially now that his days were numbered.

When they neared the fellowship, Rox pointed and said, "Park next door in front of that school."

Marty pulled in, glad it was Sunday evening and the school was closed. Butterflies in his stomach surprised him. He'd thought he was too jaded by now to get nervous about investigative work. But he'd always been a patrol officer, so the extractions and their cover stories were still new to him. And his part had always been backup or distraction—not direct engagement. Still, he'd already done this gig once at Fletcher's house, so he could handle it. "Why am I worried about this one?" he mused out loud.

Rox turned to him, staring hard. "I don't know. It's a memorial service in a fellowship hall. What's the worst that could happen?"

"You mean like stealing someone's phone and having them get murdered a few hours later?"

They both laughed, but it felt hollow. Marty reached for the door handle. "Here goes."

"Text me if we need to leave in a hurry." Rox grinned. "I'll start the engine and turn the car around."

"More likely, you'll have to come in and wake me up." Marty climbed out and hopped over the short metal railing that divided the parking spaces. The church's space was full, but a regular service probably followed Carrie's memorial, so he couldn't tell how many people had showed up to honor the victim. Marty glanced around, looking for Fletcher's red BMW, and spotted it not far from the front entry.

Three people stood on the landing outside the front doors, talking quietly. As Marty passed, he heard a woman say, "Her poor son. I wonder what will happen with him."

Marty slowed.

The man standing next to her responded, "Hopefully, Carrie has relatives. I'm sure Curtis isn't going to take him in."

Marty stopped, bent down, and fiddled with his shoe, a slip-on loafer.

"Why should he?" another man asked. "He and Carrie were engaged, but that doesn't make him responsible for her kid."

"Where is Josh?" The woman's tone was sharp this time. "Shouldn't he be here?"

"He's probably inside," the first man said. "And we should be too."

Marty stood up and hurried in ahead of them. The foyer was packed with a dozen people, but the space was quiet, with only a few whispered conversations. He glanced around, looking for Curtis Fletcher, and more broadly, for anyone who looked out of place. Particularly a male. Since Carrie had been beaten and strangled, her killer was most likely a man. Another lover? If she'd cheated on her ex-husband, she might have cheated on her fiancé too. One of the men in her life was likely the killer. With a child's custody at issue, Marty had his money on Isaac Lovejoy. He was humoring Rox by being here.

The crowd was older than he'd expected, mostly couples over fifty. Where were Carrie's friends? He would have expected a crowd of women in their forties. Marty stepped closer to a couple talking in harsh whispers. The woman said something about selling their house and the man argued about the timing. Marty moved on, shifting to a position against the wall, where he could see inside the main hall. The space with all the pews had a name but he couldn't remember it. This organization might call itself a fellowship, but it looked and sounded like a church to him.

A group of women sat in a cluster near the front, most wearing black, but none with gray hair. Carrie's female friends. More couples, a few with kids, sat across the aisle. Where was the grieving fiancé?

Marty turned to watch the foyer for a few minutes. A thirty-something man with a big beard walked in, surprising him. The guy stopped and nodded at an older couple. Marty slipped his phone out, held it up as if trying to read a text, and took a photo. He quickly put the phone away.

The crowd in the foyer moved toward the pews, so he did too. He sat in the back, amused that Rox had likely sat in this space four days earlier. Her palming of Carrie's phone to check for leads was even more surprising. The magnetic treatments were really opening up his daughter's ability to step outside her comfort zone and experience new things. He hoped the effect would last—and that she wouldn't take her new freedom too far.

Marty pulled out his cell again but kept it low in his lap while he clicked on the image he'd just recorded. He hated typing on the tiny keyboard, but he was getting better and he'd learned to use the supplied word suggestions to make things easier. He kept the message brief: *Do you know this guy?*

Rox answered right away: *No. But I'll send it to Bowman.*

His ex-partner could run facial recognition software and see if the guy had a criminal record. Behind him, a familiar voice whispered something urgent. Marty glanced over his shoulder and saw Curtis Fletcher standing in the wide doorway, a phone next to his ear.

Fletcher looked upset and spoke angrily to the person on the other end of the conversation. "You're my brother! You're supposed to be here."

A moment of quiet, then Fletcher countered, "That's not a good excuse. I'm under enough stress with my fiancé dying and the business in decline."

Was Ridgeline in serious financial trouble? Fletcher was whispering so Marty stood, as if to straighten his legs, hoping to hear better.

Fletcher raised his voice. "No, it's your fault! We blew our cash reserve paying out hush money for your aggressions. I want it back. Every last dime."

Chapter 27

Rox listened to Marty's report, frustrated that he hadn't learned anything about the transport service. It wasn't his fault; the memorial service had been a long shot.

Marty was still keyed up. "How can we use Ridgeline's money troubles to get the information we need?" He fired up the engine, finally ready to leave the parking lot. "There has to be some leverage."

"Let me think about it." Rox's brain bounced around, trying to process the new information. "We need to dig up the dirt on why Ridgeline paid out hush money. Maybe find out who the brother is. He's not listed with the business registry." She wished she could have overheard Fletcher's conversation.

"Let's not get sidetracked with investigating the company," Marty warned. "We need to get Josh out first. Then we can worry about shutting down their dirty practices."

"You're right." Rox switched gears again. "We simply need the camp's location. Maybe I can call the admin office, claiming to be a journalist, and try to pressure them with the threat of making their vulnerabilities public."

Marty pulled into the street. "Where to now? I'm in the mood—"

Rox got an impulsive idea and cut in. "Carrie's house."

Her stepdad gave her sideways look. "Why?"

"Because we haven't searched it yet. What if the transport office number is right there on her refrigerator?"

"What if the police are watching the place? Or have it taped off?" Marty laughed softly. "I know I don't have much to lose, but I really don't want to spend my final months in the county jail."

Rox wasn't worried. "I talked to Kyle, and he's pretty sure our client is guilty. That's why Lovejoy is still in jail on bullshit drug charges. They're not watching the house or looking for another suspect."

Marty shifted and cleared his throat.

She probably wouldn't like what he was about to say. *Did he always do that before bad news? Had she just noticed?*

"I have to tell you that I also think Lovejoy probably killed his ex-wife." Marty glanced over. "Don't take that personally."

"I don't." She meant it. "It doesn't matter if he is guilty. I believe him when he says he's worried that his son will kill himself in that boot camp."

Marty nodded. "Josh wasn't at his mom's service, so clearly Ridgeline has no intention of releasing him." Marty turned left, heading south. "All right. You can do a quick search while I keep watch."

Carrie Lovejoy's home sat back from the street, a small cottage with a single-car garage in a neighborhood full of similar properties. No crime-scene tape blocked the door. She hadn't been killed in the house, but the police had probably searched it. Marty parked nearby, backing into the driveway of an empty home with a *For Sale* sign.

"I'll bet her place is a rental," Rox commented.

"It's sure downscale from her fiancé's." Marty pulled

binoculars out from under his seat. "Did I describe Fletcher's house to you?"

"You mentioned that it was probably worth a million." Rox glanced at the setting sun. "I think I'll wait for a little more darkness before I go in."

"Do you suppose Carrie was into Fletcher for his money?" Marty mused.

"Maybe he was into her for her big boobs and blonde hair," Rox shot back.

"It doesn't matter now."

"Maybe it does." Rox recalled her initial conversation with their client. "Lovejoy said Carrie's fiancé probably pushed her into the wilderness-program idea to get Josh to straighten out. It may have even been a prerequisite to Carrie and Josh moving in with him."

"We'll probably never know." Marty grabbed the door handle. "I'm gonna get out and look at this house, you know, like a home buyer would."

"Makes sense."

Rox waited ten minutes while Marty looked in the windows of the sale property. When he got back into the car, she slipped out and crossed the grassy divider between the two houses. The gate to the backyard was closed, but all she had to do was reach over and unlatch it. Being tall had advantages too. When she rounded the corner of the garage, a black cat came straight at her, mewling loudly. *The dead woman's pet?* If so, it was probably starving. Rox refused to think about it. Carrie had a boyfriend. And neighbors. Her mission was to get inside the house, find what she needed, and get out—before someone called the police.

A small concrete patio held a dozen planter pots with mostly dead flowers. More after-effects of a person dying.

More evidence that Carrie had no local family and no friends who were close enough to come over and take care of her important things. Rox was grateful that Marty lived next door to her. A gut-wrenching sadness hit her. Marty didn't have much longer to live. She would be the one going over to his empty house to water his plants. Hell, she couldn't even be bothered to take care of her own.

She scanned the back of the house—three windows and a sliding glass door. Rox tried the slider first and found it locked. But the latch was as old as the house and had been well used, maybe even abused. She pulled her all-purpose tool from her back pocket, flipped out a mini-screwdriver, and wedged it behind the curved catch pin. With a hard torque, the pin popped out of place, and she slid the door open.

The cat rushed inside and scooted to its bowls in the corner of the kitchen. The home reeked of litter box and pungent perfume, a combination that tested her resolve. A few lights were on, giving her just enough illumination to conduct a search. Rox started by checking the fridge—just in case her tossed-off comment had been accurate. A grocery list hung from a clip magnet, but there were no phone numbers.

Rox ignored the cat's noises and headed for the desk in the dining room. If a computer had ever occupied the space, it was gone, probably taken by a homicide detective. Rox searched a pile of papers, finding household bills, junk mail, and a list of daily self-care items. No help. She yanked open drawers, looking for sticky notes. An invoice from Ridgeline or any of its associates, even a diary, might be helpful. Instead she dug through a ridiculous collection of colored markers, glitter, and glue-on fingernails. In the bottom drawer, she found tax returns but didn't have time to look through them.

Rox glanced around the living room, which was loaded with boxes. Carrie had been packing. Had she planned to move in with her fiancé while her son was in boot camp? That seemed cold.

Rox stepped into the hall, passed a bathroom, and stopped in front of a room with an open door. A messy teenage boy's space. Had Josh been abducted from this bedroom in the middle of the night? That alone would give someone nightmares for life.

Rox turned and entered the other bedroom—and was hit with the source of the perfume. A long dresser held dozens of bottles. A tall chest of drawers next to it was home to tiny animal figurines. *Weird!* Rox hurried to a nightstand, the last place she planned to check. The top drawer was crammed with sex toys, lubricants, and erotic reading. Her opinion of Carrie shot back up a notch. The bottom drawer held magazines, a computer tablet that seemed broken, and a collection of photos.

Rox thumbed quickly through. Most were of Josh at various ages and a few featured the boy with his father Isaac. Some were more recent images of Carrie and her fiancé Curtis Fletcher. She skipped most of the group photos with a lot of people she didn't recognize, but one made her stop and stare. Curtis Fletcher stood in front of a building with a golf club in his hand. He was flanked by his girlfriend Carrie and Rox's client, Isaac Lovejoy.

Chapter 28

Monday, July 10, 6:45 a.m., Central Oregon wilderness

The tent door opened, and Josh sat up, the sharp pain in his ribs still with him. Ace stepped in and tossed a package of granola into the tent. "You have to be productive today, so suck it up."

What was his tormentor doing here? Taking a break from hiking or looking for an opportunity to hurt him again? Even after everything he'd been through, Josh couldn't believe Ace was that sadistic. "I can't even walk!" Josh cried out, knowing it would hurt like hell to put weight on his ankle.

"You can split wood." Ace pointed at the walking stick Josh had been given. "We'll tape that to your leg for stability. Then we'll do some counseling while you work. Your suicide attempt is quite a setback for you."

Josh didn't bother to respond. There was no point. The sessions were a joke. Ace would ask about his life goals and give him a list of behavior corrections to work on.

"What happened to accountability?" Ace snapped. "You're still in the program, so you'll lose half your lunch for that non-response."'

Fuck! Josh ground his teeth and forced himself to say what they wanted to hear. "I'm sorry. I'll work harder."

Ace crossed his arms. "I don't like your attitude."

Josh wanted to punch him. Instead, he said, "I'll take care of it."

"Better." The bearded guy nodded. "Get rolling and I'll meet you at the log pile with tape."

Josh wolfed the small package of granola, vowing to escape. Maybe he would hit Ace on the head with a piece of wood, knock him out, then just go. At least he was at the base camp now, instead of in the middle of fucking nowhere. From here, he could get to a dirt trail and follow it downhill to a main road. He would have to be careful though. Another staff member bringing supplies to the base might see him and drag him back.

The glimmer of hope gave him the strength to get up and hobble outside. His tent partner, an older kid named Remy who was in the last phase of the program, had left earlier that morning to hike out to a unit with water supplies. The heat had turned up in the last few days, and one camper had passed out from dehydration. Josh had overhead that gossip from a conversation between Remy and Janine, the base-camp supervisor.

A bright blue sky and warm sun greeted him, but the weather had been like that since he arrived, so it didn't mean anything. Directly across the fire-pit opening was the supervisor's large tent and supply canopy. She had an air mattress in there, as well as a generator and a small refrigerator. Or so he'd heard from Remy.

Janine strolled out of her tent and yelled, "Good morning, wilderness!" Short, muscular, and lesbian-looking, the supervisor was disgustingly happy about her crappy job in the woods. Josh didn't get it. She nodded at him. "Good morning, camper." Josh nodded back. The bitch didn't even know his name.

Using his walking stick and grimacing with pain, he limped over to the pile of cut-up logs. Some guy had brought them in a little trailer the morning before. He'd heard him mention another base camp he'd just been to, and Josh wondered how many poor teenagers were out here in this hellish nightmare.

Josh looked around for Ace and spotted him rummaging through food supplies in the back of a truck—the one that had just moved the tents a few days earlier. Josh had no idea what day of the week it was. He picked up the axe, found a small log, and stood it on end. He'd seen people do this in movies, and it looked easy. It wasn't. The axe came down with a thud that hurt his hands and arms. After all the hiking and carrying and fording streams, he should feel stronger. But the lack of food had weakened him. In his old life, he would often eat a sandwich, a bag of chips, and five cookies just for lunch. He would never take food for granted again.

Ace lumbered over, taped the walking stick to Josh's leg, and barked instructions for cutting the wood. The pain eased with the added support. Every step still hurt, but he felt more functional. Ace, who had walked away, suddenly turned toward the road. Josh heard an engine and spun in the direction of the sound too. Through the thin cluster of pine trees, he spotted a dark-blue car. A man in uniform climbed out. *A cop?* Josh's heart skipped a beat. This was either really good or really bad. Considering his luck, he didn't feel optimistic.

The officer made his way along the path, and the supervisor strode over to meet him at the edge of their camp. Ace followed Janine.

Josh moved closer and overheard the officer ask, "What the hell happened with that girl you left in the woods?"

What girl? Josh took another step. She must have been with a different group of hikers.

Janine's voice was even more distinctive. "She just collapsed and died. We planned to take her to Bend, but we had to move the camp—at your suggestion. When we went back for her, she was gone." The supervisor crossed her arms. "What's the situation?"

"She's in the hospital and still alive." The cop paused, then yelled again. "You can't pull that shit! You put me in a tight spot." He sounded mad as hell. "Now you've got an issue with another student."

"I know," the camp supervisor cut in. "We got word that his mother has been killed and his father was arrested. But Mr. Fletcher wants Josh to stay here."

Curtis Fletcher? His mother's boyfriend? That meant they were talking about him . . . and his mother being dead. Josh's heart started to pound. His chest grew cold and he shivered in the shade of the trees. For a moment, the world was silent. Nothing moved and he had no thoughts.

Then Ace shouted, "Get back to work!"

Feeling numb and confused and afraid of the consequences, Josh did as he was told. Maybe they hadn't been talking about his mother. He'd suspected for a while that Curtis Fletcher ran the program, so they might be talking about someone else. Josh glanced over his shoulder. The camp boss and the cop were still talking. In his heart, he knew the truth. His mother was dead. He'd thought he hated her, but now he was freaked out. And why was his dad in jail? Did they think he killed her? That was crazy. His father was a nice guy. Too nice. And Josh had abused that soft-heartedness. He knew his behavior had been horrible, but he'd hated himself for what he'd done on that last trip. And he'd taken it out on everyone else. He still hated himself. But if his dad was in trouble . . .

He was more determined than ever to escape. His father needed him. Plus, he had to make amends to the girl. She had seemed willing, but then she'd passed out. He'd been totally drunk and confused, but his mentor had encouraged him to screw her anyway. Tommy had done it too. His friend had stopped speaking to him after that weekend, and now that he wasn't high all the time, Josh was worried about him. But he couldn't let the staff know he'd heard them talking about his parents. That would make them watch him more closely. Curtis Fletcher was an asshole who hated him. And if Curtis owned this program, Josh would be here forever. Unless he found a way out. He would cut wood and wait for his chance.

An hour later, Janine abruptly climbed in her own little truck and drove off. He and Ace were alone in the camp. For now. A group of hikers could roll back in at any moment. Ace sat in the shade in a low-slung canvas chair, reading a magazine. Even as old as he was, the counselor could still outrun him with his damaged ankle. Josh would have to knock him unconscious. There was no other way. Could he sneak up on him?

No. He would have to call him over, then grab a chunk of pine tree, and smack him in the head. Even though he'd fantasized about hurting Ace, Josh didn't really want to do it. But he had no choice.

"Ace!" he called out. "I need your help, please."

"What?" the bully yelled back, not moving.

"You have to see this." Josh turned his back on him, hoping to spark Ace's interest. He picked up the piece of wood he'd just split off. It was big enough to do the job, but small enough to grab hold of. Josh listened for the big man's footsteps. When he was right behind him, he would act.

Ace took his time. He started bitching halfway across the

fire-pit ring. When the counselor's voice blasted near the back of Josh's head, he spun around. With both hands on the rough bark, Josh swung the wood up and around, striking Ace on the side of the head.

The man blinked and reached up. "What the fuck?"

Oh no! He hadn't fazed him. Josh's pulse hammered so hard he couldn't breathe. He swung again, low this time, aiming for Ace's shin. But the counselor was already going down, his knees buckling. Josh made contact with the bully's junk instead. Ace screamed in pain, then promptly blacked out. Josh grabbed a water bottle from the back of the supply truck and hobbled down the wooded path to the road.

Chapter 29

Monday, July 10, 9:07 a.m., Portland

Rox checked the time. It was finally after nine. She called the state office and waited through five rings. A woman with a pleasant voice answered. "This is Beth Frasier with the Oregon Business Registry. How can I help you?"

"I'm Karina Jones, a private investigator. I'm looking into a company that may be involved in the disappearance of two teenage boys." That should get her attention.

"Oh dear. Have you called the police?"

"Yes, of course. But the company operates in several states, and I need all the information I can get."

"What's the name?"

"Fletcher & Sons." Marty had found the name on an office door after tailing Curtis Fletcher, but it hadn't come up in her search of the state's site.

After a long moment, the clerk came back on the call. "That business is no longer registered, but I think it just changed names. Give me another minute."

Rox paced while she waited. Even a dance workout that morning hadn't taken the edge off. She wanted to get on the road again and find Josh. ASAP.

"Found it," the woman said, sounding pleased. "It's now Fletcher Investments."

"Does it own other businesses?" Rox keyed the name into the search bar as she talked. The company didn't come up.

"It has several fully-owned subsidiaries. Ridgeline Wilderness Health, Ridgeline Get Straight, and RWH Transport." The woman made a noise in her throat. "It also owns a fifty-percent share in Wild Girls Galore and Steelhead Bistro."

Anxiety rippled through Rox's body. The strip club didn't surprise her because Marty had tailed Fletcher to the lounge and told her about it. But the restaurant was co-owned by her client, and Lovejoy had failed to mention that his ex-wife's new boyfriend was his investment partner. But that connection explained the photo she'd seen. The business deal might even be how Carrie Lovejoy met Curtis Fletcher and had the affair.

"Is that all you need?" the administrator asked.

Rox felt rattled by her client's involvement with Fletcher. Why hadn't he told her? *Focus!* Right now she needed to know more about the damn transport company and whether it operated a local office. It didn't make sense to send vans from Nevada to pick up kids for an Oregon camp. "Does RWH list any phone numbers?"

"No, we just have the one for the registered agent."

"Thank you." Rox hung up. There had to be a reasonable explanation for how the two men had met—such as the Community Fellowship. Lovejoy had sounded scornful when he mentioned it, but he might be a disillusioned ex-member. And Tommy's mother attended the church's other branch. Or whatever they were called. Rox was more convinced than ever that Tommy's death was somehow connected to the Fellowship or Ridgeline or both. She would bet money that the two boys knew other, even if their parents didn't know about their friendship.

A dark thought engulfed her. What if Josh had killed

Tommy? Maybe even accidentally. That would explain why his personality had changed and he'd become moody and angry. But how and why? It seemed unlikely. And if he hadn't, he was still a fifteen-year-old boy in a dangerous situation. She needed to get him out.

Desperate for answers, Rox called Doernbecher Children's Hospital and tried to explain her situation. "I found the girl in the woods and took her to the hospital in Bend. Then she was transported to your facility. She was unconscious the whole time, so I don't know her name. But I'd like to follow up and find out how she's doing."

"Without a name, I'm not sure I can help you, but I'll ask the ER and see what I can find out."

While she waited, Rox went to the kitchen and poured another cup of coffee—even though she really wanted a beer. But it was a little too early.

Finally, the receptionist came back on. "Her name is Sadie Carmichael. She's still in the ICU, but she's going to recover. That's all I can tell you. And I probably just violated patient privacy, but since you saved her life—" Her voice trailed off, and the woman hung up.

Rox called Marty and told him about the connection between Lovejoy and Fletcher, a man they'd both become suspicious of. "These cases are starting to feel incestuous."

"I'm sure they all know each other because of the church." Marty didn't sound worried.

Rox decided not to share her darkest suspicion. It seemed irrational to her now. "I'm going to the hospital to see that girl we rescued. Maybe she can tell us something. Want to tag along?"

"I can't. I have a doctor's appointment. Update me when you're back."

"Will do."

As Rox reached the big medical center on the hill, her work phone rang on the seat beside her. She glanced at the ID. *Scott Goodwin.* She pressed the button on her earpiece. "Hello."

"Hi, Karina." He sounded sexy as ever. "I saw that you called last night. Do you have new information?"

"I'm sorry, I don't. But I need to return your deposit."

"I can meet you today. What time works for you?"

"Let me get back to you about that. I've suddenly got a lot going on with my other case today."

"Did you figure out where the wilderness program is? I still think Tommy might have been there. Maybe he escaped and came back to Portland, then ran into trouble."

She hadn't thought about that. "I got close to finding the base camp, but it had moved. I'll try again soon. Maybe today."

"Good luck." Someone in the background was trying to get his attention. "I'm sorry," Goodwin said in a rush, "but I have to go. I'll call you later."

Rox drove around the medical complex for ten minutes looking for a parking space. It took another ten minutes to walk to the correct building, get through the ICU's security, and find Sadie Carmichael. The door was open, and Rox saw a couple about her age, the woman standing by the bed and the man in a chair by the window. Probably the girl's parents.

"Hello?" Rox called out softly. They both turned and stared with blank looks. "I'm Karina Jones. I found Sadie in the woods and brought her to the hospital in Bend."

The mother rushed forward and threw her arms around Rox. Startled, she forced herself to relax and let the woman hug her. But she had to pull back after a moment.

"Thank you!" The woman's eyes filled with tears. "When Ridgeline called and said she'd disappeared, I was devastated."

The father came forward. "I'm Allan Carmichael, and this is my wife, Ginger. We're forever in your debt."

Warmth surfaced in her cheeks, surprising her. Rox hadn't expected this. "We just did what anyone would. My stepdad was there with me."

The mother, a pretty woman with soft curls, grabbed Rox's hand. "The ER doctors said you kept Sadie alive with CPR and body warmth."

Rox wanted to run from the room, but she needed information. She gently pulled her hand free. "I'm just glad Sadie is okay."

"She was conscious a minute ago," the father said. "Maybe she'll wake up again."

Rox shifted on her feet. "I'm trying to find the Ridgeline camp so I can get another teenager home. Can you help me?"

The mother burst into tears. Allan Carmichael put his arm around his wife. "We're so upset. We thought the program would help Sadie grow up. Instead it almost killed her."

"How did she get the pills?" the distressed mother asked. "Was she trying to get high or kill herself? The Ridgeline office won't return my calls."

Rox didn't have any answers. "I'm sorry, but I don't know what happened to your daughter. And I'm afraid something similar will happen to the young man I'm looking for."

"He's not your child?" The mother looked confused.

"I'm a private investigator. I was hired to find my client's son." Rox realized that keeping Josh's name private wasn't helping. Maybe the girl had known him or seen him in the camps. "Has Sadie talked about her experience at all?"

The father shook his head. "She's only been conscious off and on and was a little incoherent. She mentioned a river and being hungry, but that doesn't make sense."

Had these people not done their homework before they signed up their kid? "Did Ridgeline send a transport van to pick up Sadie?"

"Yes, they said we had to do it that way." The mother shuddered. "They came in the middle of the night. I felt so terrible."

"Do you know how to contact the transport company? This is important."

The father reached in his pocket. "I think it's owned by Ridgeline, but the call should still be logged in my phone. They checked in with us an hour before they showed up." Mr. Carmichael scrolled through his data. "Sorry. This could take a minute. I have to scroll back a few weeks."

"He gets a lot of calls." His wife looked back and forth, her attention divided between her husband and her daughter. Rox glanced at the girl in the bed. Her face was pink and covered with insect bites, not deathly pale anymore.

A few minutes later, the father let out a happy yelp. "I found it." He held out the phone for her to see the number. It had an Oregon area code, either Portland or Salem, the capital to the south. Rox memorized the numerals automatically, but keyed it into her phone just to reassure the Carmichaels. "Thank you." She started to leave, then turned back. "Don't let Ridgeline get away with this. Call the state district attorney and report their irresponsible behavior."

The father nodded. "We plan to sue them as well, even though our contract says we can't."

"Good luck." Rox handed them her business card. "Please have Sadie call me as soon as she can. She might be able to help me find the camp and save someone else."

"We will." The mother squeezed her hand again. "Bless you."

Rox hurried out, already plotting how she would trick the transport office into giving her its address.

Chapter 30

When she arrived home, Rox headed straight to Marty's side of the duplex. She knocked, waited impatiently for him to give the okay, then hurried in. "I have the number for the Oregon transport office. Plus an idea for getting the address."

"Excellent!" Marty hurried toward her, wiping his hands dry on a stained blue work shirt. "How'd you get it?"

"The girl's parents were in her hospital room, and the dad had the number in his phone. Her name is Sadie, by the way." Rox tried to assess what Marty had been fixing or cleaning. "Powerwashing your patio?"

"Good guess, but not quite." He grinned. "Your patio."

"Thanks." She shook her head and silently mouthed, *You're a freak!*

Marty rolled his eyes. "What's your plan to get the address?"

"An important delivery. I say I'm from Fed Ex and can't read the address on the package."

"What if they haven't ordered anything?" Marty made his skeptical face.

"Okay, it's not a package but a certified envelope—that looks like a check."

Her stepdad nodded. "That should do it."

"They might not even be leery of giving out the information." She backtracked on that thought. "The office is probably run out of a metal building with no sign and no business listing."

"Let's find out."

"Get me a beer, please."

Marty hurried to the kitchen and Rox followed, sitting down at the table. She pulled out her work phone and keyed in the transport office number. No one answered. *Damn.* She left a message. "This is Fed Ex, and we have a certified letter for you. Please call back to confirm your address." She read off her business number, which was paid for with cash and untraceable.

Marty sat down and handed her a cold microbrew. "I'll call Bowman and see if he can get an address to match the phone number. It might be in the call center database or a reverse directory." While Marty left his ex-partner a message, Rox drank her beer and raided her stepdad's kitchen, packing food for another road trip. They'd left most of the camping stuff by Marty's front door, ready to roll.

While they waited, they ate leftovers and talked about prepping for the trip. Ten minutes later, her work phone rang—from the number she'd just contacted. She grabbed it and clicked over to speakerphone. "Fed Ex."

"You guys called here looking for our address."

The man sounded big and dumb, but maybe that was just how she visualized the *escorts.*

"Who's the letter addressed to?" he asked.

Oh hell. She hadn't thought about that. Scrambling, she muttered, "It just says Manager."

"Huh? What kind of letter?"

"I think it's a check. It says *do not discard,* and it has that little window in the envelope."

"Okay. Drop it by." He named a number and street she didn't recognize.

"Any helpful directions?"

"The gray metal building at the back of the lot. There's no sign or anything, but a white van is parked out front."

"All right. We'll try to find it." Rox hung up and grinned at Marty. "I called it, didn't I?"

"On the nose." Marty stood and cleared the table. "Where is that location? It doesn't sound like Portland."

"I think it's Salem." Rox keyed the address into a map app on her phone. "It would make sense to put the van in the middle of the state with the most direct route to Sun Ridge." The address came up in an industrial area in the south part of Salem. "Time to pack for another trip to the wilderness, then hit the road."

Marty put away his unfinished beer. "We may have to watch the transport office for days before the van goes out."

"Maybe."

"And we both have to stay in the vehicle. If the van leaves, we have to be right on it. There's no stopping to pick up the other person."

"I'm prepared for that."

"It could get ugly."

What was he worried about? "You think I can't handle a long stakeout?"

"I'm not sure I can." Marty rubbed his head. "Maybe we'll get lucky and find a nearby hotel where we can take breaks. If the one on duty sees anyone get in the van, we make a quick call. Whoever is on break bolts out to the parking lot, ready to go."

"Good plan." Rox stood. "I left a bag packed, so this won't take long. Meet you out front in fifteen minutes."

Chapter 31

Josh hobbled along the dirt road, the stabbing pain in his ankle worse with each step. He worried about doing long-term damage to his body, but the taste of freedom pushed him forward. He wanted to live long enough to talk to his father again, maybe even tell him about that shameful weekend. He had to tell somebody. His mentor—ex-mentor!—had to be stopped. Josh let out a sob of relief. After two weeks without pot or Vicodin, he was finally thinking clearly again.

He wanted to stop and rest, but he was still twenty-some miles from the nearest town. And phone. Who would he call? His parents weren't available anymore. Josh fought back tears. Now that he was no longer a prisoner and could think about his real life, Josh's heart began to ache. His mom had been flaky and annoying, but he still loved her. Thinking about her wasn't helping. He needed a plan. Who would he call? His Aunt Lynn in Seattle. She would help him. She might even hire a lawyer for his dad.

A few minutes later, he reached an asphalt road. Relief washed over him, and he sank to the ground and let himself cry. When he got to his feet again, his resolve was stronger. Now that he was on a real road, someone might come along and give him a ride. An image of the camp's truck flashed in his mind. A Ridgeline employee could drive by too, so he had to be careful. If he heard an engine, he would step off the asphalt and hide behind a tree until he could see the vehicle. If it looked safe, he would run out and flag down the driver. *Hobble,* he corrected. What if he couldn't move quickly enough?

Don't think about it. Just put one foot in front of the other. Ignore the pain and keep moving.

Late that afternoon, dizziness, exhaustion, and pain overtook him. His water long gone, Josh dropped to his knees, his throat raw and his lips sunburned. He crawled into the shade of a pine tree, thinking he would rest for ten minutes, then try again.

He woke to the sound of a diesel engine chugging up the mountain. Struggling to his feet, Josh prayed for the driver to be hiker or hunter—anyone but a Ridgeline employee. He stepped behind the thick tree to watch a truck come up the straight incline. It was black! *Yay!* Not the white van that had brought him to this hellhole and not the gray truck that carried the base equipment. He hurried toward the road, limping and shuffling as fast as he could.

At the truck neared the crest, it started to slow. Josh raised his arm to wave it down, then froze. Two men were in the front cab. They both wore red T-shirts and were staring right at him. *Shit!* Heart thumping, he turned and tried to run into the woods. But his ankle flared in pain and he fell. He started crawling but it was pointless.

Heavy footsteps came at him fast. *No! He couldn't go back!* Josh looked for a rock or something to defend himself with. Big hands grabbed the back of his shirt and yanked him upright. "You little piece of shit." The man slapped him hard. "Remember your first day? You were told no one ever escapes." He laughed, an evil sound.

The driver arrived and grabbed Josh's other arm. "Ace isn't very happy right now, and you're going to pay." As they dragged him toward the truck, Josh burst into tears.

Chapter 32

As they drove south on I-5, she and Marty watched the pink summer sun drop in the sky. Rox had brought her laptop again, thinking she could do research while they sat, watching the transport office. She hoped Marty had brought something to read. The whole tactic of waiting for the van to leave, hoping to follow it to the camp was inefficient and possibly pointless. The transport service might work for other businesses too, and they didn't want to go out on a false delivery—and miss a trip to the Sun Ridge area. They should be able to tell the difference. Other trips probably wouldn't happen in the middle of the night like the program abductions. Yet even a midnight run could take them to the wrong camp. Ridgeline ran gender-based wilderness camps and a gay-conversion therapy program. The Get Straight location might be in Klamath Falls for all they knew. They just had to make good guesses at every step.

They arrived in Salem an hour later, then spent nearly twenty minutes finding the address. The street was broken into sections, and the GPS on her phone sent them to a dead end where they found a huge welding shop instead. They backtracked around the shuttered lumber mill that broke up the street and finally found a cluster of businesses, all housed in metal buildings. The upholstery-repair shop in the front had an address that was only one numeral different from what they were looking for.

They parked across the street in a mechanic's parking lot that held several other vehicles. In the twilight, they couldn't see what was behind the building on the other side, but a light was on in the back area, and they spotted a wide strip of asphalt leading to the rear.

"I'll get out and do a quick check," Rox offered.

"Be careful," Marty cautioned. "They could be on edge because of the Fed Ex delivery that didn't show up."

"Maybe not." She found a small flashlight in the truck's glovebox. "Everyone has waited for a delivery that didn't happen."

"True enough."

Rox climbed out, glad she'd worn navy-blue workout clothes for the trip—comfortable and hard to see at night. The closed shop in front hosted one night light next to its front door, but everywhere else was dark. She hurried across the narrow street, heading diagonally toward the driveway leading to the back lot. Once she turned into the alley, she hugged up against the front building, side-stepping to stay out of sight. If a vehicle suddenly rumbled out from the back business, she had few options. Hopping the chain-link fence on the other side of the driveway might be her only choice. But it would look bad. Or maybe they would think she was a meth-head burglar.

At the end of the shop wall—her only cover—she stopped and scanned the back lot. The small metal transport office was dwarfed by the massive warehouse on the other side of the back fence. A carport next to the shop covered two white vans. *Damn.* Multiple vehicles could mean multiple runs. *Probably not at night,* she reassured herself. Perhaps the company made auto-part runs during the day to keep busy, which would explain why RWH Transport functioned as a separate entity. But at least she and Marty had finally found the transport office. Lights were on inside and outside the building, so someone was still on the job.

Rox hurried back, her footsteps the only audible movement in the quiet industrial area. A mile in the distance, she could hear the freeway, but otherwise, stillness. The heat of the day was gone, and she shivered in her long-sleeved pullover. She had a jacket in the truck but wouldn't likely wear it until they reached the base camp.

She climbed in the cab and reported her findings.

Marty grunted. "If someone's working tonight, they must have a pickup scheduled."

"That's what I think. But there could be several runs. Maybe we should have brought two vehicles."

"I thought about it when I mentioned the motel, but clearly, there's no place to stay in this area." Marty sipped from a thermos of coffee. "I really doubt they would schedule two program abductions in the same night. Unless both kids are going to the same camp. In which case, we'll be fine."

Rox was less optimistic. "Unless the poor kid in the crosshairs tonight is a girl. They separate the genders into different hiking groups."

"I'm sure they take a lot more boys into the program than girls." Marty gave a shy smile. "Even I got into a bit of teenage trouble."

He'd never admitted that before. "What did you do?"

"You know my friend who lived across the street—"

"The infamous Steve Hannagin." Rox had heard plenty of *those* stories.

"Let's just say we played a prank on a neighbor that didn't go as planned, and a mailbox got destroyed in the process."

"You scoundrel!" Rox laughed. "Were the police involved?"

"Yep. But we were only thirteen, so no arrests. Steve and I mowed a lot of lawns to pay for the damage."

They were quiet for a moment, then Rox said, "The kids who get sent to these camps are a lot more troubled than that. I know the parents must feel desperate. You would have to before making that choice. Because these programs are extreme."

"They're not all the same." Marty patted her arm. "We're rescuing Josh because his father thinks he's suicidal. He needs a different kind of help."

"Let's not forget that Tommy Goodwin is dead." She sounded more defensive than she meant to.

"But we don't know why. His death might be completely unrelated. Or it could have been an accident."

They were still waiting for the autopsy results. When a body had been left outside to decompose for weeks, determining cause of death could be difficult. Marty knew that as well as she did. They talked about the case for a few minutes, then Marty said he needed to rest his eyes. Rox pulled her laptop from under the seat, opened an article she'd downloaded, and started reading.

An hour later, her eyes grew heavy and she rolled down her window, hoping the cold air would revive her. Marty was sleeping soundly, making a soft snoring noise. She had a flash of guilt for bringing him out here. An old guy with a bad heart was not an ideal extraction partner. But she would rather work with him than anyone else, and he would rather be here than at home, dying slowly in a chair.

An engine rumbled across the street, and Rox snapped to attention. She grabbed Marty's arm and shook it. "Wake up, old man! We've got activity."

He sat up. "What's going on?"

"Do you hear that? One of the vans is being warmed up."

"Good. I'm ready to roll." He reached for his key in the starter.

"Not yet!"

"Right. I knew that." The poor guy was barely awake.

"Should I drive?"

"Hell no. I'm fine."

The engine sound was coming toward them. "Get down."

They both leaned over into the middle of the bench seat, with Rox hanging off the front edge. She imagined how it would look to someone walking up. Rox giggled, and Marty shushed her.

The rumble grew louder, then headlights shone in their windshield and they heard the vehicle pull into the street. As the noise retreated, Rox eased up and watched the white van stop at the corner.

Marty sat up too. "Now?"

"Give it another block. We're the only traffic out here."

They waited to a count of five, then Marty started the truck and pulled out. A surge of adrenaline pulsed through Rox's veins. If they handled this well, they would be at the base camp in a couple of hours. Josh might be out in the wilderness, but they would find him.

"What if the kid isn't at the base camp?" Marty asked, obviously on the same train of thought.

"I'll pressure one of the counselors to lead me to him. Or I can follow someone who's hiking out with supplies. These kids can't be that isolated, can they?"

"I don't know. I'm starting to think they are."

At the intersection in the distance, the white van turned left, and they could see two large men in the front.

"My biggest concern is the local police chief," Rox said. "If he's a Ridgeline advocate and someone in the camp calls to report our interference, we could end up in cuffs."

"We have Josh's father on our side," Marty reminded her. "And with his mother dead, I'm sure the waiver she signed giving Ridgeline temporary custody is now void. We'll threaten them with a kidnapping charge." He turned to give her a crooked smile. "We're not without connections. We both know people in the FBI we can call."

Rox laughed. "It will be three in the morning by the time we get there. We'll be on our own."

"I brought my weapon."

Rox sighed. "I know."

Ahead, the van slowed and took the south I-5 exit.

Surprised, Rox mumbled, "Where the heck are they going?" The road over the mountain pass was just north of Salem.

"They must have a pickup south of here."

"I hope we don't have to drive all the way to Eugene."

"Can you imagine doing that for a living? Driving around the state in the middle of the night abducting teenagers?" Marty shook his head. "I spent my career arresting people, yet the process of confining another human being still repulses me."

Thirty minutes later, the van exited the freeway, and they followed it to a new suburb outside of the small college town of Corvallis. As the van turned deeper into the maze of side streets, Marty hung back. They were the only vehicles on the road at this hour. "I'm tempted to park and wait," he commented. "They would have to pass us on the way out."

Rox hated to let the van out of their sight. "Let's not take the chance. Shut off your lights."

When they reached a neighborhood with nothing but dead ends, the van made a sudden right. Marty pulled off the street, parking behind a big RV. The homes in the neighborhood all looked like they'd been built that summer, with no trees or mature vegetation. "I'm going on foot the rest of the way." Rox opened her door. "I want to witness how they operate." She needed to see for herself if the horror stories told by teenagers were true.

Before Marty could discourage her, Rox jumped out and ran across the corner lawn, catching sight of the van when she reached the side street. The vehicle was parked in front of a house near the end. She looked around for something to hide behind. A short hedge in front of the next home would have to do. She jogged over and squatted behind it. Peering out with one eye, she watched the two men climb out. The passenger guy opened the van's sliding side door and left it that way. Dark clothes and clean-shaven, they looked like ex-military. The escorts chatted briefly, but she couldn't hear what they said.

At the front door, they walked in without knocking. The parents had to be expecting them, so the silence was to keep from alerting their victim. *So weird!* Rox was glad she'd never had children. The sacrifices and choices people were forced to make . . . not for her. She wanted to move in closer—and watch the interaction with the kid through a window—but didn't dare. Once the thugs came out, she had to be able to run back around the corner and get into the truck before everyone got rolling again.

The big guys were in the house for less than five minutes. When they came out, they were carrying someone wrapped in a sheet. The abductee was squirming but silent and mostly likely bound. A sick feeling lodged in Rox's stomach as she watched the thugs toss the sheet-wrapped teenager into the back of the van. She straightened her legs but kept bent over as she ran back across the corner lawn. She hurried to the truck and scrambled in. "Let's get down, they'll be rolling by in a minute."

She and Marty ducked into the middle of the seat again, but this time it didn't make her laugh.

Chapter 33

Tuesday, July 11, 1:45 a.m.

Tailing a vehicle in the middle of the night on an empty road was easy—until the other driver suddenly braked for no apparent reason.

"What are they doing?" Rox was instantly on high alert.

"Either they know we're back here and are testing the theory, or they have to pee." Marty sounded calm.

"We have to go past them." As the only other visible car on the road, they had no choice. Rox strained to see ahead in the dark to why the van had slowed. "I don't see a turnoff, unless there's an unmarked private driveway." They were over the Cascades and driving through the high-plains flat land between Sisters and Bend.

"My guess is they have to pee. I sure do." Marty kept the truck moving at the same speed, and they rapidly approached the van, which had pulled off at a small turnout. By the time they drove past, one of the men had climbed out.

Rox had to use a restroom too, but she wasn't letting herself think about it. Or drink any more coffee. She'd bought caffeine pills for their last trip and had taken one earlier. "What now?"

"I'll slow down a bit now while you watch to see what they do."

Rox unbuckled to turn in the seat. The lights of the van stayed steady for a minute, then the road curved and she lost sight of the other vehicle. That had happened repeatedly on the trip over the pass, so she didn't panic. Yet. "I can't see them at the moment."

"I still think we'll be fine. We're ninety-percent sure they're headed for Sun Ridge. The questionable part comes after that."

"We can pull off the road later and let them pass us again. I need to pee anyway."

"We'll see how it goes."

They didn't see the white van again until they'd driven through Bend and stopped at a tiny rest station to relieve themselves. The other vehicle cruised by, followed by a Jeep with a canoe on top. With the transport service back in sight and her bladder empty, Rox relaxed a little.

They reached Sun Ridge twenty-five minutes later, and Rox checked her phone. Just after three, as she'd predicted. The little town was dark with only a few motel signs illuminating the highway.

"This is where it gets tricky," Marty said, slowing down. "If they see us make the turn off the main highway, they'll know for sure we're following them."

Until that point, they could have just been another car going in the same direction, headed toward Klamath Falls.

"We shut the lights off again right before we turn."

"I will, but I can't drive the whole damn mountain road that way." A edge finally crept into Marty's tone.

He had to be tired—and the hardest part was yet to come. "Want me to drive for a while?"

"I'm fine. Just a little worried that we're going to lose them at the last minute."

She was too. "If we do, we'll just keep heading in the same direction as last time. They probably didn't move the base camp very far."

They passed the last gas station at the edge of town and Marty accelerated. They were still forty or fifty minutes from the base camp, but no longer the only vehicle on the main road. She'd noticed headlights behind them when they'd driven through Sun Ridge.

"We might have picked up a state trooper," she said, trying not to sound worried.

Marty glanced in the rearview mirror. "I don't see it."

Rox looked over her shoulder again. No lights. "Maybe it was a local cop."

After a moment Marty announced, "We need a Plan B."

"I've been thinking about that." Rox reached into her shoulder bag and pulled out a wad of cash. "I brought Scott Goodwin's retainer, which I haven't returned yet. If we lose the van, we park and stop them when they come back out. Then we bribe them to show us the location."

"Maybe we should have done that in the first place." Marty laughed. "I'm not optimistic. They might be the kind of guys who will bust our heads together just for fun."

A new dread seeped into her stomach. What if the escorts hung around the base camp to sleep or rest for a while? They could be an added layer of trouble for the extraction. "We've never done one quite like this, have we?"

"And I hope we never do again." Marty didn't bother to smile at her.

On the flat road ahead, the van veered left and drove into the high-mountain desert toward the big rock formation they'd seen on the last trip. Marty shut off the headlights. They would have to rely on the moon to see the turnoff, then hang back far enough to not arouse the transport thugs' suspicion.

Thirty minutes later—with no van in sight—Marty pulled off the road. "We've lost 'em."

Chapter 34

Rox woke to the alarm on her cell phone. She sat up, disoriented and stiff. *What the hell?* She looked over and saw Marty asleep behind the wheel of their truck. *Oh, right.* They had decided to rest for a few hours and begin searching for the base camp at daylight. Rox rubbed the back of her neck, which ached from sleeping against the window. Her forehead pounded too, with the onset of a migraine. *Get out, walk around.* She forced herself to climb from the cab. The crisp mountain air made her shiver, and only a glimmer of daylight streaked through the trees. In the near-darkness, she moved toward the road and its flat surface. After ten minutes of pacing back and forth, inhaling the cold pine-scented air, the tension in her skull eased up.

Rox climbed back in the truck and shook Marty's shoulder. "Wake up, old man." He made a soft cry in his sleep. *Damn,* she should have left him home like she did for the last extraction. It wasn't fair to drag him out here into this crazy scenario. What if he had a heart attack?

"I'm awake." Her stepdad sat up, rubbing his eyes. "I was dreaming about snakes crawling into my tent. Nasty!"

"Sorry about getting you into this situation."

"Don't be. I'm fine." He shifted and groaned. "Stiff as hell, but nothing that a good soak in the hot tub won't fix." He opened his door and stepped out. "I could really use some coffee though."

"Me too." Rox considered their options. "Should we drive back into town and get some, maybe chat up or bribe some locals into giving us directions?"

"A waste of time." Marty headed behind a tree.

Rox reached into the storage space behind the seat and pulled two cans of Diet Coke out of the cooler, then rummaged through her backpack for breakfast bars. Better than nothing. She downed half the soda but waited for her partner to return before tearing open her snack.

As they ate Marty asked, "What's the plan?"

"We keep checking side roads, watching for any sign of tire tracks or trash on the ground." Rox downed the rest of her soda, thinking it had never tasted so good. "Based on where we found the camp last time—exactly three-point-five miles from an asphalt road—we can limit how far we drive on each search."

"You mean turn around after four miles on each dirt road?" Marty sounded weary but nodded his agreement. "We still have at least two paved options to explore as well."

The task seemed overwhelming, and they were quiet for a minute. But a sparkly morning sun peeked through the trees, and Rox felt encouraged. "Yes, but we only traveled twelve miles from the first junction last time, so we'll turn around at fifteen on each." She pulled the map from the glovebox. She had studied the area online the night before and needed a refresher. "I doubt if any of the artery roads are listed, but a visual reminder of the topography could help us decide where to start." She suspected that most of the roads led to old mining camps that weren't operating any more.

She started to open the map but Marty grabbed her arm. "Shhh. Listen."

The faint hum of an engine came from higher on the

hillside. Unexpected anxiety gripped Rox. "If it's the transport van heading back, we should get out of sight."

"Yep." Marty fired up the truck. "I think they knew they were being followed last night, and I don't want any trouble."

They pulled out onto the road, then put the truck in reverse. "I think I can back through those two trees."

"Only if we pull in the rearview mirrors." Rox rolled down her window as Marty eased the truck off the pavement. The sound of tires on the road grew louder, especially when the vehicle accelerated out of the curves. They both yanked in their mirrors, then rolled the windows up. Bushy branches slapped at the front window as the truck squeezed between the two pines. "We're scratching the paint," Rox warned.

"I don't care." Marty stayed focused. They mostly used the vehicle for surveillance, slapping an electrician sign on the side for cover. He kept backing until the density of the forest forced him to stop. He killed the engine, and Rox opened her window a few inches. They were a hundred feet from the road, and the dark green truck blended into its surroundings.

Thirty seconds later, the white van flew past. They waited for the sound of braking, but it didn't come.

Marty turned to her. "Now we know we're on the right artery."

Which cut their work in half. Still, they had to find the correct dirt road—a daunting task. "We'd better get started. This could take all day."

After an hour of searching, Rox's work phone rang. Was that the number from the hospital? Worried about the camper they'd rescued, she put in her earpiece. "Karina Jones."

"This is Sadie." Her voice was weak but clear. "The girl

you found in the woods."

Relief washed over her. "I'm glad you're okay." Rox gestured for Marty to stop.

"Only because of you. Thank you!" The girl started to cry.

More unexpected tears. Why were people so emotional? "Are you all right?"

"Mostly." Sadie took a moment to collect herself. "But I have nightmares every time I close my eyes."

The poor girl would need counseling, but why had she called?

Sadie cut into her thoughts. "My mom said you were looking for the base camp to rescue another student. I think I can help you."

Thank goodness! "That is great news. I'm out here in the wilderness now. Tell me everything you know."

"When we moved the camp the other day, I remember seeing a hiking-trail sign that said Quail Run. Does that help?

They had passed it a while back. "What comes next? How far out and which dirt road do we turn on?" Rox gestured at Marty to turn around.

"I'm not totally sure, but I know it's not the first one. I heard Janine say to try a new area when we passed it." Sadie started to cry again. "I had almost graduated, and they were letting me stay at base camp to prep food. Then I said something stupid and Janine got mad. She was going to make me start over!" Sadie sobbed so loudly she was hard to understand.

Her mother came on the phone. "We need to get her calm again."

"Tell her I said thank you and best wishes." That was too informal, but she was still learning. Rox hung up and turned to Marty. "After the Quail Run sign, we turn on the second or third side road."

"Good enough." Marty pressed the gas and headed back the way they'd come. "That little piece of info just saved us five hours."

At the third turnoff after the sign marker, Rox noticed a dark, unexpected spot in the dry red dirt. She squatted, stuck her finger in it, and sniffed. "This is engine oil." They'd skipped driving up the second dirt turnoff, which had been narrow and looked like a trail used for ATVs.

"We must be close." Marty stood nearby, scanning the area. "These tire tracks look fresh too."

"Let's do this." Rox stood and wiped sweat from her brow. The sun was rising in the sky, and even filtered through trees, the heat was building.

They both climbed in the truck. Marty started forward again, steering around the deepest ruts in the narrow road. "It feels weird to do an extraction without a plan."

"I know, but this is a bare-bones scenario. What kind of con could we pull off?" She looked at her stepdad. "Seriously, is there something I haven't thought of?"

"We could try to convince them we're law enforcement." He sounded doubtful.

"Not a chance. They'll ask to see our badges. Also, they have documentation that says Josh is in their custody." Worried, Rox tried to assess the situation. "How many Ridgeline employees do we expect? Five?"

"Not in the camp." Marty sounded confident.

"You're probably right. Some of the counselors, or whatever they're called, will be out on long hikes. We may only encounter one or two at the base camp."

"How many kids?" Marty asked. "Ten?"

"Fewer, I think. They keep the teenagers busy." Rox really

had no idea. The camp might be huge with twenty or more people. But that would require structures, and based on how quickly they'd picked up and moved last time, she doubted they set up anything permanent. "I'm worried Josh won't be around." She took a long slug from her now-warm water bottle. "I'm willing to hike out to find him, but it could be a fool's errand without a guide."

"We'll be as disruptive as possible." Marty shrugged. "It's public land. They can't make us leave. The longer we're there, the more distracted their students become." Marty used air quotes around the word *students*, something he rarely did.

Rox almost laughed, but this was too serious. "These programs thrive on isolation and secrecy. They're almost cult-like that way." Rox snapped her fingers. "Camera! I brought my Go-Pro. I'll strap it on my wrist and record everything. That should be intimidating."

"And I'll have my weapon."

"No, Marty." Rox squeezed his upper arm. "There could be kids in the camp, and the counselors won't be armed. We just have to be brash and insistent."

"It's your life motto."

That did make her chuckle. It also made her change her mind. "Let's run a diversion. Once we spot the camp, I'll get out and slip into the forest. You drive up closer and get everyone's attention. Pull them away from the tents."

Marty was nodding. "Then you go in and find Josh."

"We'll meet up with you down the road."

After a moment, her stepdad backtracked. "I don't know. You could run into trouble by yourself. How will I know when to drive off?"

"If I don't find Josh, I'll make myself known."

"You're kind of hard to miss." He gave her a quick grin.

Rox tried to smile back but she was too worried.

For twenty minutes, they drove slowly up a bumpy dirt road, chugging through deep ruts and rounding blind curves. The trees were often close enough that branches slapped the sides of the truck and came in through the windows. But without air conditioning, they had no choice but to leave them open.

As they entered a flat, straight stretch of road, Rox spotted a gray truck parked in the woods about twenty yards off the road. "There!" She pointed, a pulse of adrenaline surging. Beyond the vehicle were several tents, a dirty-white canopy, and a big passenger van.

"Bingo!" Marty braked.

Rox looped the camera strap around her wrist—tightening it so her hands could be free—and started to get out.

Marty reached over and grabbed her arm. "Be careful."

"This is nothing compared to the Sister Love Cult or the survivalists." Both groups had been armed, and to rescue the girl from the cult, they'd ended up in a direct confrontation. She met Marty's eyes. "You're the one who's engaging them, so you be careful. But leave the damn gun under the seat."

"Bossy."

Rox climbed out and quietly closed the truck door. In the distant clearing, she heard someone chopping wood and two other people talking loudly. Maybe the staff had spotted them already. She bent over and jogged into the forest, the dry pine needles crunching beneath her feet. Ahead, she spotted a clump of silver sage and scurried behind it. She dropped to her knees and watched the action through a gap in the foliage. As soon as the Ridgeline people headed toward Marty's truck, she would move into the camp.

Chapter 35

Marty rolled up to the spot where the Ridgeline vehicles had crushed a path through the woods. He backed into it, blocking anyone from getting out and prepping the truck for a quick exit. In the rearview mirror, he saw a bearded man in his early thirties jogging up the path. Marty climbed out and faced him.

"What are you doing?" the man called out. He wore a red T-shirt, dirty jeans, and a gauze bandage on his temple. "You can't be here."

"This is a national forest, and I can stop and pee anywhere I want."

"We have a special permit for this area. Move along." The bearded man stopped about five feet away.

Marty could see that the gash on his head went beyond the bandage. Had he fallen and hit his head or had he been assaulted? He hadn't expected to find a counselor injured. "What's your name?" he asked out of habit from his patrol-cop days. The question came out loudly and with authority, as usual.

"I don't have to tell you. Just move along."

Marty pointed at the logo on the guy's T-shirt. "I know you work for Ridgeline. I also know the owner, and I'll get you fired if you don't cooperate. Tell me your name." He was stalling, not wanting to mention Josh until he had to.

The beefy guy crossed his arms and glared. "I'm Ace. How

do you know Ridgeline's owner? What's his name?"

"Curtis Fletcher. He drives a red BMW and lives in Portland on Skyline Boulevard."

Ace blinked a few times. "What are you doing here?" On the path behind him, a woman strode toward them. She looked forty-something, had short-cropped hair, and wore shorts that revealed her muscular legs. She moved with the confidence of someone in charge. Marty waited for her to get into hearing distance. He wasn't in a mood to repeat himself. He glanced beyond the woman, hoping to catch a glimpse of Rox, but she wasn't in sight.

"I'm looking for Josh Lovejoy," Marty announced. "His father hired me to take him to his aunt in Seattle."

"I don't believe you." The woman stepped forward. "My understanding is that Josh's father in is jail."

"Who are you?"

"Janine Sanders, Ridgeline's program manager for the Cascade region." She pointed a finger at him. "Who the hell are you?"

"Martin MacFarlane, a thirty-year officer with the Portland Police Bureau." A true statement.

Ms. Sanders was silent for a moment, her eyes busy trying to decide if she believed him. She squared her shoulders. "Ridgeline has a contract with Josh's mother that gives us custody until we determine he's ready to leave, or until she submits a waiver to release him."

A surge of feistiness hit Marty. "Carrie Lovejoy is dead, so her contract is invalid. Josh's father, Isaac Lovejoy, has full custody now and he wants his son out of here."

The program manager crossed her arms. "Mr. Lovejoy will have to take it up with a judge. Josh is a minor and currently in our custody. I'm not releasing him to a stranger without a court order."

"I'm not leaving without him." Maybe it was time for Plan B—create a ruckus and get all the teenagers in the camp riled up. If there were any around. Marty didn't see much movement. The person cutting wood had stopped, but he couldn't see them. Only a thin teenage boy was visible under the canopy. He stood at a makeshift table but was watching the interaction on the road.

"You're making a mistake," the manager declared. "This is the best place for Josh."

"Let's ask him. Oregon police officers don't even return fifteen-year-old runaways to their parents if they don't want to go. A court will not take your side."

For a long moment, Ms. Sanders didn't speak or move. Finally, she said, "Mr. Fletcher's instructions are to leave Josh here."

"Curtis Fletcher isn't related to Josh, and I'm not leaving without the boy."

"I'll get my satellite phone and call Mr. Fletcher to see what he says."

Marty didn't want to let her do that. He started to speak, but the sound of a vehicle approaching made them both turn toward the road. A black pickup slammed to a stop, and two guys in red shirts climbed out.

Chapter 36

As the butch-looking woman barreled toward Marty, Rox sprinted into the clearing. A skinny teenage boy stood at a plywood table, packaging food into plastic bags. He didn't match the photo she'd seen of Josh, who was heavier and had darker hair. She ran up to him anyway. "I'm looking for Josh Lovejoy." She kept her voice low but urgent.

The boy's eyes popped at the sight of her, and he opened his mouth—but didn't speak. His green shirt was filthy, and he had dirt caked on his arms.

"This is important!" Rox let her panic show. "Josh could be suicidal."

"He already tried." The words came out as a whisper. "He's in the infirmary."

Oh shit.

The skinny boy pointed at a small beige tent that was set back from the clearing. Beyond it, a creek gurgled over rocks. Probably the same one from the first campsite where she'd found the girl, maybe only a few miles away. The normally idyllic setting and sounds made her skin crawl. Everything was so wrong here.

Rox charged over to the beige tent, spotting another kid on the way. He stood near a pile of logs, holding an axe. He too stared at her without speaking. The tent's flaps were open, and Rox stuck her head inside. A male teenager lay on his side with a walking stick duct-taped to his leg. His hair was dark, but he looked too scrawny to be Josh. Was that blood on his head?

"Josh Lovejoy?" Rox called out, just checking.

The boy rolled on his back, and she saw his face for the first time. Lips swollen and bruised, an eye with a dark shadow underneath, and a deep scratch on his chin. Rox's stomach clenched. The bastards had beat him, and they would pay!

"Yeah. Who are you?"

"An extractor. Your dad sent me, and we're getting you out of here." She stepped into the tent and kneeled next to him. "What's wrong with your leg? Can you walk?"

"I fucked up my ankle and maybe fractured my shin." He sat up. "But if you're taking me home, I'll crawl if I have to."

Rox helped him to his feet and put an arm around his shoulder. "No matter what happens out there, just stay with me. I'm working for your dad." She remembered the photo of Isaac Lovejoy with Fletcher—and the sensation of being followed earlier. It didn't matter, she was taking Josh to a relative. "Do you like your aunt in Seattle?"

"Yeah, why?"

"That's where we're going, for now."

"The farther away the better."

Rox inched toward the tent opening, supporting the boy as much as she could. He moaned with each step, but he kept moving. As they passed the fire pit in the middle, someone near the road started shouting. Rox jerked her head up.

Two big guys in red shirts had Marty pushed up against the truck.

Goddammit! She spun toward the skinny boy at the table. "I need your help!"

He jogged toward her, still watching the commotion near

the road.

"Josh is going home, so help him walk to that truck!" She pointed as she shouted. "I need to assist my partner." She transferred Josh's weight to the other boy and sprinted toward the road.

One of the big guys had his forearm across Marty's chest and was yelling at the top of his lungs. "Get in the fucking truck and get out of here." The other guy stood close by.

The butch woman and the bearded counselor had taken a few steps back and were silently watching the bruisers rough up an old man. Rage filled her chest and threatened to erupt into a primal scream. Rox raced past the spectators and darted around to the driver's side of the truck. She yanked open the door, pulled Marty's Glock from under the seat, and spun back.

The second thug was coming around the front hood, straight at her. Heart pounding, she brought the weapon up with both hands and aimed at his chest. "Back off! I'm a trained police officer and CIA agent. I will not miss!"

"Whoa!" The big guy stopped short. "Let's not get crazy."

Rox shouted at his thug partner. "Let the old man go!"

The bruiser complied and stepped back. "Hey! We're just doing our jobs."

"So am I." Rox stole a glance toward the camp and saw Josh and Silent Boy struggling along the path. She looked at each of the four Ridgeline employees. "Get over there by that big tree and lay on the ground."

No one moved.

Shit! She couldn't let anyone grab and restrain Josh, but she hated using the damn gun. Marty scooted around the truck to where she stood. She handed him the weapon, then yelled at the Ridgeline people again. "Get on the ground. My partner likes to shoot people even more than I do!"

As the four red-clad staff members slowly eased back from the scene, Rox rushed to the teenage boys. She stood on the other side of Josh and put an arm around his waist. She and Silent Boy carried him to the truck, and she was surprised by how light he seemed. Rox opened the door and gave Josh a boost to help him in. She turned to the other teenager. "Thank you."

"Take me too." Silent Boy's eyes pleaded with her.

Oh no! She'd been afraid of this. "I don't have any authority, and this is a custody issue." It broke her heart to tell him no. "But I promise to send federal agents here to investigate." After seeing the beating Josh had been given, it was obvious all the camp kids needed rescuing.

Marty was already behind the wheel, so Rox climbed in after Josh, and her stepdad hit the gas.

Chapter 37

Rox watched over her shoulder as they sped away. The thugs in red stood on the road talking with the short woman. The manager gestured wildly, and the men made shrugging motions. No one moved to follow them. Rox heaved a sigh of relief, then burst into laughter, her heart still thumping with adrenaline. She reached across Josh to give Marty a high-five. "We did it!"

"I hope you don't get arrested for waving that gun around."

A flash of anxiety ripped through her, but Rox shook it off. "Your life was in danger. I did what I had to do. The law allows self-protection." She patted Josh's leg. "Look at this kid! They assaulted him. I don't believe their contract allows for that."

The boy was quiet, his breathing shallow.

"I know we did the right thing," Marty countered. "Just be prepared for possible blowback. In fact, I think we should avoid Sun Ridge on the way out. I don't want to be detained by the local cops."

"That'll make for a longer drive, but I'm with you." She turned to Josh. "Hey, are you all right?"

"I will be." He swallowed back a sob. "Thank you! I can't believe I'm free."

"Thank your dad. This is costing him a bundle. I'm Karina, by the way. And that's Marty."

The boy cried softly. "I heard them say my mother was dead. Is that true?"

Rox gave him a shoulder hug. "Yes. I'm sorry."

"What happened?"

She didn't want to tell him, but she couldn't lie. "Your mom was murdered."

"Who would do that? I don't understand."

"The police don't know yet. She was beaten and strangled, probably by a stranger." Rox wanted to change the subject.

But Josh choked out, "Strangled?"

Curtis Fletcher popped into Rox's mind. "Any ideas about that?"

The boy was silent for a moment, then asked, "Is my dad in jail because they think he killed her?"

"Yes." Rox patted his leg again. "Cops always think it's the boyfriend or ex-husband, but I don't think they have any real evidence."

"He didn't do it. If you're a private investigator, you have to help him prove that."

Startled, Rox deflected. "We'll see. I know the detective handling the case, and I'll get an update for you when I have cell phone service again."

"Do you have any food?" Josh folded his body forward as if in pain. "I'm starving."

Poor kid. "Not much, but we can stop at a store soon." Rox reached over the seat and gave him the last soda and a breakfast bar. Josh wolfed it down in seconds.

They rode in silence for a while, still decompressing from the stress of the last few days. Rox stared out the window, wondering if she would ever enjoy hiking in the wilderness again—without thinking of how it was used to punish teenagers. She spotted something big and dark gray in a cluster of Ponderosa pines.

"Was that a car?" Fear filled her empty stomach.

"What?" Marty's head snapped toward her.

"Maybe it was just a rock. I think I'm on edge." She didn't want to sound paranoid.

"Was it dark gray?" Marty's tone was sharp.

"Yes, and I'm thinking the same thing. We were being followed, and we still are."

"By who?" Josh wiped his face with his shirt.

"We don't know." Rox wanted to reassure him, but she couldn't. A week without the magnets, and she was already regressing. "The local police might be watching us." But if it was a Sun Ridge officer, why hadn't he intervened at the camp?

"It must be about me," Josh cried out. "That's why you're here."

"You're not our first extraction," Marty cut in, trying to sound calm. "We have other people mad at us."

"I saw the gun you used back there," Josh said. "Is that why you carry it?"

Now Marty patted the boy's leg. "We're both ex-cops. It's a habit."

Rox looked back over her shoulder, but the road curved, and she couldn't see if a vehicle was following. "I'll just keep watching." She smiled at Josh. "We'll keep you safe."

A few minutes later, they started the long descent on Briggs, an asphalt road with sharp S-curves and steep drop-offs at many of the bends. Rox checked behind them and didn't see a car. "We might be clear."

"I doubt it." Marty shifted in his seat, his shirt wet with sweat. "We'll know for sure once we get back down into the flatlands."

Rox checked her phone to see if she had service. She wanted to contact Kyle about both murders, Carrie's and Tommy's. "No luck." Her throat was so dry, she felt desperate. Marty had to be dehydrated too. With his heart condition, it was worse for him. "Hey, do we have a jug of water in the back? The one you keep with your camping stuff?"

"Yep. We'll stop when we hit a flat spot and you can fill the bottles."

Rox glanced back at the truck bed with its covered tarp. Movement up the hill caught her eye. A gray sedan was rapidly approaching. "We've got a tail, and he's coming on strong."

Marty looked in the rearview mirror. "What the hell?" Her stepdad pressed the accelerator, and the truck lurched forward. "What's he doing? Trying to scare us?"

Rox stared behind them, watching the other vehicle gain speed. Dread made her queasy. "Maybe we should just stop and confront him." The car was close enough now that she could see the driver was a lone male.

"Stop where?" A note of panic in the old man's voice.

A forested slope hugged the road on the left, and on the right, a narrow shoulder gave way to a steep, rocky drop-off.

Josh cried out, "What's happening?"

"We don't know."

Rox felt the truck slow and twisted to face the front. The road ahead curved sharply to the left, creating a wide rounded view of the valley on the other side. There was no place to pull over, just a guardrail protecting the drop-off.

They went into the curve too fast, but Marty braked and stayed in control. Rox glanced over her shoulder again. The gray sedan had closed the gap, and she could see the driver's face.

No! Why him?

Suddenly the sedan slammed into their tailgate, and Rox's body lurched forward against her seatbelt. She looked up to see them plunge through the guardrail and leave the road, heading straight into the open blue sky.

Chapter 38

Josh screamed as the truck plummeted, and his stomach dropped with it. This was it! He was going to die anyway. They all were. He closed his eyes, not wanting to watch the long slow crash into the valley floor.

A second later, the truck slammed into the ground on all four tires and bounced hard. Josh flew up and hit his head on the roof of the cab. They bounced again, but not as hard this time. No glass shattered. *What had just happened?* The old man still had his hands on the wheel, and they seemed to be on flat ground. But the truck was traveling sideways, still at a rapid speed, and a big tree loomed ahead. Josh yelled, "Watch out!" but Marty was already braking.

They crashed into the tree, and Josh was thrown forward. The seatbelt caught him before he hit the dashboard and his body slammed back against the seat. He couldn't believe he wasn't dead and the truck was still running. "Holy shit! That was insane."

The old guy mumbled, "No kidding."

The woman squeezed his leg again. "Are you all right?"

"Yeah. I can't believe we didn't die." Josh stared at the narrow dirt path they'd landed on. "Is this some kind of mountain biking trail?"

Rox gulped a breath of air. "I think it's the old road that people used before the new one was built. Look, you can see concrete under the dirt in places."

That was good, Josh thought. They might still get out of here.

"Let's see where it goes," the old man said. "If the truck will still move." He shifted into reverse and backed away from the tree.

The front end was damaged, but they were moving. "Is the engine okay?" he asked.

"Seems so. I must have got her stopped in time." The old man's voice quivered.

"Good work, Marty! That was amazing driving." The woman laughed, but she sounded nervous. "How are you? You feel okay?" She was talking to her stepdad.

"Mostly. If that didn't give me a heart attack, nothing will."

Was the old man sick? Before Josh could ask, Karina said, "That was Scott Goodwin. I can't believe our client tried to kill us."

Scott Goodwin? His old mentor? A sickness overcame him. Josh whispered, "I know Scott."

The woman spun toward him, mouth open. "How?"

As Marty steered onto the old road, Josh tried to explain. "From the Fellowship. He's a youth counselor and took us on trips."

A new worry in Karina's eyes. "Do you know Tommy Goodwin?"

Dread mixed with his guilt and fear. "Yes, he's in our youth group too. Why?"

"Oh dear god." The woman rocked forward, her hands on her face.

"What happened?" Josh fought back tears. He was so tired of crying. "Is Tommy okay?"

"No." She shook her head. "He's dead too. Probably murdered."

No! Josh felt sick. And mad as hell. Scott had probably done it. Tommy had been there that weekend too, and it was time to tell the whole ugly story. These people deserved to know because they had tried to save him. But no one could.

"What is it, Josh? What do you know?" The woman had a grip on his shoulder.

The dirt trail began to climb, and they could see the main road above them to the left. Josh hoped they could get back up there. He really needed a shower. Maybe even a doctor. But he was avoiding the conversation. Some things were too shameful to talk about.

"Josh, you have to tell what you know. Scott Goodwin just ran us off the road."

"It was me he wanted to kill. Just like he probably silenced Tommy."

"You saw it?"

"No, but I saw what Scott did to that girl." Tears welled in his eyes. Tears for Brooke and for himself. "What we all did to her."

Karina and Marty were silent—waiting for him to speak.

The confession that had been building inside him for a month finally burst out. "We raped her, but didn't think it was wrong at the time. Tommy and I were drunk and flying high on ecstasy. Brooke and Scott too. The E made us all really horny. But after Scott had sex with her, Brooke passed out. He told us to go ahead and fuck her too, that it was okay. We were too messed up to know better."

A moment of silence, the woman demanded, "Who is Brooke? How old is she?"

Josh's cheeks flushed with shame. "She's fifteen, and she had been in one of the wilderness camps."

"Where did all this happen?" Karina tried to sound calm,

but he could hear distress in her voice.

"At Scott's weekend house. He made us promise not to ever tell anyone about the girl. Or what we did." Josh covered his face, his sobs uncontrollable. "I'm so sorry. And so scared. I don't want to go to jail."

"What about Brooke? Why didn't she report it to the authorities?"

Josh got control of himself. This was the part that confused him the most. "I think Brooke is still at Scott's house. She may not be allowed to leave."

Marty slammed the truck to a stop. "What are you saying?"

"I don't know! Scott acted like Brooke belonged to him." Josh was so tired and so hungry. And he hurt everywhere. He wasn't sure he was even thinking straight.

The woman grabbed his shoulder again. "Where is this weekend house?"

They'd flown over Bend in Scott's small plane, then turned south. "I think it's around here somewhere."

Chapter 39

In silence, they rolled along the bumpy road, and Rox took long, slow breaths. Her client had raped a young girl, murdered his own nephew, then hired her to lead him to Josh—so he could kill him too. And she'd gone to dinner with Goodwin! She'd found him compelling enough to want to date. Rox tried to console herself with the knowledge that psychopaths could be charming—but she was supposed to be smarter and more jaded than that. The damn magnet treatments had made her soft. She was done with them. Better to be quirky and unemotional.

"I should have let you meet with Goodwin," Rox lamented, talking to Marty over the now-quiet boy.

"Hey." Her stepdad reached across and patted her hand. "Don't be too hard on yourself. You had no way of knowing."

"What if Goodwin decides to silence the girl too? He's obviously spinning out of control." Rage and disgust burned in her belly. The full humiliation of her gullibility would come later. Right now she had to face him. "We have to get back on the main road and go after Goodwin."

"I think I can find his house if we get on the right road," Josh offered.

Another wave of frustration hit her. She'd also risked a kidnapping charge to rescue a rapist! *He's a kid,* she reminded herself. Josh had been intoxicated and influenced by an adult. He wasn't evil . . . if he'd told them the whole truth. "What's the right road?"

"It's not far from the camp where the gay kids go."

Ridgeline Get Straight. She'd seen it listed on their business registry. "Can you narrow that down?"

"The turnoff is between Bend and Sun Ridge. I think I'll recognize the name when I see it." Josh's voice was barely a whisper.

He needed reassurance and forgiveness, but she was too upset right now. He would have to get that from a *real* counselor.

Marty was more generous. "Thanks for telling us everything, Josh. The fact that you're helping us rescue Brooke will look good to a judge."

He was only fifteen, Rox thought. He wouldn't even go to jail, just to the juvenile center, then probably be released at eighteen. She couldn't stop thinking about the girl. She looked at Josh. "How did Brooke end up at Goodwin's house?"

"Her parents sent her to the conversion camp, but she wouldn't stop being gay, or bi-sexual actually, so they didn't want her back."

"Are you serious?"

"That's what Scott told us." Josh looked sheepish. "But he also said we couldn't tell anyone she was at his house."

"What were you doing there?"

"Just spending a weekend. Boating and stuff. He's Tommy's uncle. We did that sometimes."

Rox was still confused. "How is Scott Goodwin connected to the camps?"

"He's Curtis' half-brother and used to be part-owner of Ridgeline." Josh shrugged. "I'm not supposed to know that, but I overheard my mom and Curtis talking about it."

That explained how Scott Goodwin had known she was

searching for Josh. Carrie must have known . . . and told her fiancé . . . who told his half-brother. Or maybe Carrie knew Goodwin too and told him directly. A horrifying thought popped into her head. What if Goodwin had pressured Carrie to tell him where Josh was? Then beat and strangled her when she wouldn't? Rox stared at Marty, but he was focused on the road. They would talk about it later. The photo of Curtis Fletcher and Isaac Lovejoy flashed in her mind. Did that mean anything other than a business investment? Maybe both clients had duped her.

She focused on Josh again. "Do you know why Scott is no longer a Ridgeline owner?" She could make a good guess—even without the conversation Marty had overheard about paying hush money.

"No. Sorry."

"Look!" Marty shouted. "There's a short slope up to the main road."

Rox saw a tough, rocky climb over sagebrush. "It's too steep!"

Marty shifted into a lower gear. "We'll make it." He gunned the engine and took a run at the embankment. Halfway up, the truck slowed, grinding out. Marty pressed the accelerator even harder. "Come on, girl!"

Rox held her breath as the truck inched its way up and over the edge.

Finally, they made it back to the main road. "Well done again, Marty. Maybe I should call you Mario instead."

"What does that mean?" Josh asked.

They both ignored him.

"I need to call the police," Rox announced. "If I can get service."

Marty shook his head. "Not the Sun Ridge force. Call the

Bend department instead. Or better yet, the state police office in Bend."

"They're both an hour away." But he was right. If the local cops supported Ridgeline, dealing with them could be too much trouble. The young captive girl was closer to Bend anyway. Rox tried the call, but it wouldn't go through.

She pulled out the map from the glovebox. Earlier, she'd noticed a route that connected the main highway north of Sun Ridge to a road east of the wilderness. It might even save them some time. She studied the area and spotted the cut-through. "If we want to avoid Sun Ridge, we need to head left at the bottom of the hill, then take Rattlesnake Road back around to the main highway."

"That's it!" Josh shouted. "Scott's house is by a small lake off that road."

"A fitting name," Marty muttered.

A few minutes later, they stopped at Troutdale, the main road connecting to the highway.

"Oh shit." Marty was staring at the dashboard.

"We're out of gas?"

"Almost."

Damn. She didn't want to drive into Sun Ridge for anything. The police might be looking for them. If they got stopped, the chief might take Josh back to the Ridgeline camp. Or Goodwin may have called and blamed them for the accident, and they could end up in jail. She didn't want to say any of it out loud. The kid was freaked out enough. "We have to stick to the side roads."

"Except for the buying gas part." Her stepdad had a rare moment of negativity, then turned toward the town.

They drove in silence for a while, tension heavy in the air. As they got closer, an occasional home appeared, typically set back from the road and nestled into the pines. They rounded a rock outcropping and she spotted a big ranch-style house with several outbuildings. Two trucks, a boat, and three recreational quads sat in front of the metal garage.

"There!" Rox shouted. "Pull down that driveway. Those people will have gas."

"I don't know." Marty eased off the pedal anyway. "Rural people don't like to be bothered."

"This is an emergency. And most people like to be helpful."

They made the turn and bumped down the gravel driveway. An older man bolted out of the house to meet them. Rox climbed from the truck. "I'm sorry for the intrusion, but we got lost up on the mountain and used all our gas. Can we buy some from you?"

"You're not from around here?"

"No. We're just doing some hiking and enjoying the beauty." She gave him her most charming smile. "Have you got twenty bucks worth of fuel?"

"I don't know. We'll see." He headed into the metal building and came out with a five-gallon red-plastic canister. "This is mostly full."

"Perfect." Rox went back to the truck for the cash. Marty and Josh hadn't moved, and that was just as well.

A scruffy dog ran out of the house and started barking. Rox waited while the man shushed it and made it sit. She handed him the twenty, and he poured gas into their tank.

Feeling chatty with relief, Rox said, "This is a nice place you have. I'm sure it's pretty quiet."

"It used to be until they started running those damn teen camps up there. Now we have trucks and vans driving by every day, sometimes in the middle of the damn night." He spat a wad of brown chew on the ground. "Two of 'em went by last night around three in the morning and woke me up."

She and Marty had been in the second vehicle. In the darkness, they hadn't even seen the house. She wasn't about to admit it. "That's too bad. Maybe you can plant some trees out front for a sound barrier."

The old guy laughed. "I don't have the energy."

Rox thanked him and climbed back in the truck. "Let's roll."

At the end of the driveway, Rox remembered to try the state police again—while they were still close to Sun Ridge. As she was about to press the button, she stopped. "Marty, who do I say I am? I'm currently working under my PI name, and I'd like to keep it anonymous."

He stopped the truck. "I'll make the call."

"Are you sure? We don't even have Goodwin's license plate number."

"But you saw his face." Marty made a noise in his throat. "I mean *I* saw his face. We have to report the incident to cover ourselves. We have no idea what that psycho will do next."

Josh cut in. "He's probably going to his house to get Brooke. He might kill her to keep her quiet. Or he might take her and run. He has other properties."

Rox stared at the kid. "Do you know where?"

"He mentioned Florida once." Josh locked eyes with her. "And he has a private plane."

Oh hell. Goodwin could be on his way to the airstrip now.

Marty made a call to the Bend department. Halfway through his explanation of the vehicular attack, he stopped and said, "Are you still there?"

No response.

"Damn. I lost the connection."

"Let's go," Rox shouted. "We have to reach the girl before Goodwin does." But she feared they were already too late.

Chapter 40

Marty drove as fast as he could on the high-mountain road. His tired eyes blinked with fatigue and his butt ached from sitting in the truck for twenty hours. But at least the route wasn't an uphill, switchback climb like they'd been doing. The terrain featured rolling hills, rock plateaus, and patches of flat sagebrush desert. Beyond the plateau, dark-green forested mountains pushed up against a bright blue sky. At another time, it would have been beautiful. Today, his surroundings made him edgy. Kids were out there, hiking around in circles, hungry and abused. And a psychopath was trying to silence anyone who could put him in jail—maybe even including a teenage girl. The damn wilderness stretched out for miles. Would it keep him from getting to Goodwin's place in time to save her?

Rox kept asking Josh questions about his time in the program, and the more Marty heard, the more distressed he felt. Now the boy was talking about a near-death experience.

"I almost drowned crossing a stream. I had to do it on my own, with no help at all." His voice was flat, like a numb survivor. "When the water was up to my waist, I stumbled and got carried downstream, then had to climb out on my own. It was early in the morning, and I froze for hours with wet clothes."

That sounded dangerous. Were all the wilderness camps like that?

Josh continued. "One day we hiked from daylight to sundown with only a break for lunch. Guess what they gave us to eat? A bag of peanuts and some dried apple slices." Josh held his stomach again. "Just thinking about it makes me hungry. I thought we were going to stop at a store."

"We don't have time!" Marty shouted, his own hunger making him irritable.

"I know. Sorry."

"It's okay. I'm hungry too. And thirsty. And I have to pee. But we're not stopping." Marty let out a heavy sigh. "How far is this place?"

"I don't know. I've never been there this way. After going through Bend, we drove down the highway, then turned on Rattlesnake."

Rox cut in. "Going that direction, how far is the house from the highway?"

Josh groaned. "I don't know. Maybe ten miles."

A moment later, Rox announced, "This road is thirty-eight miles long, and we've already covered eight miles, leaving thirty. If the house is ten from the other side, we're twenty miles away. Check the odometer. We don't want to miss it."

"Don't worry," Josh said. "You can see the lake from the road. I'll find the driveway."

Marty tried to relax, but his chest had tightened after Goodwin ran them off the road, and he couldn't get his muscles to unclench. He hoped it was just a spasm, not actual heart pain.

The twenty miles seemed to take forever, especially after Josh quit talking and laid his head back to rest. Marty had things he wanted to discuss with Rox, but he didn't want to say them in front of the boy and didn't trust that he was sleeping. His best guess was that Goodwin had killed Josh's mother too. Maybe accidentally, but he'd probably beaten her in an attempt to find out where Josh was. Then Goodwin had targeted Rox to get specific details about the camp's location. What made him think he'd get away with assaulting Carrie Lovejoy? Did he have blackmail material on her, or had he planned to silence her all along?

"We should be close," Rox said.

A minute later, they passed a plateau of black volcanic rock. When they came out of the long curve, a small lake came into view in the distance. Marty nudged the boy, and Josh sat up. "That's it. The driveway is after that clump of oak trees, and the cabin is back behind that hill."

Marty eased off the gas, and his pulse quickened. If Goodwin was at the house, this could get ugly. He wanted to pull out his weapon, but it was too soon. There was no point in scaring Josh yet. They needed backup. Had the Bend department responded to his last call, even though it had been cut off? Probably not. He'd tried the state police too with no success. He grabbed his phone off the dashboard and hit redial. The connection went through. "MacFarlane again. I called about a hit-and-run thirty minutes ago. Is anyone on the way?"

"I'm sorry. That call got dropped and I didn't hear the location."

"Rattlesnake Road, about twelve miles from Highway 97. The dark-gray sedan is driven by Scott Goodwin. He not only tried to kill us, he may have murdered two other people. He might also be traveling with a teenage girl he abducted."

The line was silent.

"Did you hear me?" No response. "Shit! I lost the call again."

"They'll send someone out," Rox tried to reassure him. "But we can't wait for them."

Marty eased down the packed-gravel driveway, experience telling him to move slowly and not spook the suspect. Instinct made him worry that Goodwin was perched behind the bluff with a rifle and would put a bullet between his eyes when the truck came into his view. The perp had no military background, but still, in this part of the state everyone owned a gun.

They rounded the low hill and entered a wide parking area. The gray sedan sat in front of a log-cabin style home with an adjoining carport filled with ATVs, canoes, and other sporting equipment. The sedan looked unoccupied. Was Goodwin in the house? Dealing with the girl? Or sitting next to a window with a shotgun?

Marty put the shifter into neutral, then glanced around, looking for the most protective place to stop and exit. A row of solar panels on a ten-foot frame stood off to the right. *What was that shadow on top?*

"Park next to the carport," Rox said. "It'll give us cover."

A thunderous crack cut through the air, and a rifle slug slammed into the side of the truck.

"Get down!" Marty screamed, reaching under the seat for his Glock.

Rox grabbed the boy and shoved him to the floor.

Another deafening shot rang out. This time the bullet shattered the glass on the back side of the cab. Marty glanced over at Rox and the kid. No blood and no damage that he could see. "You okay?"

"Yes." His daughter sounded strong as always.

Marty slipped out, keeping low and using the open door as a shield. The shots were coming from the solar panels, so

Goodwin had to be perched on top, maybe lying down.

Time to make a move. Marty straightened his legs, stuck his gun through the window, and fired off two quick shots at the solar structure. He ducked back down, his breath ragged. He didn't expect to take Goodwin out, but he hoped the return fire would make the perp stop shooting and run instead.

For thirty long seconds, the scene was eerily silent, except for the squawk of a blackbird in a nearby tree. As Marty peeked out from behind the truck door, an engine started. Goodwin was in his car and rolling forward. The perp fired another shot as he drove past, hitting the side of the truck again.

Thank god most citizens were terrible shots.

Rox sat upright and cursed. "The fucker!'

Marty shouted, "Go inside for the girl. I'll go after Goodwin." He started to get back into the truck.

"No!" Rox yelled back. "You take Josh into the house, and I'll give chase."

She pushed the boy toward the driver's side and Josh climbed out, blocking Marty from taking the wheel. *Damn her!* She was protecting him by giving him the easy job. But they didn't have time to argue.

Marty grabbed Josh's arm and ran toward the log cabin. Behind him, Rox gunned the engine and threw gravel as she raced after Goodwin.

Chapter 41

Scott shoved the rifle onto the seat next to him. He wanted to toss it into the lake but couldn't do it without stopping and getting out. That was okay. He might need it again. He glanced in the rearview mirror. *Shit!* The investigator was still coming after him. He regretted hiring her. If he hadn't been in such a panic, he probably could have found Josh without her help. Or not. He'd certainly tried. But when Curtis pushed him out of the family business—after the bullshit sexual-assault accusations in Utah—his brother had also banned the staff from talking to him about anything related to Ridgeline. So he'd failed to learn the base camp's new Oregon location.

Scott let out a strange laugh, feeling triumphant and bitter at the same time. He'd had no reason to even think about the damn correctional programs since he'd invested in the blossoming legal marijuana business. Following Curtis in his move to Oregon had been the smartest thing he'd ever done. Financially anyway. But he'd been consuming too many pot edibles and not thinking clearly. *No,* he realized, *those weren't the problem.* The ecstasy and the synthetic cannabis—which the kids called spice—had altered his needs and his thinking. But how else could he relate to teenagers? They wouldn't hang around him unless he had money and drugs. The fellowship message he preached was only a smokescreen, a reason to get together.

Girls seemed to like his face though. He glanced at himself in the rearview mirror. *Oh man,* he was losing his looks and he'd known it for a while. Soft lines had formed around his eyes, his skin was thickening, and his nose was actually bigger. *Was it the drinking?* His cock still worked fine—as long as he didn't get too high. Brooke never complained though. She was just glad for a place to live, and sex was a fair trade. She was old enough to consent, yet young enough to still have a tight pussy and a firm body. He'd lucked into finding the girl when she'd come to a Fellowship Youth meeting and told him about her situation. The poor thing had flunked out of the Get Straight program and couldn't go home to her uptight parents who hated her bisexuality. He'd taken her off the streets and she'd been grateful. But he'd gotten bored with her more quickly than he'd expected.

Scott jerked his head back to the bumpy driveway and braked. The highway stretched out before him. *Time to decide.* Without consciously choosing, he turned left. The airfield was close by, and once he was on the highway, he could easily outrun that old truck. He glanced over his left shoulder. The bitch was still coming but she was alone now. That meant Josh and the old guy, whoever he was, had gone into the house. It was over. His sweet life of young pussy whenever he wanted it had come to an end. This chapter of it anyway.

Once he was in the plane, he would fly to his secret villa in Costa Rica. He'd bought it a few months ago, anticipating this move. Although he hadn't expected to be running from the law. *Fucking Tommy!* He'd betrayed his confidence and told Donna, his worthless drunk mother, about the weekend with Brooke. What an ingrate! After Scott had shared his home, his girl, and his drugs, the whiny little punk had felt guilty and gone to his mommy. Donna would never tell anyone else, but Scott feared that Tommy might. He no longer trusted him.

Killing the boy had been harder than he'd expected. Tommy had gotten suspicious once they were out hiking in the park and had edged away from him at the last minute. Teenage boys were fast and strong, and the struggle had unnerved him. Yet the relief of knowing the snitch could never talk about the girl—and the drugs—again had been so great, he'd been compelled to plot Josh's silence as well. Why take chances now that his life was good again? But the timing had gone south on him, and Carrie had sent Josh to the fucking wilderness! Scott slammed the steering wheel. He'd had no idea how long Josh would be gone or where to find the camp. And he'd worried about the boy telling a counselor about that weekend.

Another car flew past going the opposite direction, and Scott focused on his driving. Twenty minutes and he'd be in the air and on his way to freedom.

Chapter 42

At the end of the long lakeside driveway, the sedan turned left, surprising Rox. She'd expected Goodwin to head for the main highway. What he planned next was hard to imagine, but the highway was the fastest way out. Instead, he was traveling back into the wilderness area.

On the road, Rox pushed the truck as hard as it would go, but it was old and worn, and Goodwin's Lexus gained distance. Still, with the Bend police and state troopers on the lookout for his vehicle —she hoped—the bastard probably wouldn't get away.

From here, Rattlesnake Road looped back around the way they'd come from the base camp. *What was Goodwin up to?* Did he plan to lure her out into the forest and ambush her? Would he take another shot with his rifle or try to run the truck off the road again? The man had clearly lost his mind.

She checked the gas gauge, relieved she still had half a tank. The day was hot already, so her window was open, and the air at seventy miles an hour blasted her face. Her lips were dry and cracked from dehydration, and her stomach growled with hunger. But her adrenaline pumped so strongly that none of it mattered. She just had to keep Goodwin in sight until law enforcement caught up to them and took over.

Within a few minutes the gray sedan pulled away in the distance and she could no longer see it. *Damn!* She wanted to call law enforcement again. And check in with Marty to see how he was doing. But at this speed, all she could do was hang on to the wheel. After passing the volcanic-rock area, she spotted a sign ahead. Was there a turnoff? She hadn't notice before. She eased off the gas, then braked as she approached it.

Rancher's Airfield? Oh shit.

Josh had mentioned that Goodwin was a pilot who sometimes flew him and Tommy to his weekend house. Was the bastard planning to jump in a plane and make his escape by air? He might be deluded enough to think he could hide out at one of his properties. If he owned a home across the border in Canada, he might have a chance. Rox slowed, prepping for the exit.

What if she was wrong and Goodwin was still driving toward the Idaho border? The state police would catch him. She had to believe that and trust her instinct on this. Rox braked hard but still took the turn too fast. She pulled the steering wheel back around and corrected before she ran into the ditch. Their clunky truck wasn't designed for high speed or sudden maneuvers, but when they'd left home in Portland, she hadn't expected to be in chase mode!

The airfield quickly appeared in the distance. A metal hangar, a small clapboard building, and a single runway. There had to be planes inside the hangar, and Goodwin might own one of them. Especially since he seemed to commute between his homes on weekends. Where was the gray sedan? Had she been wrong?

Rox raced forward, a new tightness in her stomach. Maybe the vehicle was behind the little building or on the other side of the hangar. Goodwin might be trying to hide. As Rox neared the hangar, an overhead door opened and the nose of a plane eased out. A small Beechcraft. The plane rolled toward the runway, its engine sounding like a giant lawn mower.

What now?

Impulsively, Rox jerked the wheel and lurched across the strip of grass separating the road from the runway. She turned again and headed straight for the plane. The aircraft had to come this way to power up enough speed to take flight.

The plane gained speed, heading straight at her. Rox kept her foot on the gas. She needed to reach the craft before it retracted its wheels and got air underneath. *Oh god, this was crazy!* At the last moment, Rox jerked the wheel again, skidding diagonally. She smashed into the nose of the plane just before it lifted off. The impact threw her forward, but her airbag deployed and slammed her back. Hurting and shaking, Rox dragged herself from the truck.

The damaged Beechcraft had come to a stop on the edge of the tarmac. Rox sprinted to the plane, wishing she'd brought the Glock. Marty sure wouldn't need it. From the tarmac, she couldn't see Goodwin, but he couldn't have had time to get out. She jumped on the aircraft's landing board and peeked into the cockpit. Goodwin was slumped over, his head bleeding, and no weapon in sight. A siren wailed in the distance, and Rox heaved a sigh of relief.

Chapter 43

Marty grabbed the front doorknob, realizing he still had his gun in his other hand. He shoved the weapon into the back of his pants—a move he usually hated—so he wouldn't frighten the teenage girl if she was inside the house. The door was unlocked so he pushed it open, then glanced over at Josh. The boy looked deathly pale.

"What's wrong?" Marty asked.

"Uh. I just have a bad feeling about this place."

Marty didn't blame him. If a young girl was being kept hostage as a sex slave here, then he hated the place too. As he stepped inside, the house was quiet. Brooke could be locked inside a back room or maybe even in a space under the house. "We have to search everywhere," he whispered to Josh, not sure why he was keeping his voice low. Instead, they needed to let Brooke know they were there, so she could knock or call out her location.

"Anyone home?" Marty yelled.

No response.

"Check the kitchen and backyard, and I'll do the bedroom." Marty gestured at Josh to get moving. The boy stood just inside the front door, looking pale, thin, and beaten. The poor kid had been through enough already, and maybe this was too much for him. "Never mind. I've got this." Marty hurried toward the hall.

A young girl stepped out from behind a china cabinet.

The pretty teenager held a small silver gun aimed right at him. "Get out!" she screamed.

Whoa! Marty took a step back as he scrambled to make sense of the situation. "Are you Brooke?"

"It doesn't matter. This is my house, and I want you to leave." Except for her long hair, she looked lean like a boy, and her blue eyes were glassy and unfocused.

Was she high? Or just not right in the head? Marty was at a loss for what to do. "Put down the gun. We're here to take you home."

"This is my home."

Marty recalled what Josh had said about the girl's trip to the gay-conversion camp and her parents not wanting her back. How could he convince Brooke that she could have a better life than this? Maybe he didn't need to. He could just walk away and let Children's Services deal with her.

But she had a weapon and was blocking the hall. Something wasn't right here.

"Brooke, I know you've had a rough time, but you need to put down the gun."

"I'm not going into foster care!" Her eyes sparked with anger and fear. "Just get out!" She waved the little weapon in a threatening move.

Marty took another step back and realized Josh was right behind him.

The boy spoke up. "Brooke, you don't have to go to a foster home. You can come with me to Seattle to my aunt's house."

"No. Scott wants me here."

Poor girl. She had no idea who Goodwin really was. Marty tried again. "Scott is a murderer. He killed Tommy to keep him quiet and tried to kill Josh too. He's on the run and not coming back."

Brooke was silent, her eyes jumpy as she tried to process the stunning information and decide if she believed it.

In the stillness, a thumping sound echoed from the back of the house. *Was someone knocking?* Marty's heart did a triple beat, then sped up. "What is that noise, Brooke?"

"Nothing. Go away." Tears filled her eyes.

He took a step forward. "Is there someone else here?"

Brooke started to whimper. "I can't let you back there. Scott will get mad."

Josh suddenly rushed forward, grabbing the gun from the distressed girl. He tossed it aside and took Brooke into his arms. Josh stroked her hair and whispered, "It's going to be okay now."

Still stunned, Marty ran down the hall. Two doors were slightly ajar. A bathroom and bedroom. A third door at the end was closed and locked. He called out, "Is someone in there? I'm here to help."

"Yes! But I'm trapped." A young female voice.

Could he kick the door open? Probably not. He rushed back into the living room and grabbed the heavy flashlight he'd spotted on the fireplace mantle. When he approached the door again, he yelled, "Stay back!"

Using the long flashlight as a battering ram, he smashed the doorjamb again and again until the lock gave way. He kicked the door open, then reached for his weapon—just in case this teenager had a gun too.

But the only thing in the young girl's hand was a rope that looped around her waist and secured her to a clamp on the wall. She burst into tears at the sight of him.

Chapter 44

Wednesday, July 12, 8:45 a.m., Portland

Rox glanced at the sleeping boy on her couch, then turned to Marty. "Let's take our coffee outside." They headed to her back patio, both moving slowly, like people who'd run a marathon the day before. Rox ached everywhere, as if someone had been punching her too. But it was over. They'd rescued Josh—plus three teenage girls—and hadn't been arrested. She was getting good at this business.

"I hope Josh is going to be all right," Marty said, slumping into a patio chair.

"I think he will." Rox sat down too and sipped her second round of java. "He seems pretty steady, considering what he's been through." The last twenty-four hours had been rough on all of them. The state police had interrogated everyone for hours, then they'd had to limp home in a badly damaged truck. But her business and alias were intact. She'd managed to persuade the officer handling Scott Goodwin's arrest to use her investigative name in his reports. As a fellow cop, he'd understood the need for her services. But first she'd had to convince him to contact the Portland Police Bureau and talk to Kyle Wilson. Her ex-boyfriend had vouched for both her and Marty.

"Kyle really came through for us," Marty said, obviously thinking along the same lines. He gave her a probing look. "Maybe you should go out with him again."

"Maybe." On the drive home, Rox had called Kyle to thank him, then begged him to drop the charges against Isaac Lovejoy—so her client could go home and give his son a place to live. "Children's Services might still get involved in Josh's life, but we did everything we could to prevent it."

"I hope he gets some counseling." Marty glanced at the sliding door.

Rox laughed. "Listen to you. Since when are you a fan of shrinks?"

"Since it'll be someone else talking to them." Her stepdad grinned.

"I'll suggest it to his father when I see him." Isaac Lovejoy was being released later this morning and she planned to take Josh to meet him. She hoped they both were through with the Community Fellowship. But she wasn't done trying to put Ridgeline and its camps out of business. She'd called her buddy at the FBI, and he'd started an investigation into their blackmail-style recruitment for the conversion therapy program.

The back door slid open and Josh stepped out, his eyes puffy and his hair wild from sleep. "Is there more coffee?"

An hour later, Rox parked her SUV on a side street across from the Multnomah County Jail and shut off the engine. The boy in the passenger seat asked, "What now?"

"We wait." She pointed at a large overhead door on the back of the white-brick building. "Your dad will come out that exit, most likely with a group of other inmates. They tend to release people in batches." The county ran the facility, so her experience here as a city officer was limited to booking suspects in. This was the first time she had waited for an inmate to come out.

"Thanks for all this." Josh gestured at the jail, then himself. "I mean, bringing me here and giving both of us a home. I can't wait to sleep in my own room."

"You've thanked me enough."

They were quiet for a moment, then he asked, "What's going to happen to Brooke?"

The girl had gone from angry to relieved to scared as the officers questioned her at Goodwin's house. Rox hadn't seen her since a social service worker arrived at the scene to take both girls into state custody. "If they can't find a relative who wants her, she'll end up with a foster family." Rox hoped the state wouldn't force Brooke's parents to take her back. The poor girl needed people who would accept her the way she was—and probably a lot of counseling. The other captive girl, named Ashley, had a family in Bend. She'd run away after a fight with her father and had been hitchhiking south when Goodwin picked her up and promised her a house in the country and all the pot she wanted.

"I can't believe I'm not in juvie jail right now." Josh rocked back and forth, obviously nervous. "But I'll find a way to make things up to Brooke."

"You already did." Rox touched his hair. "You helped us find her, and you kept her from making a huge mistake." Brooke had claimed she didn't even remember that night with Josh and Tommy at the house, so the police had no reason to charge Josh with anything. They'd harassed him about not reporting Goodwin's sexual relationship with a minor, then chose not to hold him accountable for it. But adults pulled that crap all the time and got away with it!

The young man was still dealing with grief though.

Josh shook his head. "As happy as I am to be home—and with my dad soon—this is still fucked up. I can't believe Scott strangled my mom. Are you sure about that?"

"They'll compare his DNA to trace evidence they found on Carrie. If it matches, then we'll know for certain. The police wouldn't release your dad if they weren't sure about another suspect."

"But why would Scott do it? Just because he wanted to get to me?"

"Mostly, yes. If he was doing drugs like you say, he may have been out of control and not thinking clearly." The piece of breath mint she'd found in her parking lot flashed in her mind. Had Goodwin broken into her office looking for notes about Josh's location? It seemed crazy, but he'd also given her two grand as a retainer for a made-up case—just to see if she had located Josh. Goodwin had also tried to kill all of them to keep them from finding the girls in his cabin. So he'd gone over the edge, for sure.

"What is it?" Josh asked, concerned.

"Excuse me, I have to make a call." Rox stepped out of her vehicle, pulled out her phone, and pressed Kyle's contact icon.

He answered almost immediately. "Hi, Rox. I only have a minute, but I'm glad to hear from you."

"A funny thing." She explained the break-in at her office and added, "I found a piece of breath mint in the parking lot, and I'm sure Scott Goodwin dropped it. Can you take it and turn it into the lab for DNA testing?"

"No shit?" Kyle made a breathy sound. "The technicians found something similar in Carrie Lovejoy's car. I'll make sure they test it for DNA as well. This could be the trace evidence that nails him for that crime."

She needed that bit of good news. "Have you questioned Goodwin?" The state police had said they would transfer him to Portland—eventually.

"He's not here yet. But the Bend detective says the suspect claims the incident on the road with you guys was an accident and that everything that happened between him and the girls was consensual." Kyle let out a snort. "Even if that's true, it's still statutory rape. But don't worry, we'll get him on Carrie's homicide."

"Good luck. Let me know if I can help." Rox hoped they would charge the bastard with Tommy's death too, but they might never have any evidence for that crime.

A pause. "You could agree to have dinner with me soon."

Rox looked up at the bright sun, still not sure how she felt, except angry at herself for being charmed by a psychopath. That would have never happened before—when she was herself. "I'm not going back to the treatments. But for now, I want to wait and see what changes for me as the effect wears off."

"Can I ask again in a few weeks?"

"Please do."

"See you later."

They hung up, and she climbed back in her vehicle, then patted Josh's arm. "I'm sorry you missed your mom's funeral."

Voices echoed across the street, and Rox looked up. Inmates streamed out of the now-open door. "Here they come."

When Josh saw his father, he jumped out.

"Wait," Rox said. "Let him cross over here."

Isaac Lovejoy spotted them and broke into a run. When he reached his son, he wrapped his arms around the boy and hugged him hard. Their joy was palpable.

Rox smiled. That was why she did this for a living.

L.J. Sellers writes the bestselling Detective Jackson mysteries—a five-time Readers Favorite Award winner. She also pens the high-octane Agent Dallas series, the new Extractor series, and provocative standalone thrillers. Her 22 novels have been highly praised by reviewers, and she's one of the highest-rated crime fiction authors on Amazon.

Detective Jackson Mysteries:

The Sex Club
Secrets to Die For
Thrilled to Death
Passions of the Dead
Dying for Justice
Liars, Cheaters & Thieves
Rules of Crime
Crimes of Memory
Deadly Bonds
Wrongful Death
Death Deserved
A Bitter Dying

Agent Dallas Thrillers:

The Trigger
The Target
The Trap

Extractor Series

Guilt Game
Broken Boys

Standalone Thrillers:

The Gender Experiment
Point of Control
The Baby Thief
The Gauntlet Assassin
The Lethal Effect

L.J. resides in Eugene, Oregon where many of her novels are set and is an award-winning journalist who earned the Grand Neal. When not plotting murders, she enjoys standup comedy, cycling, and zip-lining. She's also been known to jump out of airplanes..

Thanks for reading my novel. If you enjoyed it, please leave a review or rating online. Find out more about my work at ljsellers.com, where you can sign up to hear about new releases.
—*L.J.*

www.ingramcontent.com/pod-product-compliance
Lightning Source LLC
Chambersburg PA
CBHW030331200626
46816CB00006BA/2007